# BETWEEN
# DARKNESS
## AND
# LIGHT

### AN ENVIRO THRILLER

## PATRICIA McCONKEY

BPS
books

Toronto and New York

Published in 2012 by
BPS Books
Toronto and New York
www.bpsbooks.com
A division of Bastian Publishing Services Ltd.

ISBN 978-1-926645-92-6

Cataloguing-in-Publication Data available from
Library and Archives Canada.

Cover: Gnibel
Cover photo: Paulo Brandão
www.flickr.com/x/t/0147002/photos/paulobrandao
Author photo: Liesa Noonan
Text design and typesetting: Daniel Crack, Kinetics Design
www.kdbooks.com

Printed by Lightning Source, Tennessee. Lightning Source paper, as used in this book, does not come from endangered old-growth forests or forests of exceptional conservation value. It is acid free, lignin free, and meets all ANSI standards for archival-quality paper. The print-on-demand process used to produce this book protects the environment by printing only the number of copies that are purchased.

*To my children,*
*Benjamin and Gabrielle:*
*You are life's greatest gift.*
*I am eternally grateful that God*
*sent me two of his very best.*

*To my parents:*
*You have shown me what is required to*
*be a parent and what true love looks like.*
*Thank you from the bottom of my heart.*

# Chapter *1*

*W*ill opened his eyes. Without moving his head, he looked down at his feet. A bead of sweat rolled into his right eye. He blinked hard and tried to focus on the river far below the stony ledge. The river remained a blur. Perhaps it was the distance – or the lack of food, water, and sleep.

He fought to clear his mind by breathing deeply, but every breath intensified his pain. He looked down at his solution. One step – that's all it would take. He knew it was the right thing to do. It was his training that held him back. As a decorated fireman, he had made a career of saving lives – and preventing suicides. Now he could understand those tortured souls. He wondered if he had done the right thing interfering in their choice.

In another time, he would have thought it a perfect autumn day. The sky was clear, and the cool air held the musky scent of plant decay. In the ravine below, gusts of wind blew crisp leaves in circles. Will could see miles of river valley, full of autumn colours, snaking through the Alberta countryside. A few luxurious houses hugged the edges of the valley.

In another time, he would have thought it a perfect day, but the world now bore little resemblance to anything in human history. As Will took his last look at life, he was forced to see how still-raging fires were scarring the vista. He shook his head at the thought, dropping his eyes, wondering at the senselessness of it all. He thought of the many beautiful cities burning around the world. But it didn't matter now. It was his own nightmare that had him teetering on the edge of this cliff.

Will couldn't believe he was running through all the old rationalizations yet again. He recognized with some shame that he was still trying to make sense of the past month, trying to find someone else responsible for the madness in his life. In a conventional war, there was always an enemy. There was comfort in having someone to blame, a shared foe to denigrate as inventively and profanely as possible. Regardless of which side you were on, each thought only of their own survival as they plotted the death of their enemies in whatever way they could. Killing women and children was an acceptable loss if it advanced your cause.

In this case, however, there were no sides. One massive attack had probably killed billions of people, changing the face of the earth. Will couldn't see how anyone stood to benefit from it. What was the purpose of creating hell on earth?

~

It had been a ruthless global assault, an indiscriminate killing of men, women, and children of every race, colour, and creed. On a more personal level, Will had lost every-thing. There were no words to describe the insanity of the past month, no way to make sense of anything that had happened.

*Patricia McConkey*

She had been so beautiful, smart, and idealistic, but now she was gone. Will had no answers, only rage and heartache. He looked at what he had become in just a few short weeks. His life was over. It hadn't amounted to much, but he grieved for her. She had such potential. She could have achieved so much more than he ever had.

He inched closer to the edge, reminding himself why he was here. It was the only way to make it all stop – the pain, the hunger, the horror of everyday life. He hadn't saved his family from the madness, and in his current state he wasn't much use to anyone else. The world would be better off without him.

A wave of dizziness overcame him and he flung his arms out to steady himself. He closed his eyes and waited for the freedom death would provide. But his athletic instincts and many years of hard training snapped his body back into perfect balance.

Will caught a flash of her striking face before him, and his heart lifted with joy. She seemed so close he could almost touch her. Then reality slammed into him like a locomotive. He grasped his chest as if he could tear out the pain. He thought about her and knew he should have done more. He should have taken better care of her.

He looked back down at his feet. He had to force himself to take that one step. Even though he longed for death, some small part of him still resisted. A tiny shred of logic tried to make itself heard above the roar of his madness. The voice of his warrior self was saying, "You have been through tough times before and you have always found a solution. You can do it again. There *is* a solution."

He had said something like that to coax a young woman off a ledge and it had worked. But now the words were empty and meaningless.

The battle in his brain continued. Each thought of her death and of his family brought a rush of pain. Will felt a strange sensation. He shifted his weight from left to right and back again.

Darkness overtook him. He felt his head and chest collapse inward under great pressure. He relinquished all control and let himself fall over the edge.

# Chapter *2*

## Summer 1974

*Dieter* ran his fingers through the sandy soil as he leaned against the shed, waiting for the verdict. It was almost midnight. Though the air was slightly cool, he could still feel the warmth of the earth, thanks to the long daylight hours of summer in northern Alberta.

The science of sun and soil and how they worked together had always fascinated him. At the time he couldn't have known how this fascination would help him achieve his mission. But one thing was clear: He must make things right for the sake of his mother and sister.

Dieter had been chosen, like the other six young men, to make a change. Two babies had been born horribly disfigured. One of them was his sister, Amara, who lived only a few brief days. If that wasn't enough, his mother had died from the hard birth. His small community feared that an unseen killer was targeting the community's women and children. Could it be something that was floating in the air? It was hard to know what was happening, but the whole community feared their way of life was going to end forever.

Seven young men had been chosen to do something, but what?

Over the past few years, pollution from the nearby refinery had clearly spun out of control. The elders of the colony requested a meeting with the refinery executives. After months of delays, a date was finally set.

The elders brought to the meeting oddly shaped vegetables coated with light gray dust, clearly from the smokestacks. They pointed out the irregular shapes and explained that deformities had occurred in two babies and a number of farm animals.

Distanced by their crisp linen shirts and pinstriped suits, the executives saw only the potential for liability suits in the multi-millions. Deny, deny, deny – that's what every good executive is taught. These were no different. They dismissed the concerns of the men from the colony as preposterous. They threw out all kinds of scientific jargon to show why such a thing could never happen. They denied any responsibility whatsoever.

After the meeting, the elders came to Dieter's father, Gunter, to tell him they had failed. The oil executives would not take action. Gunter had expected as much, but on hearing the news he broke down in tears. He could not forget his wife and baby daughter. Dieter watched his father crumble. He couldn't offer his support. He was far too angry. He knew his community had neither the technical nor the financial resources to fight the oil companies. That was clear.

Earlier that evening, the men of the colony, young and old, argued over the true purpose of their mission. Although they had all read the same words from the ancient book, each had a different perspective on what they meant.

In a rare moment of anger, Gunter yelled at Dieter, "You can't just push them off the land. They will come back with guns, and there will be too many of them. They will just

*Patricia McConkey*

keep coming. We must find a way to keep going, to preserve our—"

"But *our way* is going to be extinct," Dieter snapped back. "Or have you forgotten how your baby struggled to breathe for two days before she died? And my mother is dead because of that horrible birth. If we can't have healthy children, how long before there is no one left?"

The fathers finally decided that they must make the decision themselves. They sent the young men outside to await their fate.

And so Dieter sat, waiting, trying not to remember his mother's screams.

He was startled when his father quietly called him and the others in. The seven young men filed into the dimly lit room. Each boy stood next to his father. One man sat at an old wooden table. A single candle sat on the table, barely lighting the room.

"It has been decided," the old man at the table said. "You will not return until you have accomplished your task."

Dieter sighed. He had a great desire to fulfil his duty, but he was uncertain. How could seven young, inexperienced boys carry out a mission with an impossible goal?

# Chapter 3

## September 2012

*A* ball of orange-yellow flame leapt toward the pale blue Alberta sky. Line 56 at the Baseline Road Refinery had just exploded. Within seconds an alarm blared out a warning to the entire site.

The refinery had vast quantities of flammable materials with the explosive potential to bring down a small mountain. Workers on-site knew this well. When the alarm sounded, they were nearly paralyzed with fear. Except for Will; disasters were his business. It was his job to remain calm.

Will calmly toggled his computer screen to find the location that had triggered the alarm. He pulled up video surveillance and saw flames raging in one of the main lines leading to reservoirs holding millions of litres of oil. His mind raced as he considered the ramifications. If the fire made its way down to the tank farm, the effect would be like a small nuclear explosion.

In the midst of the chaos, Will barked out orders, detailing the men to cut off the supply of oil feeding the fire. Will's composure steadied the workers. His confidence reassured them that the job could be done; all they had to do was follow his lead.

The refinery was equipped for this type of mishap with special fire hydrants containing fire retardant rather than water. Will and his team had conducted drill after drill in preparation for just such an eventuality. Hoses were positioned and the hydrants were switched on. The retardant flowed over the flames like giant globs of gooey marshmallow fluff. Once the flames were smothered, cheers went up all over the plant.

As Will was tidying up the last details of the blaze, he thought about the upcoming investigation. As Fire Chief at CanPetroleum, he would be responsible for the entire investigation, presenting a report to management on the fire's cause. It was important to Will to deliver a report with clear evidence and an undeniable conclusion. He would gather all the evidence he could, but he already suspected this one was out of the ordinary. Few of the usual elements were present.

He went over the facts. The fire had started in an unlikely spot. There was no obvious source of ignition. In spite of twenty-odd years as a firefighter, he couldn't remember anything like it.

He had investigated fires set by arsonists or ecoterrorists, and it had been quite easy to determine that the blazes had been deliberately set. It was quite a different matter, however, to convict the guilty parties. Any evidence linking them to the incident usually went up in the flames. Unlike murder investigations, which collared culprits based on physical traces, fire investigations usually had to rely on rare eyewitness accounts.

In the cases Will had seen, no charges were ever laid even though it was clear who the culprits were. This soured him on the many groups claiming to be green and environmentally friendly. To him these terms were just euphemisms for "ecoterrorist." He suspected some such earth-friendly group had intentionally set this blaze, too.

Will was startled when Tom McLaren, the General Manager, called from across the yard and motioned him over. Will gave some final commands to his staff and joined him.

Tom slapped him firmly on the back.

"That was impressive work, Will! I knew there was a good reason I pay you so much to sit around for months on end. I'd like to introduce you to Simon Bridgewater, Executive Assistant to the Prime Minister. He just happened to be on-site when all the excitement broke out."

Simon looked at Will, impressed by his six-foot height and muscular frame. He noted the hint of gray at his temples and guessed him to be forty-five to fifty, but his striking face and black skin hid his age well. The soot and dirt on his face was streaked with perspiration, adding to his aura of rugged masculinity.

Simon held out his hand and did his best to cover his lustful thoughts. Will's handshake was strong and firm and sent a quiver up Simon's arm.

"I'll be sure to tell the Prime Minister how your expertise saved the plant and the lives of everyone here," he said.

"Well, I'm glad it didn't reach the main tanks," Will said. "It would have looked like a nuclear explosion if the fire had made its way down to the tank farm."

"Do you know what caused the fire?"

"It started in a strange spot, so we'll definitely be investigating it closely. Too early to tell, but once I give my report to Tom, I'm sure he can tell you all about it."

Will knew information must flow through the proper

channels, and failure to do so would lead to a whole heap of trouble he didn't need.

"Well, I'm sure you have a lot to do. We'll get out of your hair," Tom said.

Will scarcely noticed Simon climb into a cab and drive off. He was preoccupied with the fire. There was something very strange about it; he could feel it in his gut. And his gut was usually right.

# Chapter *4*

*Will* loved his bike ride home. He often took the longest route to extend his workout.

Normally the harder he pedalled the better he could sort through his thoughts. Today, though, he couldn't stop running through every detail of the fire.

Aside from the suspicious details, something else was bothering him. Will was hired as Fire Chief a little over a year ago. During that time, not much had happened. He had had reservations about taking the position, but the amount of money they were offering was hard to turn down.

In his previous position, Will was always in the thick of things – car crashes, suicide attempts, train wrecks – you name it. He had rescued someone from every type of disaster imaginable.

On the plant site, there were a few close calls rescuing workers from dilapidated scaffolding or potentially dangerous situations, but nothing that required heroics. Nothing that got his adrenalin pumping.

Although he had kept busy at the plant, he had become more and more restless over the past few months. Beside the lack of excitement, he felt his leadership skills were being questioned. He was like a captain whose ship was docked. He thought this nagging feeling would disappear once he demonstrated his firefighting skills, but he was wrong.

To get rid of his nagging feelings of inadequacy, Will practiced and drilled with his makeshift crew. They seemed ready, as ready as part-time firefighters could be. The crew consisted of staff whose primary job was to keep the refinery running. Fire protection was a secondary duty. This makeshift crew would be used only as a temporary measure in a real-life situation. Full-time professional firefighters from the county would be called in for anything serious.

Today's success should have left him feeling exhilarated. His makeshift crew handled themselves like experts and had everything under control well before the real firemen arrived. He was being called "hero" and "top gun." All the staff admired him and thought the situation couldn't have been handled better. He should have felt on top of the world. Instead he felt hollow and empty.

He tried to pin down the source of his frustration. He had a beautiful wife who loved him, despite his growing indifference toward everything around him. His beautiful, highly motivated daughter was in her final year at high school and headed for the best pre-med program he could afford. His tall, gangly son was a sore spot, though. The only thing he put any effort into was fixing cars. And then there was his aging father, who lived with them. Will was coming to the realization that George had some sort of dementia. He often blurted out a random comment followed by a chuckle. It was getting worse. It was frustrating and heartbreaking at the same time.

Despite a few family issues, Will had the perfect life – beautiful family, big house, successful career, and the respect of his peers. Perfect, except for the feeling eating away at him.

Will coasted into his driveway and was greeted by Finnigan, whose whole body swayed side to side from his vigorous tail wagging. As soon as he opened the front door, he knew he was alone. The house was too quiet. He walked through the front hall and found a note in the usual spot – taped to the frame of the family portrait. He looked at the smiling faces in the picture as he pulled the tape off the frame.

His wife, Lauren, was radiant with her long black hair, creamy coffee complexion, and her exotic features, inherited from a mix of East Indian and African parentage.

His daughter, also stunning, looked like her mother, but most of her personality genes (a.k.a. extreme stubbornness) came from Will. She was tall, athletic, and confident.

And then there was Matt, standing in the back, almost blending in with his surroundings. He was handsome but didn't look like either parent. You could say he looked a bit like his grandfather, George, but even that was a stretch.

The note gave details for dinner and explained that Lauren, Emma, and George were at a meeting for their upcoming conference. Will rolled his eyes at the thought of the God's Green Earth conference they were organizing. It was going to be a live videoconference involving many different churches and organizations around the world. The goal: to use the power and influence of the church to promote a greener lifestyle and perhaps slow man's destructive effects on the earth.

Lauren had been talking to spiritual leaders from many different religions, and while they all seemed to agree that God had instructed man to look after the earth, they couldn't agree how it should be done. What actions were needed to save God's green earth?

Lauren had been working on this for months. She had obtained grants for the production, organized musical entertainment, and firmed up commitments from a number of high-profile celebrities and politicians to add their support on camera. She had spent a great deal of time on this project, on top of her full-time job as VP Marketing for the Cancer Society. The conference was scheduled to take place in less than a month.

Will couldn't shake the thought that all this time and effort would prove futile. More selfishly, he dreaded the thought of eating frozen dinners and take-out for the next month. He preferred Lauren's cooking to restaurant food any day.

He wondered where Matt was. He was rarely at home. When he was, the two of them argued about anything and everything. Matt had barely finished high school and wasn't pursuing any further education. He didn't make enough money to get his own place. He continued to live at home but spent as little time there as possible.

Once he was sure no one was home, Will went down to the basement into Matt's room. He had caught Matt with dope but after many heated arguments had given up on him. Now it was Will's little secret. He knew where his son hid his stash. When the opportunity presented itself, Will took just enough for a joint or two but not enough for Matt to notice.

Will headed through the back yard and out the gate leading to some nature trails. After jogging a couple kilometres down the trail, he found a secluded bench and lit a joint. His tensions seemed to drift away with each puff of smoke. He leaned his head against a tree trunk and closed his eyes.

Why did he feel alone? His wife was as committed to

him as ever, but her devotion to saving the world, helping cancer victims, and all those other higher purposes seemed to be coming between them. It was ridiculous to be jealous of her charity work and relationship with God. He shook some of the dope-induced euphoria from his brain and admitted to himself that he envied Lauren's sense of peace and well-being. That clearly had nothing to do with him; he had been neglecting her lately. If Lauren's happiness had nothing to do with him, then maybe she didn't need him. How had he let things get this far?

He quickly puffed the last bit of joint until it just about burned his fingers.

His mind floated into the foggy state he craved. He focused his attention on a beetle crawling up his leg. For a few moments there was nothing in the world but him and the beetle – nothing he had to think or worry about. He brushed the beetle off and walked slowly down the path toward his house. He wanted to examine the flowerbeds in his front lawn.

Coming up the street, he could hear the rev of his neighbour's Hummer. It was like time stopped, just for a second. Will felt the warm September sun on his back and he could hear children laughing, neighbours talking, and a dog barking. It was perfect. A moment that would stick in his mind as his last experience of normal life.

*Patricia McConkey*

# *Chapter 5*

$E$*arlier* that same day, Simon had been waiting in the CanPetroleum boardroom on the sixth floor. His anxiety kept him from taking in the boardroom's bird's eye view of the whole refinery.

Phil Dubois, CEO of CanPetroleum, came in with Tom McLaren, the General Manager. After the usual pleasantries, the three men got down to business. Simon sat on one side of the long, highly polished table and Phil and Tom on the other. Simon always looked for non-verbal cues, but he didn't need them today. The message was clear.

Phil exhaled a long slow breath, considering how to get his message across without actually saying it. Phil knew there was a slippery slope between environmental stewardship and profitable business practice. He knew he was entering some dangerous areas.

"It was too bad that Stan couldn't attend with you," he said.

Simon knew Phil was using the Prime Minister of Canada's first name to demonstrate his own power.

"But I'm sure you'll convey the important issues of our meeting to him," Phil continued.

He lowered his chin to look over his reading glasses at Simon, trying to gauge his reaction.

Simon was the PM's Executive Assistant. The public wasn't aware of it, but everyone in business knew it was a powerful position.

Simon smiled and gave the appropriate nod.

After a long pause, Phil said, "I met with the directors of the Canadian Oil Producers last night, and all agreed that we must have representation in Ottawa that will look after our needs. It is important that the Prime Minister know our concerns with the Kyoto accord."

Simon knew the CEO of CanPetroleum would not come right out and say they were against the Kyoto Accord because that would be un-environmental of them. But that was definitely the case. He had seen private correspondence between Phil and the PM with cost estimates of the required changes and how these would drastically cut into earnings.

Phil gave assurances of the company's commitment to the environment but stressed the tough realities of the economy.

The PM knew all too well the nature of business and how the world revolved around money. To secure money from the COP for his upcoming campaign, the PM would have to delay any Kyoto implementation policies. These delays would provoke a massive outcry from the environmentalists, but unfortunately they did not contribute to his campaign and therefore had relatively no say in policies. Money was the only way to stay in power, and right now COP was telling him where that power was coming from.

Simon understood Phil's message. The Prime Minister knew it was coming. There were no surprises. But as Phil continued on about the importance of having a leader who

*Patricia McConkey*

understood industry, Simon's mind raced ahead to how the delay would play out.

The environmentalist movement was gaining support from all areas of the general population. Delaying pollution control would not just stir up bad press; it would create some potentially dangerous situations. Simon would have to boost security because hard-core fringe groups among the environmentalists were known for more than just making idle threats in the media. They were acting out their rage.

So far their stunts had been little more than public annoyances, but the stunts seemed to be escalating in frequency and severity. There was no telling how they would react once they heard about the delay.

The meeting was just finishing up when the fire broke out. The three men could see everything from their vantage point in the boardroom. The ball of fire rose high above them. Fear gripped Simon's gut as the sirens began to blare.

Phil and Tom directed Simon to the fire stairwell. They went into the other offices to oversee the evacuation of the building.

Simon was joined by hundreds of office employees, all panicked by the mass of fire spouting from the other side of the refinery. He overheard workers talking about what would happen if the fire reached the massive oil reserves.

The stairwell was so packed, the crowd moved at a crawl. Finally the flood of employees poured out into the sunny parking lot and quickly walked east. Simon heard something about a muster point and followed the crowd.

Simon had just reached a sign with a big yellow "A" when spontaneous clapping and cheering erupted from the crowd. From what he could gather, the fire was under control. Simon headed back to the parking lot. He was already dialling a taxi when an attractive young woman took his arm.

"Are you Simon Bridgewater? Tom McLaren just phoned me and asked me to escort you back. We can catch up to Tom just over there. Would you like to walk this way, please?"

As they walked along, Janine thought Simon was checking her out and smiled in pleasure. Actually he was admiring her outfit. Simon was an impeccable dresser, and he loved high fashion, both men's and women's. He often thought he would have made a successful designer. Right now he was wondering where she had bought her shoes – and if they came in his size.

# *Chapter* 6

*S*imon didn't start to relax until his cab pulled away from the refinery. Although the fire appeared to be out, Simon didn't want to hang around, just in case there was another explosion.

Simon thought about Will. He was an interesting find: the ultimate in tall, dark, and handsome. Simon suspected he might have a dark, moody side. Bad boys are always more appealing, to both women and men. But Will was probably straight and married.

Straight *and* married, he thought. Hmmmmph. I don't know which is worse.

He must have spoken the words. The cabbie looked back at him. Simon waved his hand and stared out the window.

As the cab approached the legislature buildings, Simon's heart began to beat faster. The number of protesters had more than doubled since he had left, and their chants had now turned to yelling. The cabbie stopped a fair distance from the entrance.

"You want me to get out *here*?"

"If you want me to drive through that crazy bunch, it's going to cost you a whole lot more," the cabbie said.

"What if I double the fare?"

The cabbie frowned. "Yeah, right. And what if they break my windshield? Who's going to pay for that?"

"The Prime Minister will certainly reimburse you for any damages," Simon said, handing him his card.

Now the cabbie was all smiles. "Two hundred plus damages."

"Done!" Simon said, before the cabdriver could up his bid. He didn't care about the expense. Your tax dollars hard at work, he thought.

The cab inched its way up the front drive. They would have to go through a horde of angry demonstrators before the cab could pull around to the back to let Simon out. As they got to the outer edge of the crowd, Simon slid into the centre of the seat. The demonstrators didn't know who he was; it was enough that he was trying to drive through them. They pounded their fists on the windows.

"What are these guys protesting?" the cabbie asked.

Just then Zain Bedow slammed a fist down on the hood of the cab. In his other hand he held a sign that read, "Save the Environment, Make the Oil Companies Pay!" He locked eyes with the cabbie.

Zain was well known as the leader of the Green Movement. The movement had just made a huge discovery on the North Saskatchewan River. They had uncovered a big pipe on the bottom of the river. It was connected to an old underground tank that contained oily sludge from forty years ago. The tank was now releasing toxic pollutants into the water.

No one could say who was responsible because the original companies had folded and reformed under different names.

"I have to agree with them," the cabbie said. "Look how

much I have to pay for gas? And those oil companies steal my money and lie about everything they do. I'm backing up. Are you getting out here?"

"What? You can't let me out here. Look at these people."

"Fine, you can get out on the street."

"No, no. I have to see the Prime Minister. Here, that's all you get."

Simon threw a hundred dollar bill at him and pried the car door open. He took a deep breath for courage and squeezed out of the cab. So many people were yelling at him, he couldn't hear any one insult.

Simon yelled back with all his might, "I'm here to give the Prime Minister news on some environmental programs that could reduce emissions. I am pro-environmental, too."

Zain's hand landed squarely in the middle of Simon's chest. His nose was about one inch from Simon's.

"I know who you are," he said in a low grumble.

"Then you know I have to go and talk to the Prime Minister about emission reductions," Simon said, trying to hide his fear.

"You're not going to tell the Prime Minister to proceed with emission reductions. You are going to tell him to delay the Kyoto requirements, aren't you? You just came from a meeting at the refinery, didn't you? I can smell the oil on you."

The cabbie had said the same thing when Simon got into the car. Zain had Simon's Gucci tie wrapped around his fist. Simon's mouth hung open while he tried to come up with something conciliatory.

"Do you need any help, Mr. Bridgewater?"

One of the security guards had pushed through the crowds and was standing behind Zain.

"Thanks Roger, I was just trying to get to my office."

As he walked away, Zain shouted, "The oil companies aren't the only ones with deep pockets. We have financial supporters, too, Mr. Bridgewater. Be sure to tell the PM that."

Simon shivered at the thought of what Zain could do if his pockets were lined with money.

Simon and the security guard pushed their way back through the angry crowd.

He straightened his tie and tried to pull himself together. It was his father's idea for him to get into politics, and now he was questioning the sanity of that decision. Simon went straight to the Premier's office, where he would find the PM. Simon's outstretched hand made it clear that nothing was going to stop him as he breezed past assistants and other office roadblocks.

While the Premier sat at his desk, Prime Minister Stan Hartley stood at the window, looking out over the crowd of protesters. He turned and saw Simon.

"You made it. I think that crowd is getting a little nasty."

Simon's nerves were shot. He really wanted to sit down and cry, but he never let this side of his personality show to the PM; that would be political suicide. Even though he was gay, he always tried to be a "manly man" because, after all, the PM was really just a cowboy from Calgary.

"Yes, it got a bit ugly, but nothing I can't handle," Simon said. His voice cracked only once. "We've got to talk about COP and the Kyoto Accord. They want some big concessions, and that crowd is definitely not going to get any happier about it."

Simon started to recap the meeting with Phil Dubois and Tom McLaren at CanPetroleum. The Prime Minister pretended to listen, but turned his attention back to the window. Zain was now standing on top of a car holding a

*Patricia McConkey*

sign with a big red X through a picture of an oil company and shouting, "Give them what they deserve." In a way he envied Zain. His style of leadership was clear. He was free to say exactly what he felt. He was standing up for what he believed in. And in a way, he agreed with him, too.

"I'd like to tighten the screws on those damn oil companies, but they've got my balls in a vise," the PM said. "If I don't do exactly as they say, I'll be out in the street before you can say environmentalist."

The nagging pain in the Prime Minister's gut had started acting up again. It was the same old war being played out in his body: his conscience versus his job. The most pressing casualty in this war was a nasty ulcer brewing in his stomach.

The Premier pointed to the TV in the background.

"Simon, weren't you just there?"

The three men watched as cameras focused on burned equipment and a flurry of activity at CanPetroleum. Will was in most of the images, clearly in charge, giving orders for clean-up. The announcer made the point that but for Will Connors, who was able to mobilize his men and get the fire out quickly, the blaze could have been a massive tragedy. Will Connors, Fire Chief at CanPetroleum, was a hero.

The PM looked at Simon and asked, "Can you get me this guy's phone number? I want to call him personally."

Simon tried to contain his excitement and maintain some level of composure. Not so easy to do when the hairs on the back of your neck are standing up.

# Chapter 7

## May 2010

*D*ietrich lay on the king-size bed and ran his hands over the silk bedspread. Its softness brought back an old memory of the fateful night that started this whole insane journey. He remembered how he had sat outside the barn letting sand slip through his fingers and thinking it was as soft as silk. He smiled at his naïveté. That night seemed like a million years ago.

Now, lying in his luxury suite at one of the biggest hotels in Las Vegas, he went over the events that had led him to this point.

It was almost thirty-seven years since the night he and six other young men were rounded up and driven into the city. The driver had dropped them in front of an old hotel and handed them each an envelope as they filed out of the van. Inside each envelope was a sum of money and a slip of paper with the same sentence – the one task they were to fulfil.

Other than that, there were no directions or instructions on what to do next. The only thing their fathers had agreed on was that they must go and live in the modern world and become modern men. Only then would they have any hope of changing their situation.

The group of seven had spent a couple of days together trying to formulate a plan, but only one thing was clear. They had no idea how they were going to accomplish their monumental task. Each young man had such different ideas about what was needed. In the end, they all agreed that they must go their separate ways and make a name for themselves, each in a separate discipline. Perhaps someday they could combine these talents into some sort of team that would lead to the answer.

Now, Dr. Dietrich Schmidt, Head of Agricultural Sciences and Agrology, had summoned the group to meet – to tell them he had a plan to accomplish their goal.

Dr. Dietrich Schmidt, he repeated to himself. He sighed. He wished it could have been his real name, Dieter Ansgar, but he and the others had given up their real names the night they left the colony.

It seemed almost unreal to him that *he* was the one who had researched and developed an idea that could accomplish their task. He thought he was probably the least likely member, given the accomplishments of the others.

After all these years, the others had become successful in their respective fields, including one of the top Canadian Space Agency engineers, a VP of one of the world's leading media companies, a medical researcher specializing in viruses, a financial mastermind in the stock market, an oil executive, and an engineer in weapons development.

But Dietrich thought that success had gone to their heads – that they truly had become modern men, forgetting their roots. They had done little to reach the one true goal given to them so long ago.

His pulse quickened as he thought about announcing

his plan to the group. He knew their brilliant, critical minds would question every minute detail. He thumbed through his notes with sweaty hands. He would let the facts speak for themselves. He would show the others the years of research and convince them it was the ultimate solution.

Dietrich's heart skipped a beat when he heard the knock on the door. Adrenalin pumped through his fifty-four-year-old veins like never before. This would be his greatest achievement.

# Chapter 8

## September 2012

*Will* was jolted out of his utopia by a tremendous explosion. His neighbour's Hummer had exploded in the middle of their suburban street.

Against a backdrop of pastel houses with neatly manicured lawns, he could see his neighbour, completely covered in flames, struggling to get out of the vehicle. But the explosion had jammed the door.

Will's wife and daughter had been in the car behind the Hummer and were now in the street screaming hysterically at him to do something. He knew it was too late for Dr. Gentry. Nothing could save him now.

Will took a rake and smashed it into the driver's side window, breaking the window and accidentally hitting Dr. Gentry in the head. This was probably a blessing in the end.

He crawled toward the car, staying as low as possible, below the shooting flames. Using the wooden handle of the rake, he forcefully jerked the Hummer door open. When the door swung open, Dr. Gentry fell out onto the payment, still burning.

A bystander threw Will a heavy packing blanket, and he

tossed it over the burning body. He used the rake and some quick thinking to wrap Dr. Gentry in the blanket and drag him away from the burning vehicle.

Dr. Gentry's body was now covered, but the putrid smoke seeping from beneath showed that he was still smouldering. Will worked to extinguish the flames, then gingerly pulled back the blanket to reveal Henry's charred face and blackened teeth. Emma vomited, and then Lauren did, too.

As a professional firefighter, Will had seen all this before. However it was very disconcerting to have his wife and daughter at the scene, both hysterical. Although Will was a decorated fire chief, he certainly was not on top of his game at the moment. Smoking that joint just moments before didn't help either. The smell of charred flesh and vomit made Will's gut heave and his body shake.

He shook his head and tried to return to the take-charge hero he was earlier that same day. He turned his head and gulped in some fresh air. He then staggered a few feet from the body and fell to his hands and knees. Topmost of the thoughts racing through his mind was embarrassment at his behaviour. He needed to get control, of himself and the situation.

Lauren saw her husband struggling and at once went to give him support. She lovingly laid her hand on his back in a comforting gesture. Without thinking, in a state of confusion, Will's arm swung back and landed a full backhanded slap across her face. She screamed and fell flat on her back.

Will stared at her in disbelief. He had never meant to hit Lauren; it was a reflex action. He knew he should reach down and comfort her, but in his state of shock, he only stood and stared.

The confusion in his face looked like anger to his neighbours. They thought he might take another swing at her and

*Patricia McConkey*

within moments two men had jumped him and wrestled him to the ground. Will's screaming protests only made things look worse.

Will's father, George, had also been in the car with Lauren and Emma. He quickly came to Lauren and knelt beside her. He put his arms around her, and she hid her face in his coat and sobbed.

George cooed soothing words and tried to calm her down. He got her to her feet and supported her as they walked toward the house.

Emma had seen what had happened and was heading straight for her father screaming, "Stop hitting Mom. She didn't do anything to you. Quit hitting her!"

George managed to catch Emma by the wrist as she lunged toward her dad. He pulled her close as well. He understood she was just a scared little girl. He looked deep into her eyes and tried to transfer a sense of calm to her. He told her gently it was time to come home. Her rage turned to helplessness, then to surrender, and she melted into the arms of her grandfather.

With one arm around Lauren and one around Emma, George led the sobbing women into the house, away from the horror and drama in the street.

# Chapter 9

*After* Lauren and Emma were settled in the house, George stepped onto the front porch. He saw Will being questioned by the police. He started to head toward the group of men but Will stopped him with a hard glare.

George acknowledged his request and headed back into the house. After everything that happened, he preferred a moment to himself.

He walked through the back yard to his favourite retreat, the shed in the back corner. This was his secret hideaway. Will's house backed onto a cornfield, and it gave George great joy to watch the miracle of the growing process from his La-Z-Boy in the shed. His talented grandson Matt had cut a hole in the fence and installed a window in the shed so his grandfather could enjoy the view.

It was the perfect spot for George to watch the soil, the seeds, the sun, and rain and how they worked in such perfect harmony: one small part of God's handiwork here on earth.

George sat and watched the men and boys from the Jacob colony, an old-fashioned farming community, as they worked the fields. For many years they had used nothing but horses and hard work to grow their produce. Recently they had started using tractors and other farm machinery. George had come to appreciate the farmers' simple life-style, regardless of whether they used horses or tractors. He thought their family-based community was truly remark-able. He was saddened at how modern life had strayed so far from family values.

I shoulda been a farmer, he thought.

George took a deep breath and let his mind slip into that nowhere space – a place where he gained insight into events and an occasional glimpse of the future. George had always had this power, though he never spoke about it. His son already thought he was senile. Admitting to out-of-body experiences would be a one-way ticket to an old folks' home with doors that locked from the outside.

As George slipped deeper into meditation, he saw things that disturbed him. He saw the neighbour's car explode and the ensuing chaos earlier that day. He saw Will, Lauren, and Emma and how they were all affected by this event. He moved through time to see events in the future. He saw large numbers of people who were lost and suffering. He saw his own family sitting at a table, but with nothing to eat. One chair was empty.

George knew one family member had gone on to the next stage of this great adventure we call life. This didn't disturb him. He believed death was a natural transition and that there was great joy ahead. He continued his journey over the vast cornfields. Suddenly he knew why he was seeing this vision. He knew he had to complete his task while there was still time.

# Chapter 10

## June 2010

*T*he debate continued long into the night. A tinge of bright orange on the horizon was announcing daybreak when the last of Dietrich's colleagues left his suite.

Dietrich collapsed into a big leather recliner. What a night! The discussion had volleyed from the true purpose of their mission to the proposed solution and back again. Would his plan meet the lofty goal outlined so long ago? At times Dietrich had to step in to keep the debaters from making their points with their fists. But everyone agreed that his solution was the most powerful idea they had ever heard.

Dietrich was exhausted. The adrenalin rush of the evening had taken its toll on this university professor. He fell asleep in one of the big easy chairs.

At some point in the morning, he crawled over and got into the king-size bed. Embraced by its heavenly comfort, he slept well into the afternoon. When he came to, it was only because he was hungry. He ordered a sumptuous meal from room service and ate every crumb of it.

Dietrich tried to keep his mind off the details of the

night before. It was agreed that each member of the group would leave an envelope at the checkout desk for him. They would either pledge their support for Dietrich's project or reject it outright.

There was no point fretting about the outcome just yet. He would just have to wait. Ignoring the Las Vegas nightlife just outside his suite, he stayed in his room emptying the mini-bar fridge and watching old movies on the big-screen TV.

In the morning, he gathered his few belongings and headed to reception. As he approached the front desk, his heart began to beat faster and faster.

"Don't forget your messages," the clerk said, processing the last piece of paperwork. He handed him the six envelopes.

Dietrich got into a cab and told the driver to head to the airport; his flight left in about two hours. His hands were trembling so much he could barely hold the envelopes. He couldn't decide whether to open them now or wait for somewhere more private. He knew his life would change forever if the group wanted him to proceed. If they didn't, all his years of research would be in vain.

When the cabbie asked for the airline he was taking, Dietrich realized he'd been staring at the envelopes for some time. The cab had already almost reached the airport. The envelopes would have to wait.

Dietrich checked in at a kiosk and headed for the security line. His plan was to read the messages in the lounge for first-class passengers.

Dietrich stood in line watching the security staff scan each person and every item they had brought with them – bags, purses, briefcases, and shoes. It all seemed a bit ridiculous. If someone really wanted to smuggle something on board, they'd figure out a way around these relatively simple security procedures.

Every couple of minutes, he put his hand to his chest to see if the envelopes were still inside his jacket. His line was moving slower than any of the others. He wiped the sweat from his brow and breathed deeply. Finally, he was at the front of the line.

The security guard at the front of the line had been watching Dietrich for some time.

"Excuse me, sir, you'll have to step this way for a special screening."

"But I have to catch my flight," Dietrich said, glancing at his watch.

"That's not my concern, sir."

Dietrich opened his mouth and snapped it shut. Arguing would only make it worse.

"Take off your jacket, shoes, and belt, please, and place them in the tray."

Dietrich set his jacket in the plastic bin so the envelopes wouldn't fall out. He passed through the metal detector without a beep and stood waiting for his belongings.

The security guard asked if they could do a special test on his items.

Dietrich agreed.

"Can you step into this room?"

"Why?"

"We would like to ask you some questions."

Dietrich tried to compose himself. His constant fidgeting wasn't helping matters. He was sure he looked like someone with something to hide.

The security guards scrutinized his passport and searched his carry-on bag. They found nothing unusual in his bag and nothing suspicious in his answers. Still, they were reluctant to let him go.

*Patricia McConkey*

Dietrich looked at his watch for the thousandth time. The guards rummaged through his personal items and checked and rechecked their tests. Finally they said he was free to go.

Dietrich swore in German under his breath as he tried to repack his belongings. He hated things being messy but he didn't have time to put things back where they belonged.

He made it to the gate just seconds before the door to the plane was closed. He must have looked a sight. A flight attendant brought him some cold water as soon as he took his seat in the last row of the first-class section.

Once the plane was in the air, Dietrich opened each envelope with a pen, putting the pieces of linen-like paper into a neat pile. His hands shook as he began to tally the results: No, No, No, No, No, and Yes. He closed his eyes. Only *one* of the other six members had agreed with his plan. How could that be?

Was there a flaw in his plan? Did the others doubt his ability to carry it out?

No, the problem was brainwashing. His former companions had been seduced by the modern world. They had become entrenched in their hi-tech lifestyles. Like most North Americans, they thought jobs, money, cars, and the fast life equalled success.

Without their support, he didn't have the resources to put the plan in motion. His entire existence for over thirty years had been concentrated on the task of setting things right for his mother and sister, lost so many years ago. Now his life's work was being rejected – by a group of renegades drunk on the enemy's wine.

He looked out the window and imagined his body falling from the plane and splattering into a million pieces on impact.

# Chapter 11

*Kurt* Mulner was CEO of the largest brokerage firm in Canada. His life was focused on one thing: amassing wealth, both for himself and for others. And he had been very successful in his pursuits. His financial strategies, not for the faint of heart, had made him and many of his clients millionaires many times over.

One of his most successful tactics was investing in weaponry and military equipment. Kurt knew military conflicts around the world would never end. Governments would continue to spend billions every year on the newest and deadliest weaponry. He bought stocks in initial public offerings of start-up companies with a new type of weapon. He bought them for a song just before the companies landed lucrative government contracts.

Besides his own sixth sense, Kurt also had a secret weapon: a financial private detective. The detective used whatever means necessary to get the information he needed. This cloak and dagger stuff seemed to suit Kurt. With his slicked back hair and small close-set eyes, he looked like a slippery character himself.

Kurt was attracted to weaponry because he hoped to find something to use against the oil companies. He had always wanted to mount a full-out offensive attack against the refineries in the Edmonton region. But that would not only be suicidal, it would fail to accomplish what he was after. If the refineries were levelled, the oil monsters would use the rebuilding process to spread their tentacles farther and wider. But he enjoyed entertaining the fantasy every now and again.

Kurt's deep hatred for the oil companies dated back to his brother's death. Wilhelm was born with deformities and lung problems. He wasn't yet three years old when he died of pneumonia. Everyone in the colony knew the poison from the smokestacks of the refinery was to blame.

After his brother's death, every time Kurt saw the smokestacks just west of their fields, his anger grew. He remembered Wilhelm as a happy baby, gurgling and chattering, even though he was sick most of his life. Kurt used to carry him on long walks through the forest. Wilhelm laughed and pointed at all of nature's wonders. He loved ladybugs, puffballs, and the squirrels that bounced from tree to tree. Kurt didn't connect easily with people. Wilhelm was the exception.

To Kurt, Dietrich's plan seemed like a dream come true. He pictured the devastation as if he was watching an action movie. All the weapons he had considered were so obvious. Even some of the less traditional weapons, like chemical and biological warfare, were still too recognizable. Deploying any type of traditional weapon against an oil company would trigger alarms all over the world, and the offensive would be quashed in a matter of hours.

But Dietrich's scheme was far from traditional. It was both brilliant and insidious. It could be implemented over a long period of time without anyone suspecting. In addition, it could be deployed on a small scale or even globally.

The sky's the limit, Kurt thought.

He had decided, even before Dietrich had finished presenting, to fund the plan, whatever the cost. However, like most people he'd become accustomed to the conveniences of modern life. He had no intention of giving up his luxuries. That was for the rest of the world. Kurt already had a plan for how he would take care of himself.

Kurt was headed to the airport for an unscheduled trip to Edmonton. He couldn't wait to talk to Dietrich about moving forward with the plan. However, he also thought about his own future once the plan was implemented. He had already purchased a large plot of land for development purposes on a beautiful remote lake in northern Alberta. It cost him a bundle but was well worth it when you considered its little-known feature: a natural hot spring coming out the side of a rocky cliff.

Kurt had already started building an exclusive spa to feature medical and beauty treatments, exquisite cuisine, and a spiritual healing centre. He had intended to bill it as an eco-friendly spa for its many environmentally friendly technologies. To his mind the eco-friendly aspect was just another reason to charge exorbitant guest fees. It was also a perfect getaway for rich and famous celebrities because no paparazzi would ever find it.

But after hearing Dietrich's plan, he decided to make the property his own private retreat. The main building, which had almost been completed, would be his home. It would be self-sufficient through photovoltaic panels and micro turbines: eco-gadgets that would generate electricity for appliances, lighting, and anything else that would make his life easier.

*Patricia McConkey*

The hot spring had more than enough water to heat the building using in-floor heating; he could walk around in his shorts in the dead of winter if he chose to. The four hundred acres surrounding the spa would be his personal forest from which he could hunt and gather whatever he needed.

Kurt also planned a large greenhouse. It would be heated by the hot spring and supply him with fresh vegetables year round. In the summer, the large windows could be cranked open to allow natural ventilation. In the winter, banks of fluorescent lights would augment natural daylight and ensure optimum growing conditions. The greenhouse would also harbour a small beehive to pollinate the plants, and half a dozen or so large tanks of trout and perch to ensure a good supply of fresh fish.

He considered his ultimate one-time shopping list. One chance to get everything he would need – for the rest of his life. He'd buy staples like flour, sugar, and oats, in huge quantities and seal them in large plastic vats to last the rest of his lifetime. He would stock delicacies like chocolate, wine, and coffee, too. He planned to order a dozen parkas and pairs of winter boots in his size. Kurt couldn't wait to get started but there was one small problem: the other members of the group. They were horrified at Dietrich's plan. One or more of them would inform the authorities of the attack. Kurt had to talk to Dietrich as soon as possible.

"Is this seat taken?"

Dietrich just continued to look out the plane window.

"Old friend, you may be interested in what I have to say."

Dietrich's spine tingled. He turned to see Kurt sitting next to him. He couldn't even manage a simple hello.

"Well, we have a lot to talk about, you and I," Kurt said. "Since you seem to be lost for words, I'll start. I assume the votes from the other members were against?"

Dietrich nodded, still not knowing what to say.

"Well, that's a small hurdle," Kurt said. "It should be taken care of within the week. I've set the wheels in motion already."

He told Dietrich he had phoned his operative and arranged fatal "accidents" for the other five members of the group. He had done this sort of thing before. It would be looked after by his man.

Dietrich still couldn't summon any words.

"Now we need to talk about how much money you'll need for your new company," Kurt continued. "What was your estimate? Thirty-four million? Let's go over that number in more detail. I want to make sure you're well funded from the outset."

Dietrich could feel the blood rushing through his body. His prayers had been answered. Of course they were answered. He was, after all, a disciple of God. God must view his plan with favour. His brain and tongue finally reconnected.

"Kurt Mulner. *You* were the yes vote. I have the business plan in my briefcase. Let me ask the stewardess to get it from the compartment."

"While we're at it, I think we should have some champagne," Kurt said.

"What shall we toast to?" Dietrich asked, once they were settled in with document and drinks.

"Justice for your mama, Amara, and Wilhelm."

"Yes, we will toast to our lost family members, but also to the new order in the world."

"A great change is upon us," Kurt said, raising his glass. "You will herald in a new era. To Dietrich!"

# Chapter 12

*June 2010*

*D*ietrich sat in his office at the university fidgeting with office supplies. There was so much to think about, so much to do. Obviously, he would resign from the university but not before he had erased all traces of his experiments over the past thirty years. He listed the small tasks he'd need to complete before leaving. Just then his phone rang. He didn't recognize the number on the call display.

"Professor Schmidt speaking. Can I help you?"

"I need to talk to you right away. It's very important."

"Who is this?"

"It's Eric. I'm coming to Edmonton tomorrow. I want to meet with you."

It was more a command than a request.

Dietrich knew it was critical to talk to him, so he arranged a time and place. He also knew he had to talk to Kurt and find out what was happening with his plans. He rang him on his cell.

"Kurt, Eric just called and wants to meet me tomorrow. What's going on? I thought Eric would have been—"

Kurt cut him off.

"Eric hasn't been home yet and my guy hasn't been able to find him. You need to meet with him and find out what his plans are. See if he's contacted anyone about the plan. Most likely he'll try to kill you. Do you have a gun?"

"What? No, I don't have a gun. What do you mean he might try to kill me?"

"Well, think about it. If he kills you, there's no way for the plan to be implemented. You're the only one who knows how everything works. Listen, you probably shouldn't go home tonight. Go to a hotel and I'll call you later on your cell. I'll have someone come to your room and drop off a gun. Then go to the meeting tomorrow with Eric and do whatever's necessary."

Dietrich thought this all sounded a bit farfetched, but Kurt could be right. Dietrich's hand shook as he hung up the phone.

After a sleepless night and distracted day, Dietrich drove into the empty parking lot near the meeting place. No sign of Eric. It was almost eleven p.m. but still twilight. Red and orange streaks lingered in the western sky even though the sun had already dipped below the horizon. Dietrich walked down the trail toward the river, as agreed. He saw no one along the way. He sat on the bench.

The river valley was in full bloom with fresh green leaves and new growth everywhere, but Dietrich hardly noticed. His heart was pounding and his palms were sweating as he waited for Eric to arrive. He closed his eyes and prayed silently.

"Father, give me courage to do your will. Look into my heart and know what I am doing is for you and you alone." His meditative state was cut short by footsteps on the trail. It was Eric.

Eric's expression was cold. He sat down at the far end of the bench.

"How can you think that your idea is anything less than the complete extermination of the human race?" Eric said. "How many people do you think will die in this plan of yours? You make Hitler look like a schoolgirl."

"Don't you remember our task? This will achieve the goal we were given. Isn't that what we've been working toward for thirty years? Or have you forgotten? Maybe you're just too accustomed to living in the modern world and don't want to go back to the colony."

As Dietrich thought about the family he had not seen in over thirty years, his anger and confidence grew.

"And what is *your* line of work again, Eric? Oh yeah, building weapons. You're a weapons engineer for the government. Haven't you been creating killing machines all your life? How can you judge me?"

"Because I've never seen anything this powerful in my life. What I do is a small annoyance compared to what you're suggesting."

Eric continued on about how he felt the plan went well beyond the goal set out by the Elders.

Dietrich was only half listening; he was concentrating on his next move. From the sound of it, Eric was not going to sit by and let them implement the plan. Dietrich knew what he had to do.

When Eric sat down, he had placed his cell phone and keys on the bench between them. Dietrich snatched up Eric's keys and threw them into the forest behind them. The perfect diversion.

Eric exploded. Within seconds, he had punched Dietrich, thrown him to the ground, and kicked him in the guts. Dietrich curled up, praying for the torture to end. When Eric headed into the foliage to look for his keys, Dietrich pulled himself to a sitting position and reached into his pocket. He aimed and shot Eric in the back.

He went to where Eric was sprawled on the ground. Eric had a punctured lung and couldn't speak.

Looking down at Eric, Dietrich felt an unaccustomed sense of power. Eric's eyes were wide in panic. Dietrich squeezed the trigger again.

Now it was unanimous: there were no dissenters.

Dietrich dragged Eric by the feet to a hole he had prepared earlier in the day. He rolled Eric into it and covered his body with earth. He scattered rotting leaves from the previous fall over the freshly turned earth. Dietrich walked back to the river and threw the shovel in.

Then he sat on the bench to catch his breath for a few moments before heading up to his car.

"Beautiful evening," said an old man who was walking his terrier. "You'd better be careful, you never know who'll you meet on these old trails. Good thing I've got old Duke to protect me."

The old man chuckled as he gave the half-crippled dog a pat on the head.

Dietrich forced a smile. He hoped he looked calmer than he felt.

"Thanks for the warning."

The dog started to growl and headed into the bush in the direction of Eric's grave.

The old man hushed the dog.

"C'mon, now. It's just a squirrel or something."

Dietrich thought he was going to have a heart attack right then and there. He hadn't bargained on killing bystanders. But he would if he had to.

"I saw a weasel go in there not too long ago," he said. "You'd better call your dog back. They can be nasty."

After the old man left, Dietrich clutched his heart and tried to breathe. Yet, as he limped back to his car, he felt a strength he had never known before.

# Chapter *13*

## *November 2011*

*The* lab was in full production with over 150 employees working around the clock. Global Enviro Oil – GEO for short – was well on its way.

Dietrich stood in his office and smiled as he surveyed the production floor. The small seed of power planted in him seventeen months ago, the night he met Eric by the river, had taken root. Now he stood and surveyed his new kingdom. The quiet, introverted professor was gone. In his place was a confident man who ruled his kingdom with an iron fist.

Joe, the plant manager, came into the office.

"The UK shipment is ready to go," he said. "Is our warehouse there ready?"

"Yes, I spoke to them this morning. The sales force is in place and they're ready to receive product."

After reviewing a few more details with Joe, Dietrich dismissed him like a servant. He stood in front of his global map and thought about the launch of GEO. Canada, France, Germany, and Italy had fully stocked warehouses and sales agents ready to go. The UK would be in the same position once this order went out. China and Japan both had product but still needed a sales team.

Dietrich was sure the plan would fall into place shortly. The product was enroute to Russia and should arrive within the next week.

Of course, the US was a prime target, and those orders would be complete in about two weeks.

But the most important target was the OPEC nations. Dietrich had paid an obscene amount of money to see that the OPEC sales teams had the finest distribution system of all. They produced almost eighty percent of the world's oil reserves and they were key to his strategy.

Timing was everything. The global launch was set to go in about three weeks' time, on October 1, 2011. His experiments told him he could expect to see results in approximately nine to twelve months. He wanted to get as much product as possible in the field during the first nine months of the plan, before it reached the critical point. Each sales manager had a detailed schedule of how many sites must be covered each month. Generous bonuses were based on getting product into the field, incentive enough get sales mangers and agents moving quickly.

Dietrich smiled. He had worked hard here but soon he would walk out that door and never look back. At the beginning of August 2012, he would be home again, for the first time in thirty-nine years.

# Chapter *14*

*September 2012*

*W*ill sat in his office reviewing photographs from last week's fire. He was stumped. He had never seen anything like this. So far there were no indications that any accelerants were present. If this fire had been somebody's handiwork, he would have seen evidence of an accelerant or some sort of detonation device. But so far there was nothing: no evidence that anyone had planned this fire.

A movement caught Will's eye and he turned just as Tom McLaren, GM of the site, stepped into his office.

Will knew Tom wouldn't venture all the way to this part of the plant unless it was something serious.

"Will, I just got a call from Detective Meyers asking all kinds of questions about you," Tom said. "He wanted to know how well I knew your wife, and if she was having an affair. What the hell is going on?"

"The police think I may have had something to do with my neighbour's Hummer exploding – some love triangle thing. I was there last night answering all their stupid questions. It's nothing. It's just that it happened practically on my front lawn and I was the one to pull the burning body

*49*

out of the car. They just want to find some easy answer. They have no idea what the hell made that SUV explode."

"Do you need a lawyer? These guys sounded pretty serious."

"Naa. They're just fishing around. There's no connection, so I don't really give a shit. But while you're here, take a look at this. Here's something that does concern me."

Will gestured to the top of his desk, which was covered with photos and splices of pipe from the fire.

Tom wondered how Will would be so dismissive about a murder investigation but turned his attention to the fire.

"Do you know what caused it?" he asked.

"That's what I want to talk to you about, Tom. I'm stumped on this one. There's no evidence of foul play and there's no way employee error caused this one. I keep going over all the facts but can't find anything that leads to an answer. I'm going to need to do some extensive lab tests."

"Hold on there. What you really mean is expensive, not extensive."

"Tom, don't tell me you haven't seen the big picture in all of this? What would've happened if that fire had made it to the tank farm?"

Tom frowned, causing his thick Irish eyebrows to meet in the middle.

"I get it. Spend whatever you need. I'll see you get the money."

Charmaine, Will's assistant, poked her head around the corner.

"Mr. McLaren, Peggy is trying to get hold of you. She told me to tell you to charge your BlackBerry."

"Umph, thought it was awfully quiet today."

"Peggy says you need to call her right away."

"Use my phone, Tom," Will said. He dragged it out from under the photos on his desk.

Will stood up to leave to give him some privacy but Tom motioned him back.

"This won't take long. Peggy, what's up?"

"I am so glad I caught you. I thought you might've left for the airport already. There's something I think you should know."

"What? What happened?"

"A 737 just in from Toronto exploded on the runway. It was waiting to pull up to the gate, and it exploded – and it was full of passengers. I just heard it on the radio."

Tom's face went white and his knees buckled. Will pushed a chair behind him to stop him from falling.

The phone was on the floor, but Will could hear Peggy chattering on: something about one big mass of flames so they didn't expect any survivors. Will picked the phone up and told Peggy that Tom would call her back.

"I was about to go to the airport to meet my wife," Tom said. "She's coming in from Toronto."

He staggered to his feet and headed toward the door. Will ran after him.

"C'mon. My truck is parked right outside. I'll drive you."

# Chapter *15*

*W*ill broke every speed limit and traffic law on the way to the airport. Tom didn't seem to notice. He stared into space twisting the gold ring on the fourth finger of his left hand. Will knew how devoted Tom was to his wife and family.

"Tom, reach in the glove box and pull out that red light."

Tom did as requested. He held up a toy labelled Freddy Fireman and looked at Will.

"The kids gave it to me as a joke on my last birthday, but I'm getting the last laugh now. Turn it on and set it on the dash."

Tom found the switch on the bottom and set it on the dash. The red light flashed on and off and Freddy's fireman song played on the speaker. Will turned the radio up to drown out the annoying lyrics.

As they approached the next intersection, Will saw the traffic light turn red and said, "Hang on, we're going through."

Brakes squealed and tires skidded, but they made it. The familiar flashing blue and red lights appeared behind them and for a moment Will thought about ignoring them. Then he slowed down and started to pull over, but the police cruiser went whizzing past, motioning him to follow.

"Can you believe it? He's giving us an escort. Hang on."

The policeman assumed Will was another emergency worker heading to the airport. Will stayed about twenty feet back from the police cruiser, but went through every red light and stop sign. He tried to keep his exhilaration from showing.

The roads were jammed with cars. Everyone in the city seemed to be trying to get to the airport. Will kept a close eye on the officer and followed right behind him when he pulled off the road to take a short cut through a hay field.

About halfway through the field, the cruiser hit a soft spot, and mud started to fly. The officer tried to swerve out of the mud but ended up doing a one-eighty and now was headed straight at Will's truck. Will swerved left while the cruiser swerved right, right back into the mud and now up to its axles.

Will pulled up just to the left of the cruiser.

"If you're not trying to ram us, I'll give you a ride to the airport."

The officer jumped out of the cruiser and ran to the passenger side. Tom scooted into the middle of the seat to make room for him. Will snatched the Freddy Fireman siren and threw it in the back seat.

"I'm the Fire Chief at CanPetroleum," Will said. "They just paged me and told me to get to the airport as fast as I could because of the fire."

"I thought I recognized you; I just couldn't place where from. You were on TV. I saw you fighting that fire at the refinery."

As they drew closer to the airport, they could see the blaze clearly.

"What do you know about that?" Tom asked the officer, pointing to the fire. His voice cracked with strain.

"Not much. A plane just went up in a ball of fire. I'm here to help secure the area."

"My wife—"

"Ohhh—I see," the officer said. "Hey Fire Chief, turn here. We're goin' in the back way."

The officer pointed to a road leading to the back of the airport. Will stepped on the gas and headed toward a little road leading to the fence line.

"There's a gate; you'll have to stop to—"

But Will gunned the engine. "You might want to duck," he said, just before the crashing sound of metal against metal drowned out his voice.

Will pulled up to the back of the terminal. The three men jumped out and ran through a catering door and up the stairs to the main floor. People were screaming and scattering in all directions. Some were running to get away from the chaos while others were running toward the burning plane to look for survivors.

The officer joined a group of police trying to keep people away from the plane and directing them away from the area.

The plane was close enough to cause the terminal to go up in flames at any minute.

Tom thought his wife had mentioned something about gate thirty-nine. He yelled the number to Will and started running in that direction. Will followed.

They rounded a corner and there, in front of gate thirty-nine, was the plane, engulfed in a huge ball of flames. Tom fell to his knees.

"Shannon," he cried in a long, mournful moan. He crumpled to the floor.

Will saw a woman at the far end of the terminal swivel

around, looking for the man who cried out. He waved to get her attention. He hadn't seen Shannon in quite some time. He wasn't sure it was her.

The woman ran toward them.

"Tom, Tom! I'm here. I tried to call you to tell you I got an earlier flight, but I couldn't get through on your BlackBerry."

A moment later, Tom and Shannon were holding each other, sobbing "I love you, I love you" to each other.

Will was about to break up the joyful reunion and suggest they get back to the truck when a man tapped him on the shoulder. He swung around to see a man in a black suit and tie and wearing an earpiece. He was obviously security for someone.

"The Prime Minister of Canada would like to see you."

Will nearly made a smartass remark.

"The Prime Minister saw you running through the airport and asked if he could have a word with you."

"You take Shannon to the truck," Will said to Tom. "I'll be there soon."

"Shouldn't the Prime Minister be getting out of here?" Will asked, as he followed the black suit.

"We need to secure a route; right now traffic is tying up all the exits."

They continued through some security doors and passed half a dozen more guys with similar suits and earpieces. The security guide opened the door to a meeting room with a one-way glass window looking out onto the concourse and motioned Will in.

Simon held his hand out to greet Will.

"We met at the refinery last week when the fire broke out – Simon Bridgewater."

Will nodded and shook his hand, wondering if the man was nervous. He had extremely sweaty hands.

"As I am sure you know, this is the Honourable Stan Hartley, Prime Minister of Canada."

Will held out his hand.

"Will Connors."

"Yes, I know. I wanted to congratulate you on your work last week in getting the fire out at CanPetroleum. It could have been very serious had it not been for you and your team. Do you know what started the fire?"

"Well, nothing's definitive yet—"

Will thought they suspected a connection between the fire on the plane and the one at the refinery. He had no idea if the two were linked. And if you counted the Hummer, it was three fires. Could they all be related?

"I don't have any firm evidence yet, just some theories we are working on. Once I get the results back from the lab, I should have a better idea. If it's possible I'd like to get some data on this fire to rule out the possibility that they might be related."

"I think that would be a good idea," the PM said. "Simon, make sure Will gets all the information he needs. There could be some pretty serious implications if the fires are linked. Of course we have to keep a very tight lid on this. Can you assure me that you'll be the only one in your office with access to this information?"

The way the PM looked at Will reminded him of a keyed-up moment in a soap opera.

"Yes, of course."

Will knew this was serious business but fought to hold back a smirk. He always seemed to have inappropriate emotional responses.

"I may be in town for a little longer, so please get back to me as soon as possible. Thanks very much, and please keep this conversation to yourself."

"Absolutely."

Will shook the PM's hand and tried to look serious.

Simon handed Will his card and said he'd be in touch. Will avoided shaking his hand again.

When Will reached his truck, he found Tom and Shannon in the back seat doing a little more than the I'm-so-happy-to-see-you hug he saw earlier. He knocked on the window, his face averted. By the time he had got into the driver's seat, Tom and Shannon had adjusted their clothing. After a moment of awkward silence, the three of them looked at each other and burst out laughing.

"Will, the least you could have done for a lady is wait outside a minute longer," Shannon said.

"What do you mean, a minute longer?" Tom said. "He'd have been waiting out there for a couple of hours."

As Will drove out the back exit he saw a man with a suitcase walking through the field. He slowed down to give him a lift and was pleasantly surprised to find it was someone he knew.

"Keath – hop in."

Keath was equally surprised to see Will. He threw his bag in the back of the truck and joined them.

"Tom and Shannon, this is an old friend of mine, Keath Summers," Will said. "Keath, this is Tom McLaren, my boss, and his wife, Shannon."

Shannon looked a little embarrassed as she tried to make her hair presentable.

"Keath and I go hunting every year," Will said. "He has a great spot, way up north."

"I hope you're not planning on bringing that toy you had last year," Keath said.

"My crossbow? Of course. Someone's got to give the deer a fighting chance."

"Will usually tries to scare them to death by sending arrows over their heads."

"Where's the camp located?" Tom asked. "Maybe I could book it sometime. I love hunting."

"It's a private camp that's been in my family for over fifty years, so we don't rent it out to the public. It's a really beautiful spot. It's got about half a dozen cabins around a quiet lake. But it's so remote you'd never find it unless I took you in. Will's got himself lost a dozen times trying to get there. Maybe you could come up with him some time."

Will really didn't want to go hunting with his *boss*. He thought about giving Keath a look but decided against it.

"Hang on, folks," he said. "I'm going to cut across the median so we can make it home before dinner."

# Chapter *16*

*L*auren had the TV on in the kitchen as she made dinner. The news showed shot after shot of grieving families with the plane still smouldering in the background. The PM came on to declare he would personally see to it that whoever was responsible for the cowardly act would be caught and punished to the full extent of the law. He seemed to be at the same airport. Lauren thought she saw Will in the background of one of the shots, but dismissed it. He had no reason to be there.

George saw how distressed Lauren and Emma were over the news.

"You know," he said, "many people believe that transformation is always preceded by a great crisis. Maybe we're on the edge of a new social consciousness. Perhaps these troubles presage the birth of a new society."

George hoped this perspective would help them cope with the pain.

Emma was shaken and tearful. The disaster had triggered her own secret sorrow. She was trying to shake it off because it was next to impossible to keep secrets from George. A diversion seemed be the best tactic.

"Just think if Daddy was on that plane," she said. "In one moment your family is ripped away from you. Think of all the families grieving tonight."

George knew there was some other reason for Emma's reaction but couldn't pinpoint it. She had been moody for some time lately.

Before he had much time to think about it, Lauren had engaged him in a debate about how societies change after serious conflicts.

Emma was pleased. She needed a moment to collect her thoughts.

She had felt terrible ever since the night she'd been so stupid. Her parents didn't know she'd been dating Drew. She particularly didn't want her father to know, because she knew how critical he would be. No boy could ever be good enough for Daddy's little girl. So she let her parents think she had never had any serious boyfriends.

She was crazy about Drew. They had been dating about six months. It all went wrong the night she went to Anna's party alone because Drew couldn't make it. She'd been flirting with a cute guy, and he kissed her. She returned the kiss, and then stepped back, realizing she had gone too far. Unfortunately, Drew had arrived at the party just in time to see the kiss. He left immediately. Emma ran out after him but he was too upset to speak to her.

Now Drew wouldn't have anything to do with her. She had tried to apologize every way she knew how – text, e-mail, voicemail, Facebook, letters, and even the old fashioned way – in person. But he wasn't interested.

"Violence is never acceptable," Lauren was saying to George. "There are always other ways to get your point across. Anyway, we have no idea if this was a terrorist act or just some weird accident. I've been watching the news and no one seems to know what caused the explosion."

*Patricia McConkey*

"Well, it *could* be some freak accident," Emma said, "but when you combine it with the Hummer explosion and the plant fire, maybe there is something bigger going on here. We still haven't heard what caused Dr. Gentry's Hummer to explode. The police seem to think Dad had something to do with it."

"You know that's nonsense, don't you, Emma?"

"Yes, Mom, I know—"

"We know your father had nothing to do with that," George said. "But think of it: maybe we're at the beginning of something bigger, something that'll cause us to rethink everything in our day-to-day lives. Remember, the world wars were ultimately brought on by unrest in the greater social consciousness."

"What are you trying to say, George?" Laura said. "Do you think there's going to be more violence? Who's doing all this? Do you think this is the beginning of another world war?"

Lauren couldn't tolerate violence of any kind. Ironically, just the thought of it made her seriously angry.

George looked away and tried to think what to say. He knew the violence was going to get worse. He wanted Lauren and Emma to be prepared.

"This just in from our news correspondent in the UK," the TV announcer was saying. "It appears that a similar explosion has just occurred in London, England. A petrol station on a busy, inner-city street suddenly went up in flames, igniting the underground tanks and causing a massive explosion. The death toll is in the hundreds. Firefighters at the scene are trying to quench secondary fires in the adjacent buildings.

"No one knows if this incident in London and the tragedy at Edmonton Airport are related. No one has claimed responsibility for either event. And we continue to report on the breaking news in Texas, where a serious explosion has just been reported at a refinery."

George got up and switched off the TV.

"Let's just concentrate on dinner in our own little kitchen, OK?" he said.

Lauren was an amazing cook. She combined her Indian and Moroccan culinary roots to unique advantage. George peeked into her favourite tagine and saw a beautiful crimson-coloured beef stew cooked with figs and spicy red wine. A mixture of curried vegetables was sizzling away in a pan next to a covered pot. He was about to lift the lid when Lauren shrieked at him.

"Don't touch that! It's wild rice and needs to cook a little more. If you take the lid off it now, it'll be sticky. George, how about you and Emma set the table while I finish here?"

George quickly took her up on her offer.

"Mom, who's coming for dinner? It looks like a feast," Emma said.

She was hoping she wouldn't have to put on a smiling face for guests. She just wanted to go to her room to mope over Drew.

"Do I need a reason to cook a lovely dinner for my family? I'm going to be very busy with the global tele-conference and I just wanted to have a nice dinner with everyone here. Matt promised he'd be home, and your dad should be here soon."

Right on cue, Finn ran to the door leading to the garage and barked.

"Finni, cut it out," Matt said, pushing the tail-wagging, slobbery animal off him.

"Hi, Mom. I'm just going to grab something out of my bedroom and I'll be up in a minute."

Moments later Will came through the front door. He paused to take in the amazing smells of ginger and curry. Whatever it was, it smelled superb.

He surveyed the domestic scene before him. The recent events made him feel very grateful his family was safe.

Matt came bounding up the stairs, two at a time, and ran right into him. Will caught him in his arms at the top of the stairs, as close as they had been to a hug in a long time.

Lauren smiled at seeing her two men connect, even if it was just by chance.

"Hey, long time no see, Matt. How you doin'?" Will said in his best homeboy accent.

Matt snorted a laugh.

"Good," he said, heading toward the kitchen.

"What's for dinner, Mom? It smells crazy."

Lauren shook her head and smiled as she gave her tall, gangly son a squeeze.

"I guess that's a compliment," she said. "Well, the menu tonight includes Moroccan stew, wild rice, curried veggies, and a special treat for you, Will – samosas."

"Who's coming?" Will and Matt said in unison. Everyone laughed.

"You guys are terrible. I'm making this dinner just because I love you all, no other reason. Now all of you, go wash up before dinner! You have about fifteen minutes. Will, you smell like smoky airplane fuel."

Will rolled his eyes. How could she have known he was at the airport? He could never, ever, have an affair. His wife had the best nose ever and would smell another woman's perfume a mile away. He wanted to use her for hunting, but she was insulted whenever he suggested it.

When they were finally sitting around the table, George started in on saying grace.

"We are eternally grateful for our many, many blessings, including the family we have gathered at the table tonight. Please send a guardian angel to watch over each one as we move through these difficult times, and please send a special guardian to watch over Will. We need him so much and want him to stay safe."

Then, after a pause, and to stifled laughter, he said, "And may the best man win. Amen."

Sometimes Will thought George had an uncanny insight into life, but most of the time he wondered if he was going senile. When Will thought about the unusual connection between him and his father, he often questioned his own sanity. But he was absolutely not going to say anything about that to anyone. *That* would be crazy.

The family chattered about inconsequential matters over the clinking of china and Will tossed a hunk of meat to Finn. Lauren looked radiant. She loved having her family around her and things going well. When Will gave her a seductive look, she sent one back that said, not now, but try me later.

Will remembered the faces of the grieving parents and spouses at the airport. He couldn't bear the thought of losing a member of his family. He made a mental resolution to change his attitude, to put things right with everyone in his family, including Matt. That relationship would take the most work, but it was something he really wanted.

Just as they were scraping their plates clean there was a loud click and a squelching sound as all the power went off. The candles on the table were the only source of light in the whole house.

"Matt, get a few more candles from that shelf behind you," Will said. "The rest of you stay put for a minute. I'm going to check to see how far the outage extends."

Will scanned the neighbourhood from the front porch. No lights for as far as he could see. Not a good sign. He headed back to the dining room.

"Hey guys, stay right where you are. I have a surprise for you. I hope you saved room for dessert?"

He went to the freezer and pulled out three flavours of ice cream.

"Your mother made an absolutely fantastic meal, but it looks like the power is going to be out for a while so we don't want all this good stuff to go to waste. No one is leaving this table until every bit of ice cream is gone."

He looked around for some more toppings and found bananas, frozen raspberries, strawberry jam, chocolate chips, marshmallows, and peanuts.

"Here's the challenge: I'll give twenty bucks to the creator of the most delicious sundae."

With money on the line, both Emma and Matt rummaged through the cupboards to add a few extra ingredients.

By candlelight they all made the biggest, gooiest sundaes ever concocted. George was declared judge of the competition. He went around the table and took a spoonful out of each bowl, but when he got to Matt's he had second thoughts.

"Matt, you know I love you, but I'm not sure if I want to try *that*."

George was referring to the sardines that Matt had smothered in chocolate sauce and peanuts.

"C'mon, Grandpa, you have to."

George reluctantly took a bite.

"Hey, not as bad as I thought," he said. "Sweet and salty."

Looking out the dining room window, Will saw it. A large red glow on the horizon. It wasn't the sunset. It had to be the power plant. His father's words came back to him. A blaze that big would need every fire fighter in three counties.

Just then his pager went off.

The family was debating the merits of originality versus taste, trying to determine who won.

"I have to go help with a fire at the power plant. It's a big one, so don't expect me back any time soon."

Will put his arms around Lauren and held her close. He wanted to say so much in that one moment but knew this embrace was all he could manage right now. He slipped his hand under her hair and cradled the back of her head. He thought about all the times he had been a sorry excuse for a husband and wished he could make up for it in this one moment.

"Save my spot," he whispered.

She nodded with understanding as tears welled in her eyes. It was their own special line they had used throughout the years when tough situations arose.

# *Chapter* 17

*Will* arrived at the outer fence line of the power plant. There were no words for what he felt in his heart.

The power plant was fuelled by coal, and there were large piles of coal surrounding the plant to be processed into coal dust for feeding the boilers. It looked as if the initial explosion was so powerful that the entire plant went up at once and then the heat of the blast ignited the reserve coal piles.

Nothing could be done. The fire trucks were lined up in rows about a kilometre from the actual blaze because they couldn't get any closer due to the extreme heat. Dozens of firemen stood idly by as the structure was engulfed in flames.

Will turned and headed back toward his truck. He wasn't needed. He was surprised to hear someone call his name.

"Will, I had you paged. You have to come and see this. Get in."

It was Rick Sandhurst, Chief Fire Inspector for the county.

Will jumped into Rick's truck and they drove around to the back of the plant.

"This was one of the first trucks on-site. Everyone thought it went up because it got hit with a heat blast from the coal fires. I would've thought that, too, but I saw it firsthand."

Will couldn't see what Rick was talking about. There were half a dozen ambulances and coroner's vehicles on the site.

"I told them to wait until I could do a preliminary investigation before touching any of the bodies. That's why I need to talk to you. I hear you may know something about this type of fire from the refinery incident."

The two men got out of the truck and pushed their way through the crowd of emergency workers.

Will's face went blank when he saw it. Directly in front of them was a fire truck that looked as if it had been incinerated. Charred bodies were only a few feet from the truck. They must have had only a second or two before they were overcome by the flames. Will knelt down beside one of the bodies. He looked into the victim's face and the first thought that came to his mind was Dr. Gentry, the dentist who had burned up in front of his house. Anger surged through him as he remembered he was the prime suspect in that murder investigation.

"I was following them in my truck, about a kilometre behind," Rick said. "There was no warning, no sign of anything out of the ordinary. The truck just exploded into a huge ball of flames. They never had a chance. The flame was too intense. I couldn't even get close. I think they were dead within seconds. I've never seen anything like it in my life."

"Unfortunately, I have," Will said. "There was an incident with a man in a Hummer right in front of my house. Same type of thing. It just went up in flames like a rocket."

"I know I'm not supposed to talk about this with you," Rick said, "but aren't you a suspect in that death?"

"Shit – only because it happened practically on my front lawn. The fire crew knew right away there was something odd about the explosion. Because I'm a fire expert they think I had something to do with it. If it had happened in your neighbourhood, they'd be lookin' at you instead of me. You saw it for yourself – no warning, no explanation, just a huge explosion."

Rick waved at the forensic team to start processing the bodies. Ten bodies, with no survivors, meant a lot of paperwork. And that was just for this one incident. No telling how many bodies they'd find once the fire died down, but it had to be over one hundred. That is if they found bodies. The fire was so hot there'd be very little left of most of the victims.

Will told Rick about some of the tests he was running on the fire at the refinery. Rick agreed to run the same analysis to see if there was anything to connect the incidents. They were discussing how to coordinate transferring data between their departments when Rick paused in mid sentence.

"Do you think this is the end of these fires?"

Will looked down to avoid eye contact.

"I think it's just the beginning," he said.

# Chapter *18*

*J*ust then a police cruiser pulling up to the site exploded. Firemen, police, and emergency medical people stood by helplessly as the two constables burned alive. There was no way to get them out. Some of the men – tough, experienced men who had seen their share of horrific fire-related deaths – fell to their knees and cried.

A hysterical police constable ran to the scene and shouted that two more cruisers had just met with the same fate.

"It's the end of the world; it's the apocalypse!"

"You might want to walk home from here," Will said to Rick. "I'm going to take my chances. I'm driving my truck home, but after tonight I'm parking it. I don't trust it anymore."

Rick nodded. He looked stunned.

"Rick, I'm going to get all the info I have at my office from the plant fire and plane explosion and I'll bike it over to your house tomorrow. We're going to put all the pieces together and figure out what the hell is going on."

Again Rick nodded, as if in a trance. Will could see he

had tears in his eyes. He clamped his own emotions firmly down and left as quickly as he came.

Crises brought out the best in Will. He was thinking clearly and logically despite the chaos around him. He jumped in his truck and started speeding home. He was starting to think of the ripple effects. With the power plant burning like a meteor, it was obvious the power could be out for some time. Whoever or whatever was behind this, they had probably targeted other utility sites. It was anyone's guess what would be next. He had to think ahead.

He thought about the water supply. Water was pumped in from the river and purified in the water treatment plant. But their emergency power supply would last only a couple of days. After the water treatment plant stops processing, water would still flow to houses from the fourteen reservoirs around the city, but again there was only about a forty-eight-hour supply. Fresh water would soon be a priority.

And the sewers – they'd be the next problem. All the sewers flow by gravity to a lift station. Under normal circumstances, the pumps in the lift station pump the sewage uphill to another set of pipes where it flows by gravity until it reaches the next lift station and so on until it reaches the wastewater treatment plant. Of course the plant wouldn't be processing anything without power, and the lift stations would fill up very quickly. Sewage would start backing up into people's basements. Without sanitation and fresh water, things are going to get pretty bad.

With no water or sewers, people are going to want to get out and go somewhere else – but with no power, there'll be no communication. How will they know where to go?

A better question was how they would get there. Every vehicle seemed to be a ticking time bomb.

And what about other cities? Without communication

it would be impossible to tell if this was happening only in Edmonton or if other places were experiencing the same hell. Will swallowed hard, but the lump in his throat wouldn't go away.

He thought about his family. How would they survive? That was his first priority. There, on his right, was his first stop: Super Supermarket, the largest grocery store in the area.

It was late and the parking lot was empty. The employees had probably been sent home due to the power outage. He paused and looked at the scene.

He had been in many life and death situations and fear was not part of his personality. Any time he had felt a twinge of something that might be fear, he quickly pushed it out of his mind and dived right in. But now, in the parking lot of Super Supermarket, fear gripped him. His thoughts had led him to some life-altering conclusions. This thing that was happening was for real. How was his family going to get through this? He didn't fear for himself, but the fear of not being able to provide the basics – food and water – for his family was more than he could bear.

He gripped the steering wheel, stepped on the gas, and drove straight through the front doors of the store. The sound of breaking glass and twisting metal cut through the quiet night air like a knife. Will pushed his way out of the truck and grabbed a cart.

He headed down aisle six: canned foods.

Normally the police would be here in a couple of minutes, but Will knew better. There was no power to the alarm system so there would be no signal to alert them. Plus they'd be afraid to get in their cars. Three police cars had just blown up. The entire police force must be thinking about how they could do their jobs without using cars. After tonight, they might be off duty permanently.

He loaded the cart to the brim with canned meats and vegetables, dumped this load in the box of his truck, and went back for a load of bottled water. He made five or six trips before his truck was filled and he thought he should move on. As he got in his truck, he remembered another important necessity. He went in and took a display of chocolate bars for Lauren and threw it in the back. She loved chocolate and he knew he would need to mend some fences. He backed out almost as quickly as he pulled in and headed home.

Will opened the garage door and backed the truck in. He took a shovel and started shovelling the cans of food out of the truck onto the floor. The noise of the cans hitting the cement floor was like the sound of a small pellet gun popping tin cans off a fence. It only took a couple of bangs before Lauren was standing in the doorway in her housecoat, looking at him as if he'd lost his mind. He did look like a madman shovelling food into the garage in the middle of the night.

Will went over to Lauren and put his hands on her shoulders. He didn't know what to say. He wanted Lauren to comfort him, to hold him and tell him that everything would be all right, but he was afraid to let his emotions show because he might lose control. He knew that his fear about the future would come out full force and he would crumple to the floor like a baby. Although his head was swimming with emotions, all he could manage to show was anger. His hands gripped her so tightly that her face grimaced with pain.

"Don't question me on this, Lauren," he growled. "I'm going to unload the food and I want you and the kids to carry it into the basement storage room. Do it! Now! Before morning! I have to go back out."

He went back to shovelling, barely glancing at her. She looked at him and knew that whatever reason he had for doing this, it must be important.

She had never seen him like this before. She thought there was fear in his voice, something she had not heard for a long time. When Matt was only four, he got badly hurt in a tobogganing accident. She had phoned Will at work and told him to meet them at the emergency room. Before she had time to explain, Will's voice was trembling with fear.

Matt needed several stitches in his hand, but was otherwise OK. That was the last time she remembered hearing fear in Will's voice. She was sure she heard it again tonight. Instead of questioning him, she nodded and got the kids. Will finished shovelling the food out of the truck and pulled away. He headed for Hunter's Haven.

Will thought about the coming food shortage. He needed to stock up on arrows because they could be reused, and secondly he needed to get a handgun. A gun would be a necessity if his assumptions were correct. Breaking into the Hunter's Haven store would be a little more challenging. It was on the second floor of an old building, and the only door was heavily armoured to deter thieves.

Will went to the back of the building and eyed the fire escape, about thirteen feet off the ground. He parked the truck right under it and by standing on the hood was able to jump to the bottom rung. His rigorous physical training came in handy as he pulled himself up the ladder with only his arms. He finally got far enough up the ladder to get a foothold and climbed parallel to the office window. He wrapped his jacket over his hands and face and leapt through the glass. He got away with only a few minor cuts to his shoulder.

Once inside, he found everything he needed: lots of

*Patricia McConkey*

arrows that would work with his style of bow and some night vision goggles. He went to the case that held the handguns. He decided the best gun would be the one with the most ammunition. He found three cases of nine millimetre bullets for a Smith and Wesson, so that was the obvious choice.

He picked up the Smith and Wesson and held it in his hands. It was cold and heavy. He used both hands to steady his aim as he squeezed the trigger. Click. He didn't like the picture in his head as he imagined the first time he would have to use it.

Just then the bolts on the door began to click: someone was coming in. He hid behind the counter. He heard a jingle of keys and a click as each lock was turned. The door opened and a flashlight beamed around the room. Will looked under the cabinet. He would have recognized those ugly blue rubber clogs anywhere. Why the hell would a guy wear Crocs? Besides being ugly, they were kinda girly. Will knew it had to be John, the owner.

"John, it's me Wi—"

"What the f---?"

There was a heavy thump.

"John? John – relax, man. It's Will Connors. It's OK … John?"

Will gingerly peeped over the counter and saw John lying on the floor.

"Shit."

He jumped the counter and bent over John. Will checked his vital signs and laughed in relief. John had fainted. Will gently slapped his face.

"John – wake up, buddy."

"Will, am I glad to see you. Somebody broke into my store and I walked in on them. I tried to fight them, but there were too many of them."

"You sure about that?"

"Well, no, I don't really know what happened after they hit me in the head—"

"John, *I* broke in. You fainted."

John looked a little embarrassed, but soon was back to normal.

"What the hell are you doing breaking into my store?"

"John, look, I'll pay for everything I'm taking, but there is some bad stuff happening, and I'm not just talking about the power outage. Listen, you need to take all your ammo and hide in your basement. Stock up on as much canned food and bottled water as you can find. I'm serious about this. The stores won't open because they don't have power, so just break in and take what you need. Do it. The police won't bother you."

"Are you crazy, man?"

"I can't explain everything right now, but I'll check back with you in a couple of days."

Will stuffed everything in a large plastic bag and headed out the main entrance – which was much quicker than going through a second-story window.

"Hey, charge me full price for everything," he said. He ran down the stairs. He chuckled because he knew nothing would go through on his credit card without power.

John yelled back, "Full price? OK, now I *know* you've lost your mind."

*Patricia McConkey*

# Chapter 19

*I*t was early morning before Will crawled into bed. Lauren was just getting ready for work.

"Lauren, you don't have to go to work today. Come back to bed."

She raised an eyebrow and said, "I've heard that one before. You know, I wasn't born yesterday."

Will could barely move, he was so tired, but he wanted the comfort, the closeness.

"Lauren, I'm serious. There's no power and it won't come back on for some time. You won't even be able to get into the building. The power locks and security systems will all be shut down."

She sat on the edge of the bed and picked up the phone. It was dead, too.

"There's no one to call anyway. No one's at work," Will said. He pulled the covers back. "They're all taking the day off, too."

He wrapped his arms around her waist and pulled her backward, close to his aching body. He put his face into the deep brown curls of her hair and breathed deeply. He wanted to take in the smell of her and everything that was good. He reached up to gently touch her face and saw that his hands were trembling. He pulled his right hand back, balled it into a fist, and shook it in anger. He fought to keep all the emotions from flooding into the present moment.

Lauren noticed the hesitation. She flipped over and looked into his face. Will was avoiding her gaze, so she firmly gripped his face with both hands.

"Don't you do this to me. Don't retreat to that nowhere land you go to when things get tough."

Will opened his mouth to explain what he was feeling, but the words wouldn't come out. He breathed deeply; he knew she wasn't going to let him out of this. He couldn't come up with anything that didn't sound totally insane. Mostly he was afraid that he couldn't protect his family from the coming madness. A single tear ran down his cheek.

Lauren looked at Will and her heart ached for him. She had so many questions and was honestly ready to choke him for all the craziness during the night, but she put those feelings aside for the moment. She loved him deeply and had felt him slipping away from her for months. Instead of complaining about all the things that had been building up, for now she just tried to ease his burden and give him the comfort he desired.

She rolled on top of him and pinned his arms against the bed.

"Now you look here, William Michael Connors," she said, sitting up and pulling her t-shirt off. "I am going to have to torture you until you talk."

She bent her knees on either side of his chest. Her breasts dangled just above his face

Lauren smiled as she leaned down and kissed his neck and then started moving down his chest. She ran her hands down his sides to the small of his back and easily slipped her hands underneath him. He groaned in pure pleasure as she kissed her way down his body. She sat up playfully and turned on the radio. Thank God for batteries.

"Try to keep your squealing down to a minimum, will you?" she said. "You sound like a girl."

When their passion was spent, Lauren lay exhausted on top of Will, their midsections glued together with sweat. As she lifted her torso, it peeled back like a candy wrapper from a piece of sticky toffee. For a short while, neither of them thought about what was happening in the world around them. Lauren lightly stoked Will's chest and let her fingertip circle his nipple. Even though they were both exhausted, his nipple rose in response to her touch.

Will mumbled something, but Lauren couldn't understand what he said. She pulled herself up on one elbow and was about to ask him to repeat himself, but he was already asleep. She envied how quickly Will could drift off. They could be lying in bed having a conversation and he would literally fall asleep in the middle of a sentence. She put her head down again on his chest and lay there thinking about the future. She didn't know what was happening, but she knew it was going to change their lives.

Finally she went down to the kitchen and opened the fridge. It was already room temperature.

She started to unload everything onto the counter: milk, eggs, chicken, bacon, and lots of leftovers. She began to plan how to preserve the majority of the food. Luckily she had a gas stove and it was still working. She turned on the oven and got working on the chicken breasts. She'd bake them. They could be sliced and used for sandwiches. She put the bacon onto a broiler pan, which she put in the oven with the chicken.

Next she thought about breakfast. The kids would sleep late because they were both up late last night carrying food into the basement, but they'd be hungry when they got up. She looked at the milk and eggs and thought that a big batch of pancakes would be just what the doctor ordered. To make it extra special, she threw chocolate chips and raspberries into the batter. She was still busy cooking when she saw Will coming down the stairs.

"Where do you think you're going? You've been asleep less than two hours."

Although it was cool fall weather, Will was dressed in bike shorts and a t-shirt.

"Don't tell me you're going on one of your crazy long-distance rides," Lauren said with a frown. "Do I need to kick your butt to get you back to bed?"

"Can't. Got to get stuff from the office and meet with the Chief Fire Inspector. We need to figure out what's happening."

Lauren knew it was pointless to argue with him. She put a heaping stack of pancakes and some bacon on a plate and set it on the table.

"Well, at least eat before you go."

As they sat at the table, Lauren thought about how to frame her first question. She needed Will to talk, but she had to be strategic. The wrong approach and he would close up like a clam and run off on his bike.

A sixth sense exists between a husband and wife after they've been together for many years. Will knew Lauren was going to start asking questions. He took a deep breath and thought about what to say. He didn't even know what was happening; all he had were strong suspicions that it was going to get a lot worse before it got better.

"Lauren, about last night ..."

*Patricia McConkey*

Before he could finish his sentence, there was a knock at the door.

Finn went into his usual fit of barking. Will's heart missed a beat. He wondered why he was so alarmed. It could be anybody. It could be the Girl Guides for all he knew. But some gut feeling told him it was more than that.

Pushing Lauren in the direction of the bathroom, Will said, "Get in and lock the door. Don't ask why."

Lauren groaned as she nearly fell. Will ducked out of the room and was at the front door before she had a chance to argue.

Will looked through the peephole and couldn't believe who was standing there. His anger, fear, and rage boiled into a deadly combination as he unbolted the lock and swung the door open. He swiped the man's feet out from under him, got on top of him, and put his forearm across his throat.

"Give me one good reason not to kill you right now," Will said.

Zain Bedow had trouble catching his breath.

"No, you've got the wrong idea. I had nothing to do with this. Let me explain ..."

Zain was the leader of the Green Movement, a radical group of protesters that fought with the oil companies, trying to force them to take responsibility for their environmental nightmares.

Will had been trying to piece together how this craziness started and one of his prime suspects was Zain and his merry band of followers. They had been suspected of some pretty big ecoterrorist activities, but so far nothing had been proven. When Will saw him standing on his porch, he didn't really stop to think why he was there – just that it was an opportunity to mete out justice on a guy who deserved it.

Zain managed to get free of Will's grip and jumped to his feet. He landed a blow square to Will's jaw. Will went tumbling backward down the porch stairs. He had the sense to roll into a ball and straighten up at the last moment. He landed on his feet and pulled a handgun from the back of his shorts and aimed it at squarely at Zain.

Zain recognized the look in Will's eyes. It was the look of a man on the edge. It was the look of someone who was capable of anything. He took a step back and held his hands up in surrender.

"You've got the wrong guy. I came here to ask you if you knew what the *hell* was going on."

Will's hands were shaking when his thumb cocked the gun. A bead of sweat rolled down his forehead. In the many years Zain had been in this dangerous line of work, he had never felt like he could see the end of his life until now.

"No, really, it's not what you—"

"Will, what the hell are you doing?" Lauren yelled as she stepped onto the front porch, in front of Zain. "Put that gun down!"

Her voice was strong and determined, barely covering the deep fear behind it. Will looked like he was thinking about his options, but then he lowered the gun.

Zain took another look at Will and thought he better explain himself fast.

"I came because I heard you've done some research on the refinery fire. I suspect that fire was just the first of all the rest of this mayhem. If all the fires are linked, then maybe there's a way to stop them. My group has nothing to do with this. I'm sure of that. But I do have information that could lead us to the guys responsible."

Lauren now recognized him. She had seen news reports implicating him in a few drilling accidents on a nearby wildlife sanctuary. At the time she thought it was wrong for the government to issue drilling rights on the sanctuary, but she also knew that two men died in the explosion. While it was clear that whoever set the explosives was trying to protect wildlife, not hurt workers, the outcome had turned out significantly different.

Lauren looked at Zain again and tried to let her spirit guide her. Whatever his past guilt or innocence, she got the feeling he was being truthful now.

"Mr. Bedow, please come in. I'd like to hear more about your thoughts on these fires."

Here's a man who was mere seconds away from shooting me, and now his wife is inviting me in, Zain thought. He might as well see where this led him.

"Sure, if it's all right with your husband."

Will glared at Lauren, and she sent him a look back. Will nodded.

"It smells heavenly in here."

Zain closed his eyes and breathed deeply through his nose, partially for effect but mostly because it did smell great. He was as charming as he was good-looking.

"Well, if you would like some breakfast while we talk, it's already prepared," Lauren said in her best hostess voice.

Will looked as if his head might pop off.

"Mr. Bedow, please have a seat here for a moment while I have a word with my husband."

Zain walked around the kitchen table and sat with his back against the wall, just in case. If Will was going to change his mind about shooting him, he wanted to see it coming.

Lauren pulled Will out of earshot. She squeezed his forearm as hard as she could and leaned into him with her lips touching his ear.

"Your crazy behaviour is going to get someone killed, so just listen to me for one second. Have you ever heard the saying, 'Keep your friends close and your enemies closer'? Well, that's what we're doing. We need to find out what he knows about these fires. Suck it up and keep your mouth shut, unless you have something helpful to say."

When she let go, there were four little drops of blood on Will's forearm.

Lauren returned to the kitchen with Will in tow and held out her hand.

"Mr. Bedow, we haven't been formally introduced. I am Lauren Connors, Will's wife. And of course you obviously know Will."

Zain shook her hand and held it slightly longer than necessary. His firm, soft hands and handsome, crooked smile caught Lauren off guard. Flirting with the enemy took on new meaning when the enemy was a man as handsome as Zain, especially when, only moments ago, your husband was about to kill him. She knew a man like Zain must be used to flirting with danger, and sensed that he enjoyed it. It was a perilous situation – a crazy husband and a handsome, flirtatious terrorist. Lauren silently said a short prayer that no one would get killed in her kitchen that morning.

Gently releasing her hand, Zain smiled seductively and said, "I know we've just met but it feels like we've lived a lifetime in the past five minutes."

Lauren knew exactly what he was talking about. Stepping between your insane gun-toting husband and his would-be victim would count as a memorable moment in any lifetime.

"And actually, I've never met your husband. I only know him by his outstanding reputation."

"Zain, would you like some raspberry chocolate pancakes and bacon?"

Will glowered at Lauren. Food would soon be a precious resource. Feeding an ecoterrorist breakfast didn't count as a wise use of a scarce commodity.

Lauren knew it didn't matter whether you were talking to a farmer or the Queen of England. Food was a sure way to set a relaxing atmosphere and get people to open up.

"Absolutely, who could say no to that?"

Will's frustration made the prospect of breakfast all the more enjoyable for Zain.

"Will, you'll have time to finish your breakfast, too," Lauren said.

Maybe a full mouth will keep you from doing more damage was what she was really thinking.

Lauren piled a plate with pancakes and bacon and set it down in front of Zain.

"Sorry, there's no coffee. Of course with the coffee maker on holiday, we'll just have to make do with some room-temperature milk. As you can see, I'm trying to cook everything in the refrigerator to keep it from going bad."

She put a mason jar of maple syrup on the table.

"This is from my hometown in Ontario. Real maple syrup. Kind of a rarity these days."

Will took the bottle and swirled a modest amount over his pancakes. Zain took the jar and smothered everything on his plate.

No matter how old they get, boys will be boys, Lauren thought. They still had to have their stupid little pissing matches.

"This is the most amazing breakfast, Lauren. Far superior to the one I had at the Hotel McDonald yesterday."

The Hotel McDonald had one of the best Sunday brunch buffets in the city. Lauren knew this compliment was just part of the game. Will knew it, too. He wasn't going to let Zain get ahead of him.

"I'm a lucky man to have such a beautiful, talented, successful wife. Did you know that Lauren is the Vice President of the Canadian Cancer Society?"

"It's obvious that she has a great many talents," Zain said with a smile.

Lauren rolled her eyes. This had gone far enough.

"Thank you both for your kind words, but that's not what we're here to talk about. Zain, can you tell me more about these explosions?"

Zain moved quickly from flirtatious intruder to man of action. He frowned and straightened his back as he described what he'd learned.

"Well, let me start by repeating we have nothing to do with this. To be honest, I wish we had the skills and manpower to do something of this magnitude, but we don't. As you might guess, we have members in many locations, all around Canada and the US. I've had reports of explosions right across Canada, many of them right here in Alberta. My US team also reports more explosions than they can keep track of. And what is strangest to us is how random they seem. You've seen that yourself – the Hummer, the plane, the police cruisers, and now the power plant."

Zain seemed uncomfortable talking about his connections to other groups. Both Lauren and Will knew he meant other terrorist groups.

"The word on the street is that no one knows who's up to this – or why. I do have one possible suspect, but it seems pretty far-fetched."

For a fleeting moment, Zain felt vulnerable. What was happening was unsettling to him.

"That's why I came to see you. We want to figure out what's happening and stop it before …" He didn't know how to finish. Before what? What was the point of all these explosions? Where would they end?

*Patricia McConkey*

Will was still sceptical, but in his gut he was starting to believe. He continued to eat his breakfast as he thought about his next move. There was a long period of silence as each man eyed the other.

"Zain, it's pretty clear that you and I are on opposing teams. I work for an oil company and, well, you blow them up."

Zain gritted his teeth and let that slide, only because he knew that Will had a gun down the back of his shorts.

"I was just heading to my office to gather up some test results on the pipes …"

"I have a degree in chemical engineering, with a specialization in metallurgy," Zain said. "Perhaps I could help interpret the results. I could also give you data on where explosions have happened so we could plot them on a map. That could give us an indication who the target is."

Figures that a terrorist would have a degree in chemistry and metals, Will thought. But he did want to know about the other explosions.

"OK. I'd also like to hear your theories. Can you meet me at the northeast corner of the CanPetroleum fence line?"

"You mean the back entrance that employees use to bypass the security guards?"

Will wondered how he could have known about that.

"Yeah, that's the one. I'll meet you there in about twenty minutes. I'm taking my bike. I don't trust vehicles any more. They're like time bombs just waiting to go off. See you there?"

Will knew Zain would be driving and was half hoping his car would blow up on the way to the plant.

# Chapter 20

## July 2012

*D*ietrich looked out over the empty plant floor of GEO headquarters and felt a great sense of accomplishment. He chuckled at the irony of it. He had told the employees and sales team the company had failed, but GEO had actually succeeded far better than he ever dreamed.

The sales managers had been told that, since this was a revolutionary new technology, their primary goal was to give away free trials of the product. Dietrich convinced them that once clients saw the results from the trial, sales would be a piece of cake. Sales reps and their managers got bonuses based on how many clients they met with and how many trial packages were implemented.

For the sales staff, this job was a dream. They were getting paid great money to give away samples. It doesn't get any easier than that. So Dietrich's sales team was incredibly motivated, and he rewarded them well.

Sales reps in Germany, the US, Canada, and the UK blew the tops off their projections. The Canadian reps had distributed over thirty-seven percent more than Dietrich had projected even in his most optimistic moments. And the special ops team for OPEC was a huge success, definitely worth the exorbitant amount of money he had paid them. Dietrich tried to remember the thirteen nations belonging to the OPEC agreement. He got to nine or ten and gave up. It didn't matter. He knew his special ops team had succeeded in getting to them all. He called them the special ops team because so much of their work was done with bribes and underhanded deals. They were always asking for more money to pay off officials, and Dietrich happily supplied the funds because it resulted in more product in the market. He knew that if GEO successfully penetrated OPEC, his idea would be the most powerful weapon in the world.

He thought about the definition of success. In terms of meeting the objectives that were set out at start-up, GEO was an unprecedented success. But success could be measured on a number of levels, and his success would mean certain disaster for anyone living a modern lifestyle in an industrialized country anywhere in the world. To label his success as bittersweet would be an understatement.

On the surface, GEO was an extremely successful start-up company for a new rust-inhibiting product. However, as with many start-ups, eight months after sales began the new company just ran out of cash – at least that's what the cover story was. No one had the slightest suspicion what the product really was. As far as customers – and all the GEO employees – were concerned, it was a rust inhibitor that coated the inside walls of pipes.

As the August deadline grew closer, Dietrich leaked to key employees that there were financial problems. He wanted them to think the company was running out of cash.

His strategy was successful. By mid-July everyone

thought that GEO didn't have long to live. So when Dietrich announced they would be closing their doors in a couple of weeks, no one was surprised.

The hardest part for Dietrich was pretending to look devastated when he wanted to dance with joy. Closing the company was all part of the plan. Once the bacteria reached its critical state there would be no turning back.

Dietrich looked around the office for documents. He had shredded every piece of paper he could find related to GEO, but his obsessive personality forced him to do a second check. He didn't really expect anyone would connect the explosions to GEO, but he was cautious. Not that there would be anyone to come after him even if they knew where to find him. And they would never find him on the Jacob colony. All his ties to the modern world would be left behind once he returned there.

He had asked sales managers in each country to return all literature, memos, and any other documents they had to the head office. He had included a bonus cheque to each one, just to ensure that they would do a thorough job in returning all paperwork and deleting computer files. He carried the last of the shredded materials to the dumpster located in the back parking lot. The office had been totally cleared of all evidence. Tomorrow he would focus on his personal belongings.

The next morning, Dietrich looked around his apartment. The minimalist décor left very few clues about the person who had lived there some thirty years. He was raised with the belief that everything should serve a purpose. And, true to his background, there was very little technology or machinery of any kind. No TV, no radio, no dishwasher or vacuum cleaner, just a broom and a mop, and for entertainment, lots and lots of books.

*Patricia McConkey*

Books were not just possessions: he needed them to learn and develop his plan. Books had an important purpose, so he felt perfectly justified in collecting as many as he needed. He loved his books and had always kept them well organized on shelves all around the room.

Something else he was strongly attached to, the only piece of decoration, was a tiny wooden carving. He picked it up gently and held it in his palm. It was a small carving, worn smooth from years of caressing, of a newborn baby. He had made it after his sister died so many years ago. Although her life was very short, he had loved her deeply. He still remembered vividly the morning of her birth.

After a long, excruciating night of hearing his mother's screams, he had exhaled and released his anxiety. He could tell by the sounds coming from the next room that the baby had been born. Yet the sounds were not the happy ones you would normally expect with the birth of a child.

To his surprise one of the midwives came rushing out of the bedroom and gave him the baby, ordering him to sit next to the woodstove to keep her warm. She then ran from the house to get his father from the barn.

Dietrich held the little bundle close to his chest. All he could see above her blanket was a tiny face, pink and perfect. She opened her eyes and, with all the wisdom and insight of the universe, she looked deep into Dietrich's soul. They connected on an almost spiritual level and Dietrich loved her more than he thought possible. The connection was broken when Gunter burst through the kitchen door, his face so despairing it sent a chill through Dietrich. He held out the baby for his father to see, but was waved aside.

Gunter ran into the bedroom where his wife lay. The women were scurrying around his wife, trying every method they knew to stop the bleeding. Gunter knelt beside her and took her hand. She was weak, but she looked at him with tears in her eyes and asked for the baby. Gunter's eyes filled as he begged her to hang on, to stay with him. He pleaded with God to spare her. She repeated "baby" over and over. Gunter looked at the women attending her and the looks on their faces told him that she didn't have much time.

Gunter called Dietrich to bring the baby in. His wife's eyes brightened in her pale face when she saw her first-born child holding his little sister.

Dietrich's chin quivered as he set the baby in his mother's arms. She held the baby and felt a warm peaceful feeling flow over her.

"Look how beautiful she is. I dreamed she was sick."

Gunter knew that the baby was not *right*. The midwife had told him. His wife was slipping away fast. He reassured her that the baby was fine, that she looked like an angel. Mother and baby looked at each other. No one in the room breathed as they watched the two souls bond.

In the next moment, the mother was gone, and the baby cried out for the first time.

Gunter clung to his wife's lifeless body and filled the room with his anguished weeping. Dieter reached to take back the baby, but as he did so, her blanket shifted and he saw her deformed body for the first time. Something in him froze. His whole body trembled as he looked from the baby to his dead mother covered in blood. He felt as if his heart would explode.

He rewrapped the blanket around the baby's tiny body and held her snugly as he ran from the room. Standing in the kitchen holding her tenderly, he cried as much for his sister as for his mother. It wasn't her fault she had been born this way. Rage was building up inside him. He needed to blame someone for everything that had happened.

He looked out the kitchen window and saw huge black billows of smoke from the oil refinery in the distance. In that moment he knew who was responsible. Dietrich promised himself that he would set things right, no matter how long it took.

Now, almost thirty-nine years later, Dietrich was confident. Soon the oil companies would no longer exist and life would go back to the way it should be – farming and living off the land. He felt proud of his accomplishment, but somewhat disappointed because it would be a silent victory. No one could ever know who was responsible for the Great Change.

# Chapter 21

## August 2012

*D*ietrich jingled his car keys as he walked to his old Volvo. His heart was light and he almost felt like doing a dance step as he bounced along. Although it had taken years to find a solution, the day had finally come when he could look back over his work and feel proud of his accomplishments. After years of solitude, working alone in his lab, he had unlocked the answer. No one would have guessed that a tiny bacterium found in the soil would have such power, the power to change the world.

He opened the trunk and went back to gather a few belongings. A few boxes of books and a small bag of clothes was all he needed. He hummed a little tune as he started his drive to the colony. He was excited, and a little nervous, about returning home. It had been a long time.

He was so absorbed in his whistling and humming that he almost drove right by his favourite coffee shop.

One last cup can't hurt, he thought.

Dietrich considered coffee his only vice. He loved its deep rich aroma and its bittersweet taste. He knew it would not be available in the new world because no one would be shipping coffee beans and they certainly don't grow in northern Alberta. It would be a sad parting.

He stood in line waiting to get his final cup. Just in front of him were three teenage girls. Normally he wouldn't have thought twice about them, but today was different. As he stood there waiting, he could smell a fruity scent coming from their direction. Was it strawberry? Shampoo, possibly, he thought.

As a university professor, he had seen his share of beautiful young women. Still, one of the girls just ahead held his attention. She had mocha-coloured skin, deep brown eyes, and full raspberry-coloured lips displaying perfect teeth. He found himself wanting to reach out and caress her face. But contact with women was out of the question. It would distract him from his true purpose. Other than a few awkward one-night stands, he was very much an innocent in the ways of love. In spite of himself, he took a step closer and breathed deeply to inhale the wonderfully sweet smell.

"How many businesses have we got left?" he heard Ms. Raspberry Lips ask.

"I think we could ask for donations from those two places across the street and still make it to the seniors' home on time," one of the other girls answered.

"I know we started this thing as a social science project, but I'm so glad we kept it going. Since February we are almost up to thirteen thousand dollars. Just two thousand more and we're done."

"I can't believe your dad is going to fly all three of us to Ottawa so we can give the cheque directly to the charity. That is soooo cool."

"Dad says we deserve it. We've worked really hard to raise this money, and it will go to good use. The Water Group Charity will build a well and latrines at a school, and start an education program for the kids and parents. He says we could even go to Africa to see our project once it's built. My dad is pretty great. I wish he would stop calling me his little pumpkin head, though. It drives me crazy."

Dietrich was impressed that they were raising all this money to help children in Africa. He swallowed hard as he thought about their lives in the coming months. He had never really put a face on the people who would be affected by his plan. Now it was hard not to.

He looked slowly around the coffee shop. He saw a young mother with her sleeping baby, a businessman typing out e-mails on his computer, a hip young crowd chatting in the corner. It was as if everything was magnified, intensified in some strange way. Colours seemed more vibrant and the smell of coffee and sweet pastries coalesced into a thick aroma. The patrons turned toward him and their gaze seemed to penetrate his thoughts.

Oh God, they know what I've done, he thought.

Dietrich shook his head and broke the trance. For a second he wondered if he was having a stroke. He pushed the thought away and tried to return to reality. The truth was clear and there was no denying it. All of these people would suffer and many of them would die because of his plan. He looked at their faces again and felt a sharp pain.

His knees buckled. He tried to draw in a breath but his tongue felt as if it had swelled to twice its normal size. He staggered slightly as he pushed his way out the door. The bright sun hurt his eyes and he placed his hand on the brick wall to steady himself. He closed his eyes and tried desperately to draw air in through his nose. His nostrils felt much too small, but he managed to get a few breaths into his lungs.

"Are you OK?"

*Patricia McConkey*

He turned to see the girl with the raspberry lips.

"Yeah ... I'm fffffine," he mumbled, trying to get his oversized tongue to work. He focused on the ground to avoid her beautiful eyes.

"Are you sure? You look kind of pale."

He coughed a couple of times and cleared his throat.

"Yeah, I'm OK. But I want to do something for you. Just a minute."

He took a few shaky steps, unlocked his car, reached into the glove box and pulled out his chequebook.

"I overheard you talking in there. Did you say you are raising money for something in Africa?"

"That's right. We're going to build a well and a latrine at a school. There's a great charity called the Water Group we're giving the money to."

"Well, I have a business, and I want to make a donation, if that's OK."

"Sure, that's great!" she said, practically jumping with excitement.

"But I want you to promise me one thing – that you take your trip to Ottawa very soon. Within the next month."

Dietrich finished filling out the cheque. Before he handed it to the girl, he looked her in the eyes and said, "Promise?"

"Yes, of course. We're very excited to go, and as soon as we get all the money ..."

He handed her the cheque, got into his car, and drove off before she had time to say anything else. Her friends joined her and asked her what happened.

"You won't believe this. That guy just gave me a cheque for two thousand dollars!"

# Chapter 22

## September 2012

*Zain* pulled up to the agreed-on spot at the refinery, turned off the car, and released a long slow breath. There was nothing funny about Will's jab that his car might blow up on the way to the plant. Nothing was impossible these days.

He closed his eyes and leaned his head back, waiting for Will to arrive. Waiting was something he had done a great deal of in the past. Surveillance was a tedious, lonely business, but necessary in his line of work. Information was key and Zain got the necessary pieces however he could. If it meant sitting in a car for two days, then that's what he did.

He wondered what his discussions with Will would reveal. He was still jittery. He plucked his keys from the ignition and tenderly stroked the silver angel wings hanging from the chain. He felt the cold silver in his palm and smiled at the memories it brought back. He had bought the key fob six months earlier in a Mexican market.

He had been with Kabira.

Zain was training her to be his second-in-command. Although he had reservations about her, he had no doubt she could do the job. She was only five foot four but Kabira was the kind of woman who commanded respect and fear. She was a fiercely passionate woman with hellfire in her belly. She could, and frequently did, use her feminine assets to charm information out of susceptible males.

Her technical knowledge was impressive, too. But somehow the whole package seemed just a little too good. Zain suspected she was a spy for some government agency trying to keep tabs on him. But he was never able to find anything odd in her background checks. So he decided to teach her the business.

He found himself distracted during the training. He was very aware of her standing behind him as he sat looking over industrial blueprints, her long, black hair dangling over his shoulder. Her thin but curvaceous body was barely covered by her tiny t-shirts and low-rise khaki pants. He couldn't help fantasizing about her. But he had to be cautious. She was a dangerous weapon. The relationship had to be strictly business.

In addition, he had a guiding policy when it came to women – "never get too close." Zain was always on the move and in danger. He couldn't afford to have a woman know too much about him. It would be dangerous for him and just as dangerous for her. His philosophy about females worked well for him because there were so many to choose from. Why stop at just one? With his looks there were lots of easy pickings.

One morning Kabira mentioned an environmental rally located in Mexico. There would be contacts there from all over the world. She convinced him that if they attended they could firm up relationships with other international groups. They landed in Mexico on a Friday evening, took a cab to the hotel, and checked into their separate rooms. They had planned to meet some contacts for dinner.

Zain waited in the lobby for Kabira and was about to leave without her when the desk clerk paged him. He said that Ms. Maarten had phoned the desk and asked the clerk to give Zain a message. It read "Urgent matter. Please come to my room. We need to talk privately. Room 313. Kabira."

He went up and knocked on her door. She was expecting him. When he opened the door, his mouth hung open for a moment. She was wearing a silky black bra with matching panties. The black garter belt she was wearing had a tiny red rose just below her navel and lacy straps holding up her stockings. She was teetering a bit, with one foot bare and the other in a black four-inch stiletto.

"You can see the problem, can't you? I only have one shoe. How can I go out looking like this?"

They didn't leave the hotel room for two days.

On Monday morning they walked through the Mexican market, never more than a step or two apart. Like magnet to metal, they were continually drawn back together, sparks flying whenever they touched. Kabira was wearing a tiny halter-top that left very little to the imagination. Zain stood behind her so he could get a better view of her bare back. He loved her tattoo: a black outline of angel wings extending almost the full length of her back. He reached out and traced the line of the wing on her right shoulder blade. He could see goose bumps form in response to his touch even in the hot Mexican sun.

Kabira was standing in front of a table of silver jewellery, touching random pieces, not really thinking about buying anything. Zain stood behind her looking over her head. Then he saw it, glinting in the sunlight. He reached over and picked up the key fob with the silver angel wings. She smiled and nodded. They didn't need words to communicate.

When they returned from Mexico, things were strained

between them. Despite their raw attraction, they were both hardheaded and stubborn and fought like two gamecocks. However, this often turned into a form of foreplay, ending in a hot session on the desk, in the car, or wherever else they happened to be.

Then things changed. She told him she was pregnant. He wanted with all his heart to believe it was his baby, but couldn't accept it. The first thing he questioned was the timing. He'd been away for a few weeks and wasn't even sure if he was with Kabira when the baby must have been conceived. More than that, he'd been told he could never have children.

Since the day the doctor told him, he felt he had a free ticket for as much sex as possible with no long-term entanglements. But it had all left him empty and wanting more. In his line of business, however, more was not possible. So he had accepted his fate.

It was cancer that left him sterile. He was only fourteen and needed heavy rounds of chemotherapy to kill his leukemia. Although he recovered and went into full remission, his bitterness grew.

Over the next few years, he researched the causes of cancer. His research uncovered that the prevalence of cancers in his town was far greater than average. He knew he couldn't prove the link, but his home was only about one kilometre from a gas-processing plant. It was a rare day you couldn't smell them burning off sour gas. Although the plant provided copies of air quality tests, Zain looked at them with scepticism.

There was no way he could prove his suspicions about the gas plant. So, after years of trying to get answers through the proper channels, he began to look for new methods of justice – and ended up heading an ecoterrorist group.

Now he had mixed feelings about so many things. Whether it was his baby or not, he wanted it to have a chance. That's why he went to see Will. Ironically, he wanted to stop the extreme terrorists so he could get back to his routine of blowing up specific targets. No matter how extreme his views got, killing was never part of his strategy. He shook his head at the insanity of it.

In the back of his mind he hoped for a miracle. Maybe it *was* his baby?

When Will knocked on the window, Zain just about jumped out of his skin.

"C'mon. What are you waiting for?" Will said.

# Chapter *23*

*E*xcept for a few maintenance workers, the refinery was empty. The regular staff had all been sent home due to the power outage. Will and Zain walked through the empty buildings, aware of the risk they were taking. They walked softly, quietly closing doors behind them as if sound was one of the unknown detonators. As they walked, Zain fondled the silver wings.

"I'm gonna have a kid," he said, surprising even himself. Will was taken aback.

"Never thought I would ever have any. You know ... The doctor said that I couldn't because of the chemo. But then there's also a timing issue ..."

"Oh," was all Will could manage.

Will was definitely uncomfortable now. He didn't want to be conflicted about this man. So the guy's had cancer and now he's having a baby. What a sweet story! Screw that! What about those oil workers who died in mysterious explosions? Like you didn't have something to do with those? And now I'm supposed to be your best friend?

"My girlfriend is pretty freaked at the whole idea, too,

'cause she never wanted to have kids, and she thought I was a safe bet. You know, no swimmers, so no birth control needed."

Will was desperate to change the subject. Although he still despised Zain with every fibre in his body, he did understand that feeling of wanting to protect his family. Maybe that's just built into every father. But he didn't want to know the details.

They finally reached his office and could focus on the real reason they were there.

"Here are some of the chemical analyses from the refinery fire," Will said, picking some reports off his desk. "You can see there's no trace of an accelerant."

"I'm sure you know there are new accelerants that wouldn't show up on these tests."

Will took a deep breath to steady himself. It was all he could do not to take out his gun and let the man have a couple of shots right now.

Zain scanned through the test results carefully.

"But you're right. See these numbers here. Even if there were some toluene or xylene derivatives, we'd see a variation in the specific gravity of the remaining fluid."

Will tried to look unimpressed, but he never would have thought of that. He was still thinking of shooting Zain once he'd found out what he knew.

"Do you know why this organic number is so high?"

"No, but that's where I was focusing my efforts. I'm surprised it showed up at all."

Doug, one of the few maintenance guys assigned to do cleanup during the power outage, came by the office.

"Excuse me, Captain Connor, can I interrupt you for a moment? I saw you walking through the yard, so I thought I could drop these off for ya."

"C'mon in, Doug. What do you have for me?"

Doug held out some lengths of pipe cut from various spots in the plant.

"I replaced a couple of pipes like you asked, and took the old pipes and cut them down the centre lengthways so we could get a good cross section."

He laid the samples on the table. They were taken from pipes used to transport oil from one section of the refinery to the tank farm, which was home to almost a dozen huge reservoirs each holding a million litres of oil.

"Holy shit, look at this. That's our organic matter!" Zain said. His face was pale.

There appeared to be a growth on the inside of the pipe.

"Do you have a microscope?" he asked Will.

Will pointed to the corner.

Zain scraped some of the crust-like material off the pipe and put it on a glass slide. He put it under the lens and adjusted the focus. He could see tiny hard-shelled organisms, probably feeding off the fuel. He knew that a company had recently mutated Rhodococcusto bacteria so that it would eat the sulphur out of diesel fuel making the fuel more environmentally friendly. A bacterium that could live on carbonaceous materials was nothing new, but how did that result in explosions?

He took a pen and scratched the white surface to get a different view. There was a bright flash. He pulled out the slide, tried it again, and was astonished.

His heart began to race as he tried to sort through the implications. Doug and Will were still talking about the pipes. Once he understood what was going on, he interrupted them.

"I think I can explain what's happening here, but it's so fuckin' big I'm having a hard time believing it."

Will stared at him. Zain's hands were shaking.

Doug didn't really know what was going on, but he could tell it was serious.

"Maybe I should go," he said.

Will shook his head. "No, you probably need to hear this as much as anyone. Stay. Sit down."

"I'm not sure where to begin, but let's start with this piece of pipe," Zain said. "See this? It's called an oocyst – which just means a hard shell around a tiny living organism. That's what's growing in these pipes: tiny creatures that live on various types of fuel. As they grow, the old ones die and the newer organisms keep building their homes on the backs of the old shells, kind of like barnacles on the bottom of a ship. That's how this layer gets thicker and thicker."

Zain pointed to the growth on the inside of the pipe.

"Doug, tell me how you stop oil flow from one section of pipe to another."

"Well, that's easy. Most of the pipes have butterfly valves. That's just a circular piece of metal that can close off the pipe or open to let the liquid flow through."

"Got it. Is it something like this?"

Zain fished around for a coin in his pocket. Then he rolled a piece of paper around the coin, so it looked like a pipe with a valve.

"If you look closely at my rough model here, can you see that the valve would scrape against the walls of the pipe as it opens and closes?"

"Yeah, that's obvious," Doug said.

Will was wondering when Zain would get to the point.

"OK, so every set of pipes here and in every other refinery in the country has valves like this, right?"

Doug and Will nodded.

"Now here's the unbelievable part."

*Patricia McConkey*

Zain's mouth felt dry. Saying it out loud meant acknowledging it was real.

"Pretend this coin is the valve and it's trying to turn with all this crud in the pipe. It scrapes against this buildup, then watch what happens."

Zain scraped the coin on the inside of the pipe. Like magic, when the metal surface rubbed against the growth in the pipe, a little spark appeared. The spark ignited a bit of oil on the surface and, within seconds, the pipe was burning.

Will grabbed an old towel and easily patted out the flames.

He understood.

Doug stepped back from the table with his mouth hanging open. He was no expert, but it didn't take a genius to figure out what was happening.

Will spoke first.

"So ... so this little organism or bacteria or whatever it is ... has the ability to create a spark in a pipe full of fuel?"

"On its own, no. But when a valve or a piston scrapes up against it, *kerpow*! We have liftoff. They must have mutated the bacteria so that the shells contain sulphur to help create the spark. Just like the head of a match."

"And if you look at the location of these pipes, they were on the inflow side to the tank farm," Will said. "That means everything downstream is potentially contaminated with this stuff. Every litre of oil that's gone through our facility is contaminated. Millions and millions of litres of oil gets piped all across Western Canada and the northern US. How long has it been contaminated, or more importantly, where does the contamination start and stop?"

Will stopped for a breath and went on.

"But who would do this? And why? Who's going to benefit from blowing everything up?"

Zain had to sit down.

"I can't answer the why, but I have an idea of the who. And it's worse than you ever imagined. It's only a hunch, but if it is them, then we're screwed, totally screwed."

Zain was a wild-ass son of a bitch who would shoot your grandmother if he had to, but *this* scared him. He took a deep breath to try to steady his voice.

"Have you ever heard of a company called Global Enviro Oil?"

Will thought it sounded vaguely familiar.

"Some of my men joined their organization last year when they started up. They were promoting a product that had some magical anti-corrosion ability that was supposed to protect your pipes from rust. They were looking for sales reps. The cool catch was that they were giving the stuff away. It was free."

A light went off in Will's head. He couldn't remember the exact date, but he knew it was early that fall. The only reason he had agreed to take the sales call was that it would be a good excuse to get out of the office and walk around in the sunshine. He remembered the crunchy yellow leaves underfoot as they walked toward the tank farm. At the time his gut feeling told him there was something odd about the two guys, but he never gave it a second thought.

# Chapter 24

*November 2011*

*S*usan sat at her desk that day pretending to type as she listened to music on her MP3 player. She had just had her nails done and didn't want them spoiled. If she appeared busy, people sometimes did their annoying tasks themselves. Otherwise they would ask, "Could you photocopy these for me? Do you mind?" Of course she minded, but she could hardly tell them to go screw themselves.

Two men dressed in ties and sport jackets were heading right to her desk. Just what she needed. Salesmen.

"Hi, I'm Gilles Leport. We have an appointment to see Steve McIvy regarding an anti-corrosion prod—"

"Please have a seat and I'll page him for you," Susan said.

She really didn't need to know anything about them. It was ironic that, even though she was a receptionist, she really disliked talking to people.

When salespeople came on-site, they were spotted pretty fast. Nobody wanted to talk to them. So when Susan tried to call Mr. McIvy, there was no answer. She rang some of his staff and, not surprisingly, no one was available. So she flipped through the corporate phone book and saw the word "corrosion" in the job description next to Will Connor's name. She knew he was in. She'd just seen him go into his office with a cup of coffee.

There was no way she wanted these guys hanging around her desk any longer than necessary, so she told them to head to Will's office at the end of the hall. She checked out the younger man's butt as he walked past, but decided it was nothing to get excited about.

The two men showed up at Will's office and started their pitch. As Fire Chief for the site, Will's duties included monitoring water pipes for pressure, flow, and corrosion. He knew they were definitely talking to the wrong guy, so he rang Steve McIvy, the maintenance manager, on his cell. But Steve said he couldn't get away.

Steve had heard about the product from a buddy at another plant site and doubted it would do what they claimed, but wanted to try it.

"Couldn't hurt, right?" he said to Will.

He asked Will to take the men to a few high-corrosion spots and supervise them while they were there.

Will and the two men chatted as they headed toward the tank farm. The younger man was obviously pretty new and anxious to impress his boss. The older gentleman introduced himself as the president of the new company. He joked that he normally didn't get out on sales calls, but the sales manager was busy training another sales rep so he was accompanying Gilles on a few local customer visits.

"And what a beautiful day for it," he said in a slightly German accent.

Will smiled. Another office dweller just trying to get out in the sunshine.

"Where are you from?" he asked.

Gilles piped up, "I'm from Mundare, you know, just east of here? The town with the world's biggest sausage. Ya know what they say about the men from ..."

He stopped talking when he realized that Will had been speaking to his boss.

"Oh, I'm from just north of here, but my parents spoke German and I picked up a bit of their accent. We were farmers. Great place, Alberta. Great soil – that's my background. Someday I'll be a farmer again."

"Corrosion products. Doesn't seem like there's a connection to soil and farming," Will said. "How did you get into this business?"

"Kind of a long story, but the product actually grew out of an idea I had from an experiment I was working on. I spent many years in the lab and accidentally stumbled across this idea while studying bacteria that grow in the soil. An old friend in the stock market saw its potential. He raised the funding we needed to get going."

"Your friend might be right. If your product reduces corrosion like you claim, you'll have more customers than you can handle."

"I've studied this product for a very long time, and I am very confident it will perform," he said.

Will directed them up a small hill toward the tank farm. It was a sampling station that took oil from the main line.

"Steve told me to have you guys insert the sample just up here. What do you need to do?"

Gilles stepped forward in an overly confident manner. His slick black hair and purple tie didn't do much for his professional image.

"It's very simple. We're going to take a quick x-ray of this pipe as a base measurement."

He had a box slung over his shoulder that looked like

something a ghostbuster might carry. He snapped a clamp around the pipe and turned on the machine. It made a slight hum and recorded some measurements.

"See? Now we know exactly how thick the pipe wall is before we start our treatment. I'll also take the measurement of a similar pipe that won't receive the treatment. That'll give us a good comparison."

He showed Will some numbers. They were meaningless to him, but he played along.

"Now all we do is pour the contents of this gallon jug into the system and let the magic happen," Gilles said.

"The product will attach itself to the pipe walls," the older man said. "And over time it will build up a coating that protects the pipe walls from the normal corrosion process. You said that you were involved in tracking corrosion in the water system, no?"

Will nodded.

"Well, you know that when hard water flows through the pipes, calcium, magnesium, and phosphates start to build up on the inside wall of the pipe. The calcium scaling reduces the friction coefficient to help the water flow more easily and also protects the pipes from corroding. Think of our product like that. It'll create a very thin layer that builds up on the insides of your oil pipes, and it protects them in the same manner."

Will was knowledgeable about the water industry. He knew the man's science was bang on.

The young salesman stepped in again.

"So in one year's time, I'll be knocking on your door and we can take measurements of these pipes again and prove to you the value of our product. Did you have a couple of other spots in mind for a trial?"

"Yes, I do. Steve – he's our head of pipe maintenance – gave me a few other spots that he wants to test out."

Will led the men through a maze of pipes and buildings toward the next test site. They repeated the process three more times before heading back to the visitor parking lot.

"Well, if this stuff does half the things you claim, I think I would like to talk to your friend about purchasing stock in your company."

The president smiled and held out his business card and his hand.

Will took a step back. The man's hand was cold and clammy. Something was off here.

The two men headed off to their car. Will wiped his hand on his pant leg and looked at the card, which read: "Global Enviro Oil, a global solution for corrosion control."

It had a phone number, but no name or address.

He tossed the card in the nearest garbage can.

# Chapter 25

## September 2012

*Will* jumped when Doug accidentally dropped a piece of pipe on the floor. For a moment he thought it might be another explosion.

Zain found a map of North America and laid it on the table.

"Will, take a look at this."

He took a red marker and started making *x*s on the map where explosions had occurred. Western Canada was certainly looking as if it had been targeted. Now Zain started to make *x*s in eastern Canada, and the US.

"I communicate with contacts throughout North America via shortwave radio. They've been reporting explosions throughout the US. Whoever these GEO shits are, they sure got a wide distribution. When my guys started working for GEO, they told me the company seemed very well-organized. And another interesting thing is that they didn't really believe the GEO product worked. But it didn't matter because clients would try the stuff because it was free. But here's the real kicker."

Zain looked around and saw a small world map tacked

to the wall. He pulled it off the wall and laid it on the table. He started circling countries.

"Here are the thirteen OPEC countries: Algeria, Angola, Ecuador, Indonesia, Iran, Iraq, Kuwait, Libya, Nigeria, Qatar, Saudi Arabia, the UAE, and Venezuela. Ecuador had its membership suspended for quite some time, but they're back in as of a few years ago."

Will's distaste for Zain hadn't changed, but he had to admit the guy sure knew what he was talking about.

"My guys at GEO said there was a special team of men that just focused on getting GEO product to the OPEC producers. OPEC ships fifty-five percent of the world's crude oil and owns almost eighty percent of the world's oil reserves. There's not a country in the world that won't be infected with this stuff."

Zain exhaled as he sat down and ran his fingers through his hair.

"There's nothing anyone can do. I thought, maybe if I came to see you we could figure out what was happening and shut this thing down. I had no idea how the explosions were being set. Now that I know ... it's too late. That bacteria is all over the whole fuckin' world, and it's just going to keep growing and growing until ..." Zain's voice changed from angry to fearful. "What kind of world will my kid grow up in?"

He turned his back to the other men as he rubbed the silver wings on his key chain, trying to control his emotions.

"OK, we can't use any transportation to get outta here because it will explode, but for that matter, where would we go?" Will said. "It seems like this is a global epidemic. So we can't get out, but the opposite is also true – nothing can get in, mainly food. I don't know if you guys noticed, but we don't grow much food up here through the winter months. What the hell are we gonna eat?"

"Yeah," Doug said, "don't forget the whole minus forty something temperatures. We're all going to turn into popsicles before we starve. What kind of sick bastard would do this?" Doug said.

Will asked him who was working at the plant that day.

"Just me and three other guys. Why does it matter?"

"What are they doing?"

"Just making sure the pressure in the tanks doesn't get too high. If it does, they can use the emergency generator to open the release valves …"

Comprehension came about a second later, and by then he was running out of the room and turning any type of valve that could spark an explosion.

"Get everyone off-site and tell them never to come back," Will yelled to him. "C'mon, we've got to get outta here."

Will thought of locking Zain in the building and letting nature take its course. It would be poetic justice. He repressed the urge and focused on the crisis at hand. He pulled the fire alarm, and the sirens started.

Zain and Will ran through the empty buildings, kicking doors open as they went. There was no time to waste.

Will, normally the hero, was not taking any chances by stopping to round up the maintenance guys. He rationalized that he had no idea where they were. They could be anywhere from the underground tunnels to the cooling towers. He would never find them in time. He kept running.

The running helped him clear his head. It was like opening a window and filling your lungs with fresh air. Maybe it was the same instinct that had kept him alive through all the craziness in his life. He had an impulse to look behind him. As he turned, he caught a glimpse of yellow flame in the mechanical pit below. The pump room was about thirty feet deep and contained three sixteen-hundred horsepower motors.

Will and Zain had cut across a catwalk in order to get to the back parking lot as quickly as possible. Now Will was rethinking the wisdom of that move. He saw the motors explode with such incredible force that thousands of metal shards flew in every direction. Will was about ten feet ahead of Zain on the catwalk and was able to dive behind a wall before the impact. Zain didn't have a chance.

Metal shrapnel struck the wall like machine-gun spray. Will heard a piece of metal strike a soft object, then a soft gasp. It was a very familiar sound, like an arrow hitting the torso of a deer. But it wasn't a deer this time. A moment later, Will saw a ball of flames engulf the entire catwalk. There was nothing he could do for Zain.

Blood was everywhere. Will didn't know if it was his or Zain's. He just kept moving. He rolled on the ground toward the exit and pushed through the doors. For a split second, he thought about checking to see if Zain had survived, but thinking about Zain's past he decided it was a suitable ending for him. And besides, there was no way he could have survived.

Will ran across the parking lot like he had never run before, each step faster than the one before. The only thing in his mind was reaching his bike and riding to safety. He had to make it out. His family was depending on him.

He was probably three kilometres away before he collapsed onto a patch of grass next to the road. Gulping in oxygen as if it was water on a hot sunny day, he tried to get control of his thoughts. The images and possibilities that raced through his head were nothing short of a nightmare. He needed a plan. But there was no plan. It's hard to think of a solution when you realize that society as you know it will no longer exist.

Behind him the explosions continued. The whole plant was going up in flames. Huge billows of black smoke blocked out the sun. Will felt tiny particles of ash float down from the sky and cover his skin, almost like snow, except they didn't melt.

He lay on the grass next to the road. His lungs were scorched from the heat and he struggled to catch his breath. Water, what he wouldn't do for a cold glass of water right now.

He checked his body to see if the main parts were still there. He knew that, when adrenalin is pumping through you, you can be seriously injured and not notice.

Will opened his eyes – it must have been a few hours later, he thought – and stared blankly at the smoke-filled sky. His mind was overloaded. The ripple effects stretched so far and wide, it was almost unfathomable. Although he was alone, he tried to talk this through, one step at a time.

"OK, we live in a cold country. We can't grow food for at least seven months of the year, and since we can't bring in food from the south, we're going to starve. OK, even if we don't starve, we're going to freeze to death because how are we going to heat the houses? A wood fireplace is not going to keep us warm when it's minus forty degrees Celsius.

"Next possibility, can we get out of here? Obviously we can't use any form of motor transport – too dangerous. What about horses? There's no way we'd get very far with hundreds of thousands of starving people. Horses are out. What if we sailed down the North Saskatchewan River? Well, that would be a hell of long sailing trip to get to Manitoba, which is no further south, so not much use. Besides, the water is going to freeze any day now. Cycling is a possibility, but it would take a lot of calories and water, which we don't have, and then of course the snow is going to fall pretty soon which would make it really slow going."

*Patricia McConkey*

Will felt like he was in one of those survival game shows. "Today's lucky winner gets to live another day," he said in his best game show host voice. He started questioning his sanity at that point.

"We're going to have to stick it out for the winter. I have my bow and some rounds of ammo. Maybe I can get some wildlife before it gets too scarce."

Will didn't really think they would make it, but he certainly wouldn't let anyone know, especially Lauren. He sealed up his emotions and decided he had to move on.

Although there wasn't much point, he thought he should inform the Prime Minister. He got on his bike and headed down 98th Avenue toward the legislature buildings, about five kilometres away.

The streets were oddly quiet. There were a few cars driving around, but most people were staying home since nothing was open. No store would open without electricity; all the cash registers were electronic. Nobody knew what was really going on, and why should they? There were no media reports to tell them there was a national emergency, and possibly global catastrophe. Radio and TV needed electricity to broadcast.

There were people out raking their lawns, doing the last chores of fall. They seemed to be enjoying a day off with their kids home from school.

Will realized he was getting horrified stares. Until now, he hadn't thought about his appearance. When he left the house this morning he had on a running jacket, a long-sleeved t-shirt, and biking shorts. Now he looked down at what was left.

As the plant was going up in flames, his jacket started to melt from the heat of the explosion. He had pulled it off as he ran, but parts of it had melted right onto his white t-shirt beneath. He still had his shorts, shoes, and, most importantly, his Smith and Wesson tucked down the back of his shorts. Good thing the heat from the blast didn't ignite the shells or I could have lost some important stuff, he thought. There was a good reason firemen didn't carry guns.

But on closer examination, what was left of his white shirt was now mostly red and black.

Probably Zain's blood, he thought, without any remorse.

Another thing that added to his unsightly appearance was the gash on his leg. He hadn't noticed it until now, but blood was running down his right leg and had turned his white Nike shoe red. He made a mental note to stop the bleeding as soon as he got to the legislature.

Within minutes, he had pulled up in front of the legislature building. He had heard that the Prime Minister had taken up residence on the top floor of the building for security reasons. He couldn't travel until it was clear the planes were safe. Will had bad news for him. He'd be in Edmonton for some time.

He took off his shirt, thinking he could rip off a sleeve and tie it around his leg to stop the bleeding. But it was a nylon-based material and it wasn't ripping. He looked over his shoulder and saw the security team eyeing him. Surely they would have a knife.

He walked up to the guard with his shirt in his hand and said he was here to see the Prime Minister. Not surprisingly, the guard told him he wasn't going to let him anywhere near the PM looking the way he did.

"OK, here's the deal, Jack. The PM asked me to do some special undercover work for him. You just run on up and tell him Will Connor, Fire Chief of CanPetroleum, is here to see him. Now before you do that, can I borrow your knife to cut the sleeve off my shirt which I am going to tie around my leg to stop it from bleeding on your nice white floor?"

The security guard, dressed in a conventional black suit, was probably six foot six and easily three hundred pounds. He just glared at Will and continued to block the door.

"This guy was not hired for his brains, that's for damn sure," Will muttered under his breath.

The guy was as big as a gorilla and probably about as fast as a sloth. Will decided to make a break for it. He stood about ten feet in front of Mr. Gorilla and faked a run to his left, then he jumped right and was around him in seconds. No challenge whatsoever. Will hadn't really thought this whole thing through, so getting around the next half dozen guards was going to be trickier. He had seen a second guard radio his friends for backup.

Will was now in the main foyer. Guard number two stood about twenty feet from him in front of an open staircase. Will ran at him as fast as he could and threw up his left leg as if he were going to jump a hurdle in a race. The guard had no time to get out of his way, so when Will's left foot landed squarely in the middle of his chest, he fell flat on his back. Will landed, one foot on his chest and his other foot above the guard's head. But he was only able to make it a few feet before guard number three tackled him from behind.

It took three men to pin Will to the ground and get his hands behind his back. Of course, the fact that he was carrying a handgun down the back of his shorts didn't make things any better. Within a minute or two, there were four more guards with guns drawn pointed at him.

"Will you jerks just check with the Prime Minister? He'll tell you that I'm working for him."

As luck would have it, Simon had been sitting at his

desk on the fourth floor office when he saw Will coasting across the lawn on his bike. Hoping he was here to visit the PM's office, he got up to meet him. Simon could hear the commotion by the time he was halfway down the stairs. When he got to the bottom, he witnessed Will's spectacular takedown of guard number two and was thoroughly impressed. Who wouldn't be? It was a very cool move.

Simon waved to Jim, the head of security, who happened to be Mr. Gorilla from the front door and told him to let Will through. After more scuffling and swearing, the guards got off him, one by one, and let him stand. Simon approached cautiously. Talking to Will was like trying to have a conversation with a rabid wolf.

"Will," he said, standing back a good ten feet. "I'm Simon Bridgewater, the Prime Minister's Assistant."

"Yeah, I remember you. I need to tell the PM some information about the explosions."

Will stood in the foyer, bare-chested, covered in soot, and still bleeding from the leg.

"I thought as much, but if you don't mind me asking, what happened to you?"

Simon was having a hard time keeping his mind on business.

"Funny you should ask. Take a look through those windows to the east and you should be able to see a big yellow ball of fire where CanPetroleum used to be. I happened to be there when it went up."

As he was talking, one of the guards handed Will what was left of his shirt. The guard didn't want to touch it but he didn't want it hanging around in the foyer either.

"And see this?" Will said, holding up the remains of his shirt, and pointing to the blood.

"This was a guy who was with me and didn't make it out.

I took my shirt off so I could make a bandage out of it to stop the bleeding. Isn't that right, *asshole?*" he said, staring at Jim.

"Get the first-aid kit from that closet and give him a bandage," Jim growled.

"Water, too," Will said.

Jim nodded reluctantly.

Simon stood, only half listening to Will's story, trying to keep his mind focused. It was difficult with the view he had of Will's chiselled body.

"My God, Will, it's amazing that you made it out alive. Here, take my coat. You must be cold."

Simon slid off his suit jacket and handed it to Will. Will slipped into the silk Armani jacket and buttoned the first button. The view was still powerfully seductive for Simon because now Will's muscular chest popped out from the slightly too-small jacket.

Will took a moment to wrap a bandage around his leg. He shook his head at the senselessness of it all. These guys were just doing their jobs, but they really had no idea who the real bad guy was. Maybe ignorance was bliss.

As Will and Simon headed off to meet with the PM, some of the guards tried to wipe the blood off the floor. Will couldn't resist spooking them further.

"Oh boys," he called to them in a feminine singsong voice, "be careful mopping up that blood. I may have caught the bug last time I was out with the fellas. Wouldn't want you to catch something from lil' ol' me."

He laughed as he saw them drop everything and stand there not knowing what to do.

Simon's jaw dropped. Although he thought Will was just joking, it still stirred him. He was ready to rip off Will's clothes and take him right there. Thoughts raced through his mind. Maybe he's gay and the marriage is just a cover. Maybe I should make a move to let him know that I am interested. No, that's inappropriate. He's here on business. But as soon as he's done with the PM, I am going to make a move.

Will dreaded explaining the new reality to the PM. Denial and repression were his best tactics, but they had to be set aside. His guts lurched, bringing back memories of the time he had to tell a crewmember's wife that her husband would never be coming home again. Her pain was so strong. He never wanted to be in that situation again. Now he had to explain that history had come to a turning point, one that would leave millions dead. He swallowed hard and tried to brace himself for the task at hand.

Simon noticed the quick and extreme shift in Will's mood, from flaming fag to stony-faced undertaker. He remembered Will's ferociousness at the front door and wondered if he could be dealing with a psychotic personality.

Will caught the look.

"Simon, I'm here to tell them that things are not going to get better. We can't fix this problem, and what's worse, it's everywhere. The explosions that are happening here are also happening all around the world. And they'll increase in frequency. None of us are safe. Our world is over."

Simon's knees buckled, but he caught his balance by grabbing the railing.

"Are you sure? There's got to be some mistake. What do you mean worldwide? What about the US, Europe, Japan – anybody? Can't they help us fix this mess?"

"As far as I know, every industrialized nation in the world is being hit with the same random explosions. I've figured out what causes it, but unfortunately there's no cure. It's like a virus that has spread all over the world. There's nothing we can do about it."

Simon reached out and leaned on a wooden ledge to steady himself. He couldn't hold back the tears. He threw his arms around Will and started crying.

Will hadn't seen this coming, but it had been such an incredibly hard day that a hug felt kind of good, even if it was from a sobbing idiot. Will hugged him back for a moment, but then it felt a bit weird. He slowly pushed Simon back.

Simon couldn't go on. He choked out instructions to Will to keep going down to the end of the hall to the Premier's office.

A security guard was lingering in the hallway, obviously sent to keep an eye on him. Will motioned him to help Simon to his office.

"All my life – pretending!" Simon was saying. "Pretending to be someone I'm not. Now I'll never get the chance to be me. How could I have wasted all this time?"

Will understood Simon's regrets. There were many areas of his life in which he wished he had done things differently. He walked to the end of the hall, trying to think of what to say.

# Chapter 26

*The* security guards outside the Premier's office must have been warned of Will's approach because they were bristling with hostility. As Will approached, one stepped forward and asked him to wait. The other spoke into his radio, and grimaced.

Will was losing what few shards of patience he had left.

"Look, are we gonna do the dance, too? Just let me through. The Prime Minister's expecting me."

One guard opened the door to the office and stepped inside as if to confirm Will's appointment, but Will pushed past him.

"Will, come in, come in," the Prime Minister said, motioning him to sit on the couch.

"We're fine in here; thanks, Jean-Pierre," he said to the guard.

The guard stepped hesitantly back into the hallway.

The PM got down to business right away.

"Will Connor, this is Norman Boyle, Premier of Alberta. Will is the Fire Chief at CanPetroleum."

Norman held out his hand.

"Oh, Will and I have met at a couple of occasions. The Snowflake Ball or maybe some other fundraiser?"

Will nodded as they shook hands.

"Thanks for coming, Will," the PM said. "I assume you have some information that can help?"

Will's stood with his eyes cast down. He fidgeted nervously, struggling to find the words.

"I know it's a bit early, but how 'bout a shot of the good stuff?" Norman asked.

He headed to a cabinet under the window, took out three highball glasses, and filled each glass almost half full with good Alberta whiskey.

Will was up and pacing. He took the glass from the Premier and downed it in one shot.

The Premier and PM exchanged a worried glance.

"Let me start, Will," the Premier said. "We just got reports that CanPetroleum has gone up in a tremendous explosion. And there's nothing we can do with the fire trucks out of commission."

"I know. I just came from there and as you can see I got out with not much more than my ass covered. Your assistant lent me his suit coat. I was there with a couple of other guys trying to figure out what the hell is going on. They didn't make it out. I think we sorted out what's going on, but it's sick and twisted. It's hard to believe it and even harder to understand why."

Will tipped his glass back, draining the last few drops. His hands were shaking as he set his glass on the polished wooden table.

He took a deep breath and hoped that the alcohol had dulled his emotions enough so he could get through the explanation without his voice wavering. He tried to explain how bacteria had been injected into fuel supplies worldwide, where it was turning up, and how friction could cause it to spark.

"And we all know what happens when you have a spark near a fuel source. That's what happened to CanPetroleum this morning."

Will held out his glass for more whiskey.

"The real kicker is that this bacteria was injected about a year ago into many different sources: power plants, refineries, gas stations, pipelines – you name it. So it's really had a chance to spread. And what's even worse is that this crazy group injected the bacteria into fuel supplies all around the world, including all the OPEC producers."

Since no one was offering, Will went over and helped himself to more whiskey. He sat on the couch, expecting questions, but the Premier and PM said nothing for a few minutes. Their faces were blank with shock and disbelief.

"You mean the US, Britain, Japan, all the industrialized nations – they're in the same boat?" the Premier finally asked.

"Yup, as far as I know."

"What … who the hell would do this? Who is responsible?" the Premier asked.

"It looks like a company called Global Enviro Oil," Will said. "I've no proof, though."

He told them about Zain's intelligence work and about the salesmen who had visited his plant, but as comprehension set in, the culprit was less important than the outcome of the crime.

"How will Albertans live through the winter? What about power, water, and heat in the upcoming winter?"

The Premier was pacing the floor and waving his hands wildly as he spoke.

"Things are going to get crazy out there," he said.

"Looting, stealing, killing – and who's going to stop them? We don't have a mobilized police force or an army."

The Prime Minister was equally disturbed by the news but was thinking more globally.

"How can we communicate with the outside world? Not that it would help. Who could come to our aid?"

The room went quiet. Too many questions and no answers. Each man thought about the impact to their families and friends. They sat in silence, helpless.

Will looked at the two of them. They were the most powerful, influential men in Canada, yet here they were as helpless as every other man on the street. A tiny bacterium had brought the establishment to its knees; it didn't matter who you were or how much money you had.

The men drank quietly for a time.

Then the Premier doubled back to Will's suspicions about GEO.

"I know where their office used to be," he said. "It was something to do with anti-corrosion, but they went belly up months ago. So, do you think they have stopped injecting the bacteria since they're no longer in business?"

"I think the bacteria take a certain length of time to accumulate to a critical mass. My guess is they knew exactly how long it would take to activate and pulled up stakes before it happened. So that's the good news. The bad news is that we're probably at the beginning of the cycle. There'll be a lot more explosions ahead."

More silence.

The Prime Minister put his head in his hands and started to weep. He pulled himself together for a moment, finished off his whiskey and slammed the glass on the table.

"How will I get back to Ottawa? My kids are so young. What's life going to be like for them? Will I ever get to see them again?"

"I'm so glad that Louise isn't here for this," the Premier said.

His wife, Louise, had died of cancer the previous February. It had hit him hard and his staff had worked tirelessly to make it appear that he was handling it with grace and dignity. But he still hadn't really dealt with her death. He would often sit in his office and have conversations with her as if she was sitting next to him.

Norman excused himself for a moment and left the room. The PM and Will avoided eye contact. They were brooding about their families and what would become of them. Then Will heard a familiar double click in the room next door. As he scrambled to his feet, a loud bang reverberated off the walls.

Norman had decided it was time to join his wife.

# Chapter *27*

## *October 2012*

*I*t had only been ten days since Will met with the Prime Minister and told him that life would never return to normal. A new reality was emerging. It was survival of the fittest – survival of anyone with a gun. Everything had changed. Most of the things we take for granted – police, fire protection, and medical care – were all gone. More important, food was very scarce. Water was available from the river, but untreated it could lead to severe illnesses like beaver fever, or even worse, cryptosporidiosis.

The biggest difference between this new nightmare and previous catastrophes was that before people could count on outside help. When tsunamis or earthquakes or hurricanes had hit, caring people around the world did their part to pitch in. But this nightmare had no end in sight and there was no one to come to the rescue. People everywhere were experiencing the same problem.

Will remembered the chaos in New Orleans after hurricane Katrina. In just a few days, every vestige of civilization had vanished. Law enforcement was powerless. Thanks to modern technology, people around the world had ringside seats and looked on in horror as people died waiting to be rescued. But Will knew no one was watching this time. And no one would be coming. New Orleans at its worst would soon look like a day at the spa.

Random explosions continued, but no fire trucks, police cars, or any other type of official vehicle would respond. Fires spread quickly, igniting surrounding buildings. And so the city burned.

Will lay in bed and looked out the window. The sky was filled with smoke. He was sure that women and children were dying in the flames. But he had lost all motivation. There were no heroics when life was just about trying to keep yourself alive however you could.

He lay there remembering the past. At this time of year, he usually picked his favourites for the hockey pool and cheered on the Eskimos in the Grey Cup finals. But things were different now. Hockey, football – those were silly pastimes of last week. Today's reality was that he was thinking about killing the neighbour's dog and barbequing it. Even worse, he was even considering eating his own dog, Finnigan.

Will pitied the general public because they had no idea what was really going on. With no radio, TV, or newspapers, people had to draw their own conclusions. Many thought it was the second coming or some such version of the end of the world. Almost overnight, churches became the most popular places in town.

Religion aside, everyone soon realized that a major food shortage was imminent. Every type of establishment that sold food was raided, torn apart, and thoroughly searched to track down every last crumb of food. Restaurants, convenience stores, cafeterias, and even department stores that sold confectionery were all targeted. Households had stockpiled what they could, but that was just the beginning. Stealing food from one of those places was easy. Hanging on to food was the really tricky part.

The food shortage had created a new system of justice. It was very simple. The guy with the most guns wins. Gangs emerged to roam the city, taking food wherever they found it. And they had some pretty effective tactics. Will saw it play out from his perch on his rooftop. He called to Matt to warn him what to expect.

"Matt, you gotta be on your toes 'cause these guys are slick. It only takes them a few minutes to get into the house and take all the food."

Will stared hard at Matt to make sure he understood the importance of what he was saying.

"Here's what to look for. Yesterday I saw a group of young guys come up the street, all carrying knapsacks. You know what that means?"

Matt's blank look answered the question.

"The knapsacks are to carry the stolen food."

Matt nodded.

"This is how they did it. One of the little bastards lit a piece of gasoline-soaked cloth on fire. He threw it on somebody's porch while the other guys hid out of sight. The homeowner saw that his porch was on fire and opened the door to try and put it out. As soon as he was outside, the little bastard pulled a gun on him and cornered him so he couldn't move. The other shitheads ran in and stole all the food."

"So you'll be on your toes, right? Don't let them even come near the house."

"Yes, I got it, Dad."

Will didn't want to leave Matt in charge of the house but he knew he had to find food.

"Well, they should stay away 'cause they saw me sitting up here yesterday with a shotgun. But I need you to stay up here till I'm back. I'm going hunting. I want to see if I can get one of the hares that are always hopping around the neighbourhood."

When Will returned from his hunt, empty-handed, he saw that Matt wasn't sitting on the roof. He clenched his fists and ran toward the house as fast as he could.

The front door had been broken open. Will's first thoughts were for his wife and daughter. At the sight of the door hanging by one hinge, his heart leaped to his throat. His extreme ability to focus in the midst of chaos is what allowed him to be heroic in other situations. It wasn't serving him well now.

He found Emma, Lauren, and Matt in the kitchen. Lauren was wrapping a bandage on Matt's arm. Emma had a cut on her neck and was crying.

"Emma, are you OK? Lauren?"

Emma nodded through her tears and Lauren tried to explain.

"Will, there was no way to stop them. They shot—"

Before she had a chance to continue, Will started firing questions at Matt.

"Didn't I tell you what to look for? Didn't you see them coming?"

Matt felt terrible. His whole life he'd tried to live up to his father's expectations and had failed. He wanted to do something that would make his father proud of him, but things always ended up in a mess. He really wanted this time to be different.

"I saw them coming, and I cocked the gun. I know they heard it because they scattered. They yelled up to me, 'Hey man, we just want to talk to you. Chill. Just want to ask if you want to join us.'

*Patricia McConkey*

"I told them to back off. There's no way I was going to join them. Then I told them I was going to shoot one of them if they didn't back off.

"Then the leader said, 'OK, OK – we're moving on. Chill, man.'

"So they all started to head down the street, all but the guy who had snuck around the back and was behind me. He took a shot at me and hit me in the arm. That's when I dropped the gun."

Lauren picked up the story from there.

"When I heard the gunshot and saw Matt's rifle drop to the sidewalk, I thought he had been shot. Just as I turned the front door handle, one of the guys ran at the door and kicked it down.

"The force of the blow knocked me backward and I banged my head on the bench. I guess it knocked me out."

Matt said, "I jumped down from the roof and tried to recover the gun, but they were too fast. Mom was passed out and they had a knife at Emma's throat. There was way too many of them. I couldn't fight them all. They said that if I didn't show them where the food was, they'd kill Emma and Mom. We went downstairs and they took as much as they could carry."

Matt hung his head and started to cry.

Lauren held him.

"I'm so sorry Mom. I tried, but there were so many of them."

She held him close and wept, too.

"You couldn't have stopped them all. Honey, I love you. You did the best anyone could. There was no other way. I'm just glad that you're alive. It's OK, we'll get through this. Don't worry. Let's get your arm patched up."

Lauren tried to get her thoughts in order. She was upset

and her head was still pounding from the fall. She feared what Will might do.

Will didn't hear a word of what they said. He was furious that Lauren and Emma had been hurt but was more concerned about how much food had been taken. He ran to the basement to see what was left. He quickly scanned the room and concluded that they had taken all the canned meat, most of the bottled water, and whatever else they could find.

Will was seething. That was their only chance to stay alive over the winter. He bounded back up the stairs two at time. Lauren was still patching Matt's arm when Will grabbed the front of his sweatshirt and pulled Matt up, face to face.

"I told you that they would try! I told you. Didn't you hear me? You shoulda shot 'em as soon as they were in range. What do you think we're gonna eat all winter?"

Will was like a machine. He was angry, powerful, and using very few higher mental functions. It was an extremely effective combination for Will, making it a pretty one-sided fight.

Lauren knew she had to get his attention. She was almost a black belt in Tae Kwon Do but had never used her skills for anything other than sport. Will was standing only inches from Matt. She wanted to hit him without hurting Matt. If she could land a blow on the back of Will's head, it would not seriously injure him but would give her enough time to get between them and even things out. From a fighting stance, she spun around to do a back roundhouse kick.

Unfortunately for Lauren, Will had often helped her practice this kick. He saw her approach and knew exactly where she was going. Just before she landed the kick, he

*Patricia McConkey*

caught her foot and pushed it straight up. This caught her by surprise, and she lost her footing, and fell back hard, hitting her head again. She curled up in a fetal position and moaned softly. She had a concussion and wasn't going anywhere.

When Will first started his insane tirade, Matt felt he had deserved it and hung his head to accept his punishment. But seeing what his father had done to his mother, he clenched his fist and landed a staggering blow to Will's jaw.

Will swayed and fell to his knees. All was quiet for a moment as the men eyed each other. The loathing and disgust in Will's eyes were equally reflected in Matt's eyes.

"Mom, are you OK?" he asked.

She groaned in response.

"I'll look after her. Don't worry," Emma said, sitting on the floor and stroking her mother's back.

"Mom, I love you," Matt said. "I always will. And Emma, I've never said it, but I love you, too. I can't stay. It's probably better that I don't. Mom, I'll miss you."

He bent down and kissed her head. She was barely conscious.

"Matt, don't!" Emma cried, though she knew he wouldn't listen.

"Matt, Mom and I love you. I know she would say it if she could. Stay safe."

Matt snatched his coat. He didn't look back as he walked away from the only home he'd ever known.

# Chapter 28

*M*att had always known that he had never measured up to his father's expectations, but now he saw his father in a different light. His father had judged him without knowing the facts. Matt thought his father's anger was childlike and unjustified. His actions toward Lauren were cold and heartless, even abusive. Matt couldn't stand for that.

He knew that his mother was trying to protect him with that crazy move she tried. Gutsy move, but obviously not going to work on Dad, he thought. Still, he worried about her safety and wondered if his departure would leave her more vulnerable.

No, he thought, nice try. She's probably better off without me. The only reason she got in this mess in the first place is because she was trying to save my ass. He decided his departure was the best move for his mother's safety. But what about himself?

He walked the deserted streets and tried to think what to do next. Although he needed to concentrate on food and shelter, his thoughts always wandered back to Sarah. Sarah was the love of his life. She was a tiny, dark-haired, quiet-natured girl who never judged him. It didn't matter what he did, she seemed happy with who he was. He never had to prove himself in her eyes.

But things had changed a few months ago.

Matt had been seeing her for over two years, and was starting to think of long-term plans for a future with her. He wanted to buy a house, get married, and have a family – the whole enchilada. He considered how he could make this happen.

He had found a small garage that had been abandoned for a few years, and was hoping to start a small business in customizing vehicles. Put an airbrush in his hands and he was like Michelangelo. In order to get things going, he was going to have to borrow some money from his mother and a friend of the family.

But before things got off the ground, he and Sarah broke up.

Sarah had contracted a venereal disease. Matt had been tested and was negative, so the question was, how did she get it? Sarah denied any wrongdoing and Matt wanted to believe her. However, the doctor had said it was very unlikely she could have contracted it in any way other than having sex. They had a huge fight. It put a stop to every-thing – their relationship and his plans for the garage.

Will didn't know about Sarah or about Matt's business plans. Matt had sworn his mother to secrecy and she had honoured her word. He'd really wanted to get the business going, not only to make it successful for Sarah, but also to prove something to his dad. But everything went sideways. After the incident with Sarah, he didn't have the drive to keep going. His mother tried to reassure him that in time he'd feel better. But he couldn't see the point if he didn't have Sarah.

There were bigger problems now, but thoughts of food

and shelter took a back seat to those related to Sarah. He wondered what he could say to her. If he said he forgave her that would imply she was guilty, and of course she'd be offended all over again. He had to talk to her but knew her parents wouldn't allow it. They had assumed Matt was the one to infect her and she had not volunteered the truth. Matt was no longer welcome in their house.

It didn't matter which way he intended to go, he always seemed to end up near her house. Dusk was falling and the temperature was dropping rapidly. He hid shivering behind an electrical box on the neighbour's lawn, just across the street from her house. He'd wait until dark and try knocking on her bedroom window.

It was dark now and much colder. He looked at her room and saw a flicker of light, probably a candle. He had to try. He put one foot on the brick ledge and held on to the drainpipe. Within a minute, he was on the garage roof. It wasn't the first time he'd gone up this way. He crawled under the window, peeked in, and saw her huddled under her blankets, reading by candlelight. He gently tapped on the window, startling her.

Sarah looked at the dark outline hovering just outside her window and was paralyzed with fear until she realized it must be Matt. She couldn't see his face, but recognized his strangely long fingers pressed on the glass. She went to the window and slid it open.

"What are you doing here?"

"Can I come in? I really want to talk."

"OK, but you have to be really quiet. My parents will kill you if they find you here."

Matt slid through the window, landing on his hands, and pulled the rest of his long lanky body inside. Sarah closed the window, motioning him not to speak. She blew

*Patricia McConkey*

out the candle, pulled him into the closet, and closed the door. Luckily, Sarah had a walk-in closet, so there was more than enough room for both of them.

"I just wanted to see if you were OK. I've been thinking about you so much, worrying ..."

"Matt, I've been thinking about you constantly. I really, really wanted to talk to you. There's something I want to tell you."

Sarah fidgeted with her hands, then sat cross-legged on the floor. She pulled Matt down, and he sat facing her, looking at her sadly. She wanted to tell him, but didn't know where to start.

"Sarah, look, I don't care about the past. I don't care what happened. I just want to know if you still care about me."

"Matt," she said, sobbing, "I love you more than I ever have. You are the best and I, I ..."

"Sarah, let's not even talk about it. I just want you. I don't need to know what happened."

"No, I have to say it. I have to know if you can forgive me. It was at that party, the one you couldn't come to. I got really drunk, and Brandon started coming on to me. He said that we could fool around and you would never know. I knew it was wrong, but I was just so out of it, I let it happen. I am sooo sorry. I've felt so bad ever since. I wanted to say something, but I was so scared you would hate me. I was wrong, and being drunk was no excuse. Please forgive me."

Marble-sized tears ran down her face.

Matt's eyes filled with tears, too. He wiped his nose on his coat sleeve. He wasn't sure what to say. He felt betrayed but he knew he still loved her. For all he knew the world was ending, his girlfriend had just admitted to cheating on him, and here he was sitting in a closet hiding out from her parents.

His head was spinning with anger, love, betrayal, desire.

Then Sarah touched his face. It was like the warmth of the sun and a lightning bolt at the same time.

He threw his arms around her and they hugged, wedged between shoes and dirty clothes. Sarah reached under his shirt and ran her hand up his slender body. Before the Change happened, Matt was totally cut with a picture-perfect body. Now, lack of food had made him gaunt and angular. She stroked his body gently.

Matt touched Sarah's face and held it as if it was the most precious thing in the whole world. He kissed her tenderly, leaving her lips wanting more. He breathed in deeply through his nose and smiled as he remembered her sweet mango-pineapple scent. She kissed his hand and slid it down her neck to her breast. He exhaled in ecstasy.

"Wait – I just thought of something," Sarah said. "Don't move. Stay here."

She got up and opened the closet door.

Matt heard her open her bedroom door and walk down the hallway to the top of the stairs.

"Mom, I'm going to sleep now. I blew out the candle so no need to look in on me. Good night. Oh, I'm closing my door 'cause it stays warmer in my room. See you in the morning."

"Good night Pumpkin. Sweet dreams," her mom called up to her.

"Good night, Mom and Dad. Love you."

Sarah closed the door and propped a chair up against it. She went back to the closet where Matt was sitting with his legs stretched out. She sat facing him with her legs wrapped around his back. For a long time, they sat and just looked into each other's eyes, wondering what to say and do about the past and what the future would bring. Both knew that a lot had changed, but they wanted to turn the clock back.

*Patricia McConkey*

Sarah thought it would take time to build Matt's trust so she moved slowly, not wanting to rush into anything. She put her hands on his face and opened her mouth to say something, but Matt stopped her.

"No, don't say anything."

Sarah understood. She knew she had caused Matt a great deal of pain, and now she wanted him to know how sorry she was and how much she still cared about him. She put her arms around his neck and pressed her body as close to his as she could. She wanted every fibre of her being to scream "I love you," without saying it in words.

Matt closed his eyes and could feel her love in the warmth and softness of her body. He buried his head in her neck as she stroked his back.

Sarah slid her hands under Matt's shirt and pulled it off over his head. He put his hands at her waist, hesitating for a moment as he slid his hands under her shirt.

"I want you to know that I never stopped loving you and I never will," Matt whispered in her ear.

Sarah put her hands on the back of his neck and kissed him hard as tears poured down her face. She paused just long enough to pull her shirt off and unclasp her bra. Matt made a small sound of pleasure, and she pressed her naked torso against his.

Sarah gently pushed him so he was lying on his back. She kissed his chest, and ran her tongue around his nipple, flicking the nipple ring up and down. Then she put the silver ring in her mouth and sucked hard. Matt groaned with pleasure and pain.

"Shhhhhh. You have to be quiet."

Matt took a shirt from the floor of the closet and stuffed it in his mouth.

"Bedda?" he said quietly with a mouth full of shirt.

"No," she said. She dislodged the shirt. "I'll use my tongue to keep you quiet."

She applied a big wet kiss, and pushed her tongue firmly down his throat.

Matt rolled on top of her and cradled her in his arms. His left hand caressed her shoulder and then down her side.

"Matt, make love to me."

"Where do you think I was going with this?"

He reached for her hand and placed it on his bulging pants.

"It's just for you, baby."

# Chapter 29

*Matt* and Sarah made love all that night. It was close to dawn when they finally fell asleep in each other's arms. Late the next morning, Sarah awoke with a jolt.

"Oh my God. What time is it? My mom will come in here looking for me."

She found her bra and pulled a shirt from a hanger and threw it on. She pulled on her pants without any underwear.

"What am *I* going to do? Live in your closet?"

"No, I'm going to tell my mom and dad the truth, and tell them that you're living here now."

"Can I come with you to talk to them? I have a few things I want to say."

Sarah looked hesitant. She knew it would be a tough pill for her parents to swallow and thought it might be best if she tried talking to them alone.

"No, really, it's important," Matt said.

"OK, but put some clothes on."

"Yeah, right. Like I was planning to go like this."

Matt wondered what he was going to say to Sarah's parents. He wanted to tell them that he loved her very much and that he was going to do everything in his power to protect her and provide for her in this new way of life. He didn't understand what was happening, but thought that he could still open the garage as soon as things got back to normal.

Sarah fidgeted while Matt got dressed. She couldn't believe it was ten a.m. and her mother hadn't knocked on her door to wake her up yet. Matt put his hands on her shoulders.

"Everything will be all right. Don't worry. We can make this work."

They opened the door and looked into the hallway. They leaned over the railing but couldn't hear anything.

"Why are they so quiet?" Sarah whispered as she led him downstairs.

Each step they took on the carpeted stairs made a quiet squishing noise but sounded extraordinarily loud because the house was so quiet. At the base of the stairs, they saw that the front door was open. Matt's heart pounded. He jumped in front of her.

"Sarah, get back upstairs."

Sarah didn't understand. She took a few steps up toward the bedrooms just to placate him, but when he turned to go into the kitchen, she quietly followed.

Matt inched his way toward the kitchen. He saw blood-stains on the floor. He poked his head around the corner and gasped. Sarah's parents were lying on the floor in an enormous puddle of blood. Their throats had been cut. The cupboards were open and empty.

Matt sensed Sarah's approach and tried to push her back before she could see them, but it was too late. She screamed and fell to her knees. He wrapped his arms around her and held her tight. There were no words to make the situation any better so he just held her while she cried. He carried her back upstairs and put her on the bed. He sat next to her, holding back his own tears.

After consoling Sarah, Matt went down to the kitchen. He wanted to see if there was anything left to eat. He found half a dozen cans of food and some dried pasta the raiders had missed. In the bathroom he looked through the cupboards and found some extra strength ibuprofen and thought that would do the job. He rummaged around, found a can opener, and headed back upstairs.

Matt walked quietly into Sarah's room in case she had fallen asleep, but she still lay in exactly the same spot.

"Sarah, I want you to take these. It's just a couple of painkillers, but it might help you. Here, I brought a can of pears. You can use the juice to take the pills."

Sarah looked at him with red, swollen eyes and said not a word.

Matt pulled her to a sitting position and put the pills in her mouth. Then he gave her a spoonful of pear juice. She swallowed. He continued to feed her a few more bites of pear before she slumped down in bed and turned her head.

"I want you to listen to me. I love you. I am always going to be here to look after you, so I don't want you to worry. We'll get through this, together. Now I am going to go outside for a little bit. I won't be far if you need me. I'll be in the back yard."

Sarah tried to speak, but no words came out. She went back to her almost catatonic state.

October in Alberta meant freezing temperatures and rock-hard ground, so there was no way to dig a grave. Matt looked around and came up with a plan. Henry and June had a beautiful backyard rock garden with annuals and perennials carefully interlaced between thousands of rocks.

Matt remembered June proudly telling him that she had over twenty tons of rock there and had decided the placement of each one. He felt slightly guilty as he took a shovel and started to pry them loose. He knew she'd be happy to be buried with them. At this point there wasn't much choice.

He found some of Henry's old work clothes in the house. After covering himself as much as possible with old clothes and rubber gloves, he went into the kitchen to collect the bodies.

He bent down over June. Her milky eyes stared back at him with a blank expression. A chill went up his spine. He pushed her eyelids closed. Leaning this close to the bodies made him gag from the smell of urine and feces. He stepped back and took a deep breath of fresh air. Then, working quickly, he took June under her arms and dragged her toward the door leading to the backyard.

As he was walking backward toward the door he slipped in the pool of blood, landing on his back with June on top of him. He clawed her off and ran outside, heaving as if he was about to throw up. But he'd had so little to eat the previous day, there was nothing to come up.

After a few minutes, his heart rate settled down to a near normal rate, and he went back to work. Watching where he placed his feet, he managed to get June to the flat spot in the yard he had chosen. Next was Henry. He was much heavier, and for some reason smelled worse, but his body was still pliable, which made him easier to move. Matt dragged him a few feet, then stepped outside to breathe. It was a long, slow, unpleasant process, but eventually Henry was on the garden grass next to June.

Matt thought he should cover them with something before placing the rocks on their bodies. He found an old tarp in the garage and laid it over them. As he worked, he

148                                              *Patricia McConkey*

wondered if there should be some sort of ceremony before he covered them with rocks. He thought it best that Sarah not see their faces again. He didn't want her to remember them like this. He covered the bodies with the rock cairn. He and Sarah could have a proper memorial tomorrow, once she had a bit of time to adjust.

He continued his back-breaking work until he was ready to pass out from thirst and hunger. He was dreaming of water, thinking that it would be nice if he could wish it into existence. Then out of the corner of his eye, he saw a rain barrel under the downspout of the eavestrough. He said a little prayer as he peeked over the top rim. Hallelujah – it was almost full.

Matt was not a religious person, but things looked a little different after you buried your girlfriend's parents in their backyard. He felt his prayers had been answered. He drank until he felt bloated. Then he opened a can of beans and ate the entire contents in less than two minutes.

He peeled off the bloodied clothes and threw them in the garbage bin. Although he hadn't got any blood on his own clothes, he still felt dirty after handling the bodies. He thought using some of the precious water to wash up was justified. He took two jugs of water into the bathroom, used one to wet his body and get soapy, and the second to rinse off. The water was ice cold, but it felt good to get clean.

He got dressed and quickly headed back upstairs to see how Sarah was doing.

She was still lying motionless on the bed, with her back toward him. She looked so still and quiet. Then Matt's heart stopped. The bottle of painkillers had been emptied. For a moment he was unable to move.

"Matt, I decided not to kill myself, but only because I don't want to hurt you," Sarah said in a barely audible voice.

"Holy shit, Sarah!"

Matt fell to his knees and buried his head in her chest. He was shaking so hard that the bed jiggled.

"Get into bed with me," she said quietly.

"Sarah, I love you! Don't ever leave me. Say you'd never ... do something like that."

Matt couldn't say the word aloud; it scared him too much. He was shaken to the core.

She kissed him and held him close and told him how much she loved him. She would always love him, and would never leave him for another man. But she couldn't make that last promise. Today she was seconds away from swallowing that whole bottle of painkillers. She didn't want to hurt him again, but the urge was still there. She didn't want to go on living.

# Chapter 30

## September 2012

*Zain* opened his eyes to find himself lying face down on a catwalk at the refinery. The cold cement provided a slight relief for his scorched body. The metal walls and the roof of the building had been blown off by the force of the explosion. He could smell thick black smoke coming from the ruins.

He tried to remember what had happened. He vaguely remembered running for the door with Will. His body was throbbing. He couldn't think clearly. He closed his eyes and tried to focus on his breathing to get control of the pain long enough to take stock. He couldn't lift his head, the pain was too intense. Out of the corner of his eye, he saw a long metal object protruding from his back.

He had never pictured dying like this. But this looked like the end, all right.

One part of his brain wanted to surrender, to end the pain, but another part was still struggling to survive. He could feel the silver angel wings clutched in his hand. He longed for Kabira. Before she came along, he felt invincible. He had no one to care if he lived or died. His mother had died in a boating accident when he was twenty-five, and he had no other family. He felt free to lead a life of danger. Now things had changed. As he lay there dying, all he could think of now was the love of his life and their unborn child.

Zain had lived like a cat, narrowly escaping death many times. He must have used up his nine lives. He prayed, not for himself, but that Kabira's child was his and that some part of him would live on.

Just a short time ago, he would not have cared about anything beyond himself. His attitude had been that life and the oil companies had screwed him, and it was up to him to pay them back.

Now he had to admit he was no different from all of the average people he despised – the ones leading small, trivial lives in beige and green homes in suburbia. The ones who mowed their lawns in neat geometric patterns and went to work for the oil companies. They didn't care about the consequences their actions had as long as they got their paycheque every two weeks. There he was, dying on cold cement, and all he was thinking about was his girlfriend and "his" baby. He finally understood all those people who just wanted to look after their families.

As he lay there, his thoughts drifting, he heard shuffling and voices. He clutched the wings in his hand and willed himself to live so he could tell Kabira he believed her, believed it was his baby. He could barely breathe, so yelling was out of the question. He heard the voices coming closer.

"We can cut across here to the back parking lot. My house is only a ten-minute walk," he heard one of them say.

"Great, I'm freezing. That water was cold. I think my balls are the size of raisins."

It was Doug. He had gone looking for his best friend, Ken, who also worked at the plant, when he learned of the

*Patricia McConkey*

imminent danger. But just as he found him, the plant went up in flames. Luckily, they were close to the water reservoir. They jumped into the water and stayed there until the flames died down. They were fine, except for a slight bit of hypothermia. Once the explosions had stopped, they decided to make their way through the rubble to Doug's home.

"Holy shit, Doug, look at this."

Ken leaned over Zain's bloody, burnt body, skewered in the back with a huge triangular-shaped piece of metal. His face and most of his body was covered with blood. When the machinery exploded, the metal casing on the motors had splintered into thousands of pieces, many of which were embedded in the poor bastard.

"I hope he went quickly," Ken said.

Just then, Zain grabbed Ken's ankle.

"Bastard's still alive! I was just talking to this guy before it happened. He's the one who figured out what's causing the explosions."

"What do we do with him?" Ken asked. "He doesn't look like he's gonna last much longer. Do we just leave him here?"

Before they could make that decision, Zain motioned Doug to come closer. Doug got down on one knee and leaned his ear close to Zain's mouth.

Zain's words were barely audible.

"Get me out of here and keep me alive. I have enough food to feed you and your family all winter."

"Did you hear what he said?" Doug asked, looking at Ken.

"What if he's lying?"

"Maybe, but he did know a lot about this whole situation. He might have had time to prepare. Maybe he stockpiled a shitload of food 'cause he knew the mess we were headed for."

Doug looked at Zain, who attempted to nod.

"Well, I don't know if he's lying or not, but I can't just leave him here. That's not right. My wife's a paramedic. She can give him a few shots of painkillers to make him more comfortable. C'mon. Get that dolly over there and we'll load him on it. We can push him to my house. It's not far."

"How am I s'posed to grab him? He's got a hunk of metal coming out of his back bigger'n a dinner plate."

The normal way to pick up a limp body is for one person to support it under the arms while another takes its feet. That wasn't possible with Zain. They had to be careful so as not to make his injuries worse.

Doug looked at Zain and sighed.

"OK, man, we gotta get you outta here and it's gonna hurt when we move you. Hang tough."

Doug grabbed Zain's belt while Ken lifted under his arms and tried to lift him as gently as possible onto the dolly, keeping him on his stomach so as not to push the metal object in any further.

The pain made Zain pass out.

Doug checked his pulse. He was still alive so they decided to continue.

Doug's wife was an instructor for paramedics, and she also worked as medical standby at public events. She had lots of medical supplies at home. Doug thought she would know what to do with Zain, even if it meant just giving him enough pain medication to help him die peacefully.

Doug and Ken shivered as they walked to Doug's house pushing the trolley as casually as if it held a side of beef. Once in a while they took a quick look to see if Zain was still breathing, then continued talking about what they would do all winter with no hockey to watch.

They reached Doug's house and argued for a moment about how to get him inside since Doug had about six steps up to his front door. They decided they would have to lift the entire dolly into the house. This would be difficult because of the weight.

Doug called his wife out to help. She was a strong, sturdy woman. With Doug and Leslie on each side and Ken on one end, they carefully lifted the dolly up the front steps and into the living room. They gently lowered Zain onto a blanket Leslie had laid out.

She sighed as she looked at Zain, wondering if it was worth the effort.

"Help me get his clothes off," she said.

Doug and Ken resisted. They were uncomfortable with the idea of undressing another man. But Leslie was a no-nonsense Newfoundlander and would hear no whining excuses. They used scissors to cut off what remained of his shirt and pants. When they came to his midsection, the men backed off.

"What are you afraid of? That I might see somethin' bigger and better? Lord thunderin' Jaysus, get over here and help cut off his undershorts."

Once they had him totally undressed, it was hard not to comment on his tanned six foot four muscular physique. Although he had some nasty burns to one side of his body and was bloody from all the shrapnel, it was clear from the defined six-pack that he pumped iron in his spare time.

"Well bys the by, boys, he does have some pretty nice tools now, don't he?"

Doug shot her a look of anger.

"Oh get a grip. What would I do with this limp noodle anyways?" she said, poking at his flaccid penis. "I'm good for now. I'll call you when I need you. Why don't the two of you head into the basement while I get this handsome stud all patched up."

Handsome was a bit of stretch, but if you looked past the wounds, you could tell he had been a good-looking man before the accident.

Leslie was an uncomplicated woman. She always said exactly what was on her mind, and more often than not, it included some explicit sexual reference. There was no doubting her medical skills, though. She had been the first responder in hundreds of life-threatening accidents and had saved many lives with her quick thinking and skilled hands.

What concerned her most was the large metal fragment protruding from Zain's back. In a different world, she wouldn't try to remove it herself. She would just stabilize the patient until they could get him into surgery. This time it was up to her.

She assessed her patient using the standard ABC method – airway, breathing, circulation. His breathing was shallow, but steady, so the A and the B seemed OK for the moment. C was a problem. The gash on his head would need immediate attention as he was losing a fair amount of blood. Other lacerations were going to require some stitches, but those could wait.

The burns were serious enough that she was worried about infection. While some blood was oozing from the wound around the metal fragment, she thought it best to look after the gushing wounds first. She thought that in the end the hunk of metal would probably kill him.

She knew what to look for. If there were air bubbles coming through the wound, the metal had punctured his lung and it meant certain death, at least in these primitive conditions. When the time came to remove it, if there were

*Patricia McConkey*

bubbles, she would just give him enough morphine to drift off to sleep forever. That would be the best she could do for him.

First thing she needed to do was get some fluid into him along with enough pain medication to keep him unconscious while she sewed him up. She pinned an IV bag to the living room curtain and swabbed a portion of his right forearm in order to insert the needle. He was muscular so it was a bit difficult finding the artery, but once she had the needle in she gave him a hefty shot of morphine and his first dose of penicillin.

She shaved the left side of his head to expose a long arched gash from his temple all the way back behind his ear. She lost count but guessed it took about forty stitches to get that closed up. She applied a pressure dressing to help stop the flow of blood.

After patching up various smaller wounds and lightly covering the burns with gauze padding, she prepared for the main task. She looked at the metal fragment and tried to determine the best angle to pull it out. It seemed to be angling toward the left. She sat on the floor on his left side, braced her feet against his midsection and placed both hands on the jagged metal. She took a deep breath and pulled with all her strength. It came out with a horrible sucking sound. She held her breath as she leaned over to listen for air bubbles popping up through the wound.

# Chapter *31*

## *October 2012*

*A̶lton* Ladner had been the program leader at the Edmonton Universal Church for fifteen years. He was a peaceful, happy man of fifty-five who had a kind word for everyone. He was an excellent leader and provided an atmosphere where people of many different beliefs could meet and discuss anything related to God or the spiritual universe. Alton made sure that everyone got a chance to speak and that no one was demeaned. He was well respected and loved by all.

Alton rarely discussed his personal beliefs in a group setting. He wanted others to have a chance to air their concerns without hurry, so time often ran out before they got around to him. He managed to condense his philosophy into one short thought: We are one, everyone, everywhere, eternally. He even designed a tie-dyed t-shirt with this slogan. Many people snickered over it.

Alton thought it amusing that people didn't realize they were all one spirit, part of a great universal being. Man had attempted to make sense of his own existence by developing various theories on God and the unknown. Over thousands of years, these became religions, each claiming superiority and splintering the population into warring factions.

In all his years at the church, Alton had never encountered a time like the present. It was hard to understand what was happening. It had been approximately twenty days since the power went out, and to everyone's surprise, it never came back on. Although it had only been a relatively short time since the power outage, things had changed dramatically. There was an enormous increase in violence related to food. The resulting fear, anguish, and heartache were taking their toll. In his opinion, there were significantly harder times to come before a new equilibrium could be achieved. However, the new normal would be vastly different from what they were used to.

Alton thought about the changes, trying to understand what was happening so he could help his group through this difficult time. He and his closest friend, George Connor, had talked about it a lot. He knew George was an extremely gifted individual but one who was also very humble and who downplayed his gift. Although George would deny it, Alton considered him to be an interesting mix of spiritual healer and prophet.

George had been strangely quiet about the current events. Alton sensed that he knew more than he was telling. George's only comments had been about how, sometimes in history, it took a great catastrophe to bring about change and a better world.

Even for Alton, the eternal optimist, it was hard to keep positive about this new change. Alton's days were filled with presiding over small funeral services for members killed by gang attacks. Before the crisis, services were held only on Saturday and Sunday. But now people were showing up every night at seven p.m. Tonight would not be any different. So Alton racked his brain to think of a topic to give them some hope.

At six forty-five p.m., he stood at the back of the church greeting people as they came in. Every so often someone would quietly slip him a can of tuna, or fruit, or some other small item of food. He took anything that was offered and graciously thanked them. He knew it was going to be a long winter.

When George and Lauren came to the door, Alton made a point to step in front of them so he could chat to George for a moment.

"George, Lauren, always good to see you."

Lauren nodded but looked past Alton, scanning the crowd.

"Alton, have you seen Emma this evening? She was supposed to be home earlier, but she may have decided to come directly here."

"No, I haven't seen her yet. Maybe she is still on her way."

Lauren barely acknowledged his answer, and headed off to get a closer look at those already seated.

As she was searching, Doug MacDougal grabbed her arm.

"Lauren, how are you?"

It took her a moment to place him, then she remembered he worked at the refinery with Will. She nodded and smiled, but didn't stop moving.

"Can you tell your husband I need to see him sometime?"

"Sure I will," she said. She pushed past him.

Alton turned his attention to George.

"I'd like you to consider getting up and talking to the crowd tonight. We need your positive outlook."

"Not tonight, Alton. I'll be needed elsewhere."

Alton wanted to press for more details, but he could tell from George's sombre look that something was wrong. George was usually so sunny. It worried Alton to see him like this.

"Maybe we can chat later," Alton said, heading off into the small gathering.

A few minutes later, Alton stepped onto the small platform at the front of the room and held up his hands.

"As always, please take a few moments to meditate and focus on your blessings."

As the room went quiet, the tension and sorrow in it seemed to grow. Alton was always happy and confident leading the services, but tonight it felt like an immense burden. He looked around the room and saw pain in everyone's eyes. George caught his eye and nodded. He seemed to be saying, "Just focus on me. It will be OK."

"Hello, everyone," Alton said. "As you may notice, I find these sessions harder than usual because of the great suffering I know everyone is enduring. There is no denying it. These are difficult times, the most difficult times we have ever seen. Only weeks ago, we were all focused on accumulating toys – houses, cars, boats – you name it. We took the necessities of life for granted. Food and water were never an issue. Now everything has changed. I think everyone's primary concern these days is just keeping their families fed and how to stay warm this winter. But family is at the centre now, there is no doubt of that.

"Just for a moment, I want us to change our focus and think back to a happier family time. I want you to remember when your son or daughter was born. I'm betting that every mom and dad can tell a long story about how that little life came into this world – how long the labour was, how they got to the hospital, how the car stalled – or whatever the story was. Looking over this group, I can see lots of mothers, fathers, and grandparents nodding their heads. However, would anyone here say that the pain wasn't worth it?"

Alton gave the crowd a moment to pause and consider his question.

"Of course everyone would agree that the pain suffered during childbirth is well worth the prize you get in the end. Am I right?"

Lauren clapped with the rest of the crowd, but was still distracted. She scanned the crowd in earnest, but still couldn't see Emma. She shot a glance to George and he shook his head. He knew Lauren was worried about Emma, but he couldn't tell her about his vision. He wondered if his vision had been wrong. Maybe it was just a dream. His palms were clammy.

"Now, I know this is difficult, but I want you to think of these times as being like the birth of a baby. Right now we are all feeling the labour pains. At the end of the process, we will look back and see a great benefit to society thanks to our struggle.

"Just like the husband and wife who both played a part to conceive the baby, we all played a part in this current situation. Let me explain what I mean."

Alton shifted uneasily on the stage. He knew the next part of the message was going to be difficult, but thought it needed to be said.

"Think back only a month or two ago. Was anyone here seriously concerned that man was harming the earth with his relentless overuse of natural resources? We all knew about global warming, overfishing the oceans, killing the rain forests."

A slight moan went up from the crowd. Yes, a month

or so ago they vaguely thought about such issues. But now basic survival was their top priority. Alton noted their disgruntled response as they rolled their eyes and shuffled their feet.

"Well, I can see that you agree those were minor concerns, but now we have much greater problems to deal with. But don't you see? Those concerns of yesterday have created our circumstances today.

"Now I know none of you were directly responsible for the chaos happening right outside our door, but in a sense we all made it possible. Everyone used to complain about the environment, energy, and the strange weather patterns that were warming the earth. We weren't happy with the way things were going. We were saying to the universe that we were destroying our beautiful home and needed to think of a new way to live in harmony with the environment. We couldn't continue to rape and pillage Mother Earth until she could bear us no longer.

"Maybe, somehow, some way, the universe heard our feelings of unrest. And responded with the situation we are in today.

"I know this idea sounds a bit far-fetched, but try to remember your history lessons. Do you remember much about World War II and the terrible tragedy in Germany when so many Jewish people lost their lives? I wasn't there, but I can only imagine what times were like prior to Hitler setting his plan in motion. Maybe the average man in Germany looked at the Jewish community and was jealous of their prosperity. Who knows? Maybe there was a general dislike for Jews for many trivial reasons. After all, Hitler didn't work in a vacuum. He had the support of the nation behind him.

"But if you talked to the great majority of regular

German folk before the war and asked them if they wanted to kill six million Jews, they would have thought you insane. They never would have considered it.

I'm examining the past because it was a time of great tragedy and great change. World War II was devastating and took millions of lives. Yet here we all sit. We survived that great change, and went on to build a bigger and better future than anyone at the time could have imagined.

"And now we are that point again. Great change is upon us. The contractions are strong, and it's hard to see the end goal. But we must take some responsibility for where we are. For if we take responsibility for our actions we can weather the change and emerge as a stronger society. Instead of getting mired down in the sad news of today and tomorrow, we must keep our eyes on the horizon. Where are you going to lead your family?

"Maybe our lack of concern about the environment has brought us to this point. It's hard to say, I'm no expert, but let me tell you an analogy about the power of thought. An individual thought is like a snowflake. On its own, it is fragile and delicate with no power over its surroundings. But look what happens when billions of snowflakes combine to create a powerful and unstoppable avalanche. The same is true with our thoughts. They are just as powerful. Unknowingly, *we* have created this avalanche."

Alton stopped speaking abruptly and his mouth gaped open as he stared at the new arrival at the back of the church. The crowd turned and gasped in horror. George was the only one who didn't turn around. He knew what he would see.

# Chapter *32*

## *Earlier that same day*

*E*mma was worried about her friend, Beth. The two had been friends for as long as she could remember. On their first day of school, they had walked down the street holding hands, each trying to be braver than the other. Emma remembered her first sleepover at Beth's, the first time they called a boy, and when she first heard the news about Beth's illness.

Before the Change, Beth had been diagnosed with leukemia. Chemotherapy was scheduled to start just around the time of the power outage. Now, less than a month later, Beth's symptoms were getting worse. She felt sick all over, headachy and with stiffness in her joints. It was a bit like the flu.

Emma went to her house in the morning and stayed with her until late in the afternoon. Most of the time Beth didn't feel much like talking because her head ached, so she lay on the bed while Emma read the Bible to her, or they just sat silently holding hands. In those quiet moments, Emma looked at Beth and remembered the fun times they had together.

Beth had a strong Christian faith, which she tried to practice in every aspect of her life. Beth knew that, if it was her time, she would go with grace because she would meet her Maker in heaven.

Emma respected Beth's religious beliefs, even though hers were quite different. The differences were clear when Emma asked Beth if she would allow George to perform Reiki on her. Beth said it wasn't necessary, but deep down Emma thought that Beth was concerned that it would cross some line in the Christian faith.

Emma sat by the bed and felt helpless as her friend lay in pain. She searched every corner of her mind, trying to think of something that would lift Beth's spirits. Then it came to her. She was so excited she couldn't sit still.

"Beth, I just thought of something I have to do. I'm going out for a little bit but I won't be gone too long. You just rest until I come back."

"Emma, you're the best friend I could ever hope for. I just want you to know that. I love you."

Emma squeezed her hand and swallowed the lump in her throat.

"That's sweet, but I'm not going to be gone long. I have a surprise that I can't wait to show you."

She bent over and kissed Beth's forehead, then she ran down the stairs, slipping on her coat as she headed out the front door. The streets were deserted, but she was still careful to watch for gangs. The gangs had become very smart, using small children as decoys and lookouts. She thought she saw someone peeking around the edge of a fence once or twice, but decided she was just being paranoid. Luckily, the library was only about a fifteen-minute walk.

The library had always been one of her favourite places. Now she could hardly recognize it.

Emma ducked through the broken glass of the front door to find the inside of the building in worse shape than she had imagined. Shelves had been toppled over and books were thrown everywhere. It looked as if a tornado had touched down inside the building.

She crawled through the wreckage to where she remembered seeing the book. She found the pedestal on which it normally sat under a glass security case. It had been overturned and the glass broken. Her heart pounded at the thought of the book being lost forever. Scanning the room, she felt fear rise in her.

Then she saw it, tossed into a corner, left to sit among modern books of little value. The gang that destroyed the room obviously didn't know its worth. Before coming to the library, it had sold for $80,000 to a wealthy collector. But in today's economy, the only thing that mattered was food. Gold, diamonds, and rare books had no value when they couldn't buy food.

Emma carefully tucked the book under her coat and thought about getting home safely. She knew that if someone had followed her to the library they'd be waiting for her to come out the front entrance. As a precautionary measure, she'd go out another exit and take a different way back to Beth's house.

She saw a window that had been smashed at the back of the building. She peeked her head out and couldn't see anyone, but it was dusk and the low light made it tricky to really know. Carefully avoiding the broken glass, she crawled out on top of a dumpster and then jumped to the ground.

She was heading across the parking lot when she heard footsteps behind her. She spun around a saw a boy about nine years old. He was thin, blond, and had pale blue eyes underlined with dark circles. Her heart saddened at his appearance. Probably a short time ago his biggest worry was looking for a cool Halloween costume.

"Look, I don't have any food. I was just in the library."

She looked at him and saw the hunger in eyes.

A high-pitched, bloodcurdling scream was his only response.

Emma started to run toward the buildings across the boulevard. She would be safe if she could make it there. Just as she went to jump the median, someone tackled her from behind. She hit the pavement hard with her assailant on top of her. As she struggled to get her breath back, about five other young guys caught up with them. They surrounded her as she lay on the ground still wheezing. She recognized some of them from her school.

"What are you hiding?" one young man demanded, pointing to the square shape under her coat.

Emma couldn't get the words out.

She held up her hands to show that she was submitting and then slowly reached inside her coat, to prove that it was only a book.

There was a young guy standing at her feet, and he wasn't interested in taking any chances. As Emma reached for the book, he leaned down and plunged a knife into her upper right abdomen.

He justified his move by grunting, "Bitch probably has a gun in there."

He kicked her in the stomach and her coat fell open as she rolled onto her side. The book fell into plain view. The gang members grunted with dissatisfaction at not finding any food and headed off looking for their next meal.

The little guy hung back as the others walked on ahead. He looked at Emma and his big blue eyes started to water.

Emma mouthed the words, "It's OK, don't worry."

He ran off with tears streaming down his face.

Emma lay on the cold payment and smiled: not your usual reaction after being stabbed in the liver. She could feel the warm blood running down her side, but it was the blood seeping into her abdominal cavity that would ultimately kill her. She felt a strange sense of peace and was not unhappy with her fate. Only the thought of her family's grief caused her a moment of unhappiness.

I don't have much time but I want them to know I'm OK, she said to herself as she opened the Bible. She had no intention of reading it.

# Chapter 33

*T*he sun was going down in a cloudless sky, signalling the start to a cold, crisp October evening. It was the day after Sarah's parents died. Matt had organized a memorial service. He and Sarah were the only ones attending, but he wanted it to seem official.

He stood with his back to the pile of rocks that covered Sarah's parents and she sat on a lawn chair facing him. He read a passage from the Bible that he didn't really understand, but the words sounded nice. He remembered the things he liked about her parents: her mother's roast beef dinners, her father's love of hockey, the way they both had a weird, annoying laugh.

He didn't know the words, but he attempted to hum "Amazing Grace." It was kind of sad, but Sarah appreciated the effort. Then he asked Sarah to say some words.

She stood and faced the grave.

"Mom and Dad, I want to say I'm sorry for all the times you worried about me 'cause I was late, for all the times I didn't clean my room, and all the times I lied to you. I'm sorry my marks weren't better."

She paused as her emotions overwhelmed her. She could barely speak.

"I'm sorry that I wasn't the perfect kid."

Her tears flowed freely and she shook so hard she fell to her knees. As Matt put his arms around her, he felt a warm breeze.

"Sarah, listen. Do you hear that?"

Sarah stopped for a moment. She could feel the breeze, too. She stood up, closed her eyes, and breathed deeply. She didn't hear anything, but thought for a moment she could feel her parents' presence. She reached into the air hoping to get something more, some sort of sign, but there was nothing. She felt rejected and sort of stupid for thinking it might have been a sign from her parents. She collapsed to the ground and lay on the rock pile, sobbing.

Matt thought he had heard something in the breeze like voices in the distance, but didn't know if he should say anything to Sarah. He did think it was a sign, but didn't know if he could convince her.

He pulled her off the rock grave and held her close, trying to soothe her with comforting words even though he knew it wouldn't help. To prepare for the service, he had taken a picture from the fireplace mantel. It was taken at a wedding. Sarah's mom and dad were standing with some other relatives. Matt had cut out a small square that had just their faces. He pulled it from his pocket and gave it to her. Sarah held it close to her heart and cried again.

Matt looked at the darkening sky and thought that they should get going. There was no way they could stay in the house. The smell of blood was sickening. He also thought it would be better for Sarah to move on with her life. He packed a knapsack with a few clothes for her and what little food they had left. He had found two heavy sleeping bags that were rated at minus twenty degrees Celsius. It was a good start, he knew, but it would get way colder than that here. Still it was the best he could do.

Matt's plan just might work, if they could get across the city without being killed. That was the one wrinkle. By car the journey would have taken about fifteen minutes. By foot it would take them over four hours. It was slow going. They had to be extra careful. When they finally reached the sixteen-story building, they were both exhausted.

The front doors had already been broken into, so it was easy to gain access to the main lobby. Although it looked as if there were many attempts, it appeared that no one had gained access to the upper floors. The building had a large bank of elevators to the upper levels, but of course with no power they were a dead end. The stairwell door had been broken into, but Matt suspected the intruders would have given up once they saw that each landing had equally strong doors forbidding their entrance.

Matt had been here many times before with his mother. She worked in this building. He knew where the superintendent kept his magic key, the passkey to all the doors in the building. He found it in the usual spot in the broom closet.

After climbing the first two flights, Sarah said, "Matt, I'm so tired, can't we just sleep on this floor?"

"Yeah we could, but I want to go to my mom's office. It has two nice couches we can pull together. Besides, we still have to check out the cafeteria on the fifth floor and see what's left."

Once they reached the cafeteria, they were delighted to see that the snack machine had not been touched. They were soon stuffing their faces full of chocolate, potato chips, and pop. They found a cupboard full of soup and had a can each.

With their bellies full, they could face the eleven flights they still had to climb. Sarah would have given up a few times, but Matt urged her on, telling her it would be safest on the top floor.

Once there, Matt went to his mother's office. He could still smell a faint hint of her perfume in the air. His eyes watered as he thought about how much he missed her. He went to the credenza behind her desk and picked up a photo of himself and Emma when they were just kids. He remembered the day it was taken.

"It was in summer, and Mom had taken the day off work to spend it with us," he told Sarah. "After breakfast, we went for a walk in the park. There was a beaver in the river and we watched him for a while until the sun was so hot that we had to go home. We got our bathing suits on and jumped in our inflatable pool.

"Mom got in the pool with us. She would run around for a few minutes to create a whirlpool, then jump out and watch us float around in a circle. That's when she took this picture. See. We look as if we are just floating, but actually we're moving with the current."

Matt sniffed and wiped his nose on his shirtsleeve.

He busied himself rearranging the office furniture to create their bedroom. He moved the desk against the door to ensure that no one would get through there while they slept. Then he pulled the two leather couches together to make a comfy bed. Matt started zipping sleeping bags together so that they made one big sleeping bag. He smiled at the thought.

Sarah watched Matt work and looked at him as if for the first time. She knew he was only keeping busy so that he wouldn't start crying. She knew he missed his family terribly and that everything he did now was for her – to protect her, to keep her safe in this crazy world they lived in. She tried to think why he loved her. She had caused him so much pain over the past few months, and the past two days she had been like a helpless child as she tried to come to terms with losing her parents.

With a full stomach and feeling completely safe, she smiled and decided to show him how much she cared.

"Matt, are you ready for bed?"

"Yeah, look, the sleeping bags are zipped together so we can keep each other warm."

"Can you get in and warm it up for me? I want to show you something."

Matt was puzzled but did as she asked.

Sarah went over to the desk and pushed everything off with one swoop of her arm. That got Matt's attention. He sat up with a concerned look on his face and started to object. But that didn't stop Sarah. She climbed up on the desk and started to hum a song while dancing around in circles.

Matt had no idea what she was doing until she got to the chorus of the song and started to sing:

*And with a swing of her hips she started to strip,*
*To tremendous applause she took off her drawers,*
*And with a lick of her lips she undid all the clips,*
*Threw it all in the air, and everyone stared,*
*And as the last piece of clothing fell to the floor,*
*The police were yelling out for more ...* *

As she sang, Sarah stripped, but instead of the police yelling out for more it was Matt doing all the hooting and hollering. He joined in the lyrics and started to sing along as he clapped and shouted. He started to pull off his clothing as quickly as he could to be ready when she had finished.

---

\* *Patricia the Stripper, Chris 191*

Sarah did a final pirouette and stood there totally naked. Her five-feet-two frame was thin, but she still had the curves. She looked at Matt and smiled.

"I love you Matt, with all my heart."

Matt stood on the couch and took her hand so she could jump from the desk to their improvised bed. He put his arms around her tiny waist. Matt was touched by her words. He started to return the phrase, but she put her finger on his lips.

"I know how you feel about me. I just wanted to make sure you knew that I am yours, forever."

He smiled and ran his hand along her jaw, through her hair, and down to her breast. Her skin was covered in goose bumps and, to help warm her up, he pulled the sleeping bag up around her shoulders.

"Well, Miss Delicia, as an officer of the law, I'm going to have to put you under house arrest, which means you can't move from this bed for at least twelve hours. And I'll have to examine the evidence very closely."

He knelt down and started to kiss her midsection.

"OK, officer, please be gentle with me ... Ahhhhhh, hee hee. You're tickling. What are you doing down there?"

~

Matt woke up with the sun streaming through the office windows. Sarah's head was under the covers, so she was undisturbed by the bright light. She snuggled in closer to Matt to keep warm. It was a good feeling, having Sarah here with him, knowing they were safe.

Over the next week, life became a series of daily rituals that they came to enjoy.

Matt had found a small piece of fish net pinned to a cubicle wall. Perhaps a Maritimer had worked there. This came in handy for his hunting trips on the roof. He tied a paperweight to each corner and learned how to throw the net just the right way to trap a pigeon or two.

Sarah plucked and gutted them while Matt got a fire going using wooden furniture he had chopped up with a fire axe and carried up to the roof.

Sarah put the pigeon meat into a pot along with the contents of a can of soup and let it boil away until it was well cooked. It actually didn't taste too bad.

Sarah was in charge of rationing and decided that they would have two meals of pigeon soup each day then snack on chips and chocolate in the evening. This way their food would probably last until January. At that point they would raid other office buildings. With a bountiful supply of pigeons, life seemed manageable over the long winter months.

They both took up new hobbies to pass the time.

Sarah chose drawing, given that office supplies were plentiful. She was artistic and sketched moments from her childhood when she and her parents were at their lakefront cottage – when she swam or paddled around in the kayak while her father fished and her mother read novels.

Once in a while, she begged Matt to sit still long enough for her to sketch him. She liked to draw him bare-chested because he had such defined muscles, but she thought it was a bit cruel to make him sit there half naked when it was so cold. Despite this she had managed to do some great sketches of him.

Matt started a journal. He poured out his feelings. Years of injustice, insecurity, and angst came out.

On the eighth night of their stay at "Hotel Sarah," Matt tossed and turned all night, interrupting Sarah's sleep. She was about to shake him to tell him to cut it out when

*Patricia McConkey*

she noticed his expression. He looked tormented and had broken out in a cold sweat.

Sarah was concerned he might be sick, then realized he was having a nightmare. His body went into rigid spasms as he tried to wipe something off his hands and arms.

Sarah was about to wake him when he screamed and bolted upright.

"No, No! Mom!" he yelled, as he reached into the cold darkness.

"Matt, Matt, it's OK; you were dreaming. You're OK. I'm here."

Matt was cold and clammy and still shaking from the scenes that played out in his head.

In his dream, Matt had seen Sarah's mother in the kitchen where she lay covered in blood. He wanted to take her body to the backyard for burial. When he gently slid his hands under her shoulders and lifted, blood started pouring out of her mouth and ears. Matt jumped back and tried to wipe it off on his clothes, but the more he wiped the bloodier he got. There was blood everywhere.

In the dream, Matt saw June's face changing, like a picture taken out of focus. He squinted and refocused his eyes, stumbling backward in horror as he recognized the face. It was Emma. No, it was his mother, Lauren, covered in blood. He couldn't tell which.

"It's my mom or Emma. No, it's Mom. She ... she was covered in blood. I'm afraid ..."

Sarah knew Matt would do anything to protect them. But there was that small matter of his father. Just showing up at his house would start World War III between Matt and Will.

"Matt, what about your dad? Do you think it would cause trouble if you just went back to see if your mom was all right?"

"I'm going to pound him into the ground next time I see him. He doesn't deserve Mom."

"It would only make things worse for your mom if the two of you got into a fight again."

Matt growled but knew what she said was true.

"Well, what if we go see your mom at church tonight? She'll be there and he won't."

Matt threw his arms around Sarah and felt relieved. It was a great idea. He was so happy that she understood how important his mother was to him.

He held her and breathed in her scent. The thought of fighting his father got his testosterone flowing, but now he was thinking of something else and Sarah sensed it.

"Come here, my big handsome guy. I think I have a solution to get rid of your pent-up energy and then we can both have a good sleep."

She slid her hand down his back to his buttocks and grabbed a handful of flesh.

# Chapter *34*

*Matt* had been gone a little over a week. Will couldn't stop thinking about him, wondering if he was safe, cold, or hungry. Even though their parting left Will with a bruised lip, it was nothing compared with the pain and regret he felt over Matt's departure. Despite their disagreements, Will still had normal fatherly instincts. He loved Matt, even though he didn't make it obvious.

In addition to a constant gut-wrenching worry about Matt's safety, Will also felt guilty about everything that had happened.

Lauren ended up with a bad concussion. He never meant to hurt her; he was just trying to avoid a kick to the head. However, she had been rattled pretty badly and had barely moved from her bed for days.

Emma never left her side and couldn't even speak to her father, she was so angry with him. She knew that both her mom and Matt had some responsibility for the way things happened, but that didn't seem to bear any weight as she sat and watched her mother suffer. The result was that her mother was seriously injured and her brother was gone and might never return. To her mind, her father was responsible for both those events.

Emma had always been Will's favourite, even though no good parent would openly admit to preferring one child over another. He admired Emma's drive and ambition. There was nothing she couldn't do once she set her mind to it.

Matt on the other hand seemed to struggle his whole life and could never get that break he needed.

Will thought about his contribution to his children's success and failures. Perhaps his expectations for Matt were partially responsible for his failure. Lately that question had rolled around in Will's mind like a song stuck in his head. Will admitted to himself that he had never been there for Matt. More and more he recognized his failings as a father.

George and Lauren were getting prepared to walk to church for the seven p.m. service.

In a low but assertive voice, Will said, "You shouldn't go. It's too dangerous."

Lauren glared back at him with a fierceness that would make any man cringe.

"What are you going to do to stop me? I'm going and George is coming with me." She paused briefly. "Besides, if I die on the way to church, it's probably a free ticket into heaven."

Lauren looked directly into Will's eyes, daring him to say something that would give her ammunition to start a fight. She had not forgiven him for the way he treated Matt and was ready to mix it up with him every chance she got.

"So you think a seventy-four-year-old man is going to somehow protect you?"

Lauren let that slide because she knew he was right. George wouldn't be much good in a fight, but she much preferred his company these days. His Reiki treatments were magical in relieving her pain over the past week.

"Lauren, are you sure that you feel up to going?" George said. "I can tell you still have a lot of pain."

George was very perceptive. Lauren wasn't feeling her best, but she was tired of lying in bed. She needed to get out and focus on something other than her own troubles.

"Now don't you start on me, too, George. We're going, and that's final."

To Will, she said, "Emma is over at Beth's. She told me she was coming to the service tonight and would meet us there. She'll come home with us later."

Will closed the door behind them. He had managed to hold back his anger in front of Lauren, but now he was free to let loose. He picked up a clay statue and threw it across the room, shattering it on the fireplace mantle. He stomped around the living room cursing under his breath.

The members of his family were out gallivanting around when it was absurdly dangerous to even step outside your door. He couldn't believe they had so little respect for him to continue doing whatever the hell they wanted despite his warnings.

He threw on his black coat and headed out. He followed Lauren and George, hiding behind trees and fences as he went. This method of surveillance worked well until they came to a big park used for soccer, baseball, and football.

Lauren and George were crossing through the centre of this field as a shortcut to the church, which was just on the opposite side. He would have to take the street around the park toward the library and try to catch up with them on the far side as they exited the park.

Will jogged at a good clip to try making up time. As he ran, he remembered that Beth's house was in this direction and kept an eye open for Emma.

Will's stomach burned as his body tried to signal that

he needed to refuel. Will kept jogging. The pain from his stomach, in combination with his anger at Lauren and guilt over Matt, made his head spin. He stopped to catch his breath and try to block out the pain.

He was standing on the boulevard, not far from the library. In spite of the low light, he could see a body lying on the street just ahead. He looked away. He had no desire to help anyone who was hurt. This poor soul was probably dead anyway, he thought. Those sons of bitches don't leave anyone alive.

He breathed deeply and tried to release his pain, but he couldn't focus. The motionless body was too much of a distraction. He knew he couldn't just walk away without at least checking to see if the person was alive. Years of being a hero couldn't be erased in a few weeks.

Although it was dark, he could see that the body was female. He knelt down and swept the long dark hair back from her face, and fell back as if someone had stabbed him in the heart. It was his beautiful daughter's face, eyes wide open and staring at him. He couldn't breathe. For a few seconds his heart stopped. He was in shock. With his hand trembling almost uncontrollably, he reached for her neck to see if she had a pulse. Her skin was cold. There was no sign of life.

Will sat on the ground and cradled his daughter in his arms. He closed her eyes and said, "Sleep now." He rocked her back and forth, remembering how much he loved to hold her when she was just a baby. He hummed the song "Hush Little Baby," just as he had done when she was a tiny bundle in his arms. He stroked her hair, and remembered her over the years.

As he gazed at his perfect little girl, parts of the picture didn't fit together. He smiled at how tall she grown. Her long beautiful arms and legs made her such a good athlete. He picked up her cold hand, placed it on his chest, and held her closer.

You've got to warm up, baby, he thought, as he rubbed her back to warm her.

Reality crept up on Will with the inevitability of day turning to night. He couldn't hang on to his daydream of Emma in the cold Alberta air. He thought about their last days together. Emma had been furious with him. She blamed him for her mother's injury and for Matt's departure. Her anger was unrelenting. It was almost as if she blamed him for everything that was wrong with the world.

Now he didn't have the chance to set things straight and tell her how sorry he was. He wanted to tell that her that he was sorry for the way he had treated Matt and that he never, ever meant to hurt Lauren. He wanted to say all these things just to have her smile at him and wrap her long arms around him. Until now, even during their worst arguments, Emma never stayed mad at him for very long. Will desperately longed to feel that forgiveness, but it would never happen. That realization felt like a knife to his chest.

Will shivered as Emma's blood soaked through his clothing. He started to look at the surroundings and put the pieces together. He saw an old book lying nearby and thought that Emma had probably gone into the library to get it. Then he looked at her position on the road and guessed that she was heading for the church. As Will picked up the old book, his rage started to build.

Will had issues with God, and now this just topped everything. Emma had gone to the library to get a Bible and was headed to church when she was killed. This was perfect proof in his mind. If there was a loving God, how could he have let Emma die with a Bible in her hand on her way to a church service? What kind of Father in heaven could do this?

"Take *me*," he screamed. "I'm a goddamned son of a bitch, but not her. She's perfect. Why would you take her? I'm the one who should have suffered."

Just then the wind ruffled the pages of the Bible and Will saw that there was something written in blood. He picked up the book and read the words. They sent him into a rage.

"You bastard! You goddamned bastard! How could you take her? Oh, that's right. You just sit up there in your comfy cozy heaven while your little pissants down here suffer and die. Well, fuck you!"

Will knew he had failed his family in every sense – his son had left, his wife hated him, and now his daughter was gone. God had certainly failed him, if there ever was one.

He looked at the church and saw the faint glow of candlelight in the windows.

Those stupid bastards are all in there praying to their useless God, he thought.

He put the book on top of Emma and scooped her up in his arms. With each step he took, his rage boiled and the pressure built. The catalyst was only steps away.

He reached the doors of the church and kicked them open. A tall thin man who happened to be standing at the back of the church was shocked at the sight.

Will pushed past him.

He stood at the back of the room, covered in blood and cradling his dead daughter in his arms. When Alton saw him, he froze. The crowd turned to see and gasped in horror.

Will marched to the altar and gently lay Emma down for all to see, carefully arranging her hands to rest on her blood-soaked abdomen. He seemed oblivious to his surroundings as he looked down and softly stroked Emma's cheek. His anger melted away for a moment as he smiled at her beautiful face. The crowd was stunned.

A second later the silence was broken.

Lauren jumped to her feet and ran to her daughter screaming.

"No, no, no, no, this can't be true."

She bent over Emma and wept loudly.

The congregation murmured in hushed sympathy with Will and Lauren's grief. Many of them had experienced similar losses in these last dark days. They wept as mother and father knelt beside the slain body of their daughter.

Lauren wailed as she held her daughter's angelic face. When Lauren began praying loudly, things took an abrupt turn for the worse.

"My God, my God, please help me. Bring her back to me," she cried out.

That was the fuse Will needed.

He clamped his hands onto Lauren's shoulders and lifted her to a standing position.

"Don't you get it? Your God is not going to help you. Where is your God? Is he here now? Where was he when Emma was stabbed on his doorstep? Shouldn't he have stepped in then? He's not gonna help you any more than he helped Emma. Don't ask your fuckin' God to help."

Then he threw her down.

Lauren landed hard and rolled down the stairs. Some men in the crowd jumped up to help her, but George waved them off. He went to Lauren and put his arms around her to comfort her. She buried her face in the collar of his shirt.

"Look at all of you gathered here, to do what? To pray to your God for relief from this fuckin' nightmare?"

Some of the onlookers were calling out for Will to be removed. This time Alton came forward. He could see the wild rage in Will's eyes and worried that trying to remove him by force would just result in someone getting hurt.

"Let him finish what he has to say," Alton said, looking at the crowd, "Then he'll leave peacefully."

He looked at Will as if willing him to agree.

"Oh, that's right. I forgot, the Universe appointed you high and mighty to lead the crowd. And look at them. They do as they're told because they've been brainwashed by this crazy-assed lie called religion.

"Well I'm here tonight to teach you a new lesson. There is no God. Tell me how could there be? How could there be?"

Will picked up the Bible and held it in the air. He walked across the altar, showing it to the whole crowd a smug look on his face.

"How could there be a God? That's my question for you. My baby went to the library to get this book, was on her way to church, and then look what happened. Some son of a bitch decided to stab her and leave her for dead. But she didn't just die. No, no, no. She lay there and had time to suffer, had time to think of all the things that she would never see and do. The pain, I can only imagine how she suffered ..."

Will started to cry.

"She had time to write a message in her own blood, something about the One. Who knows what she was talking about? She believed in this bullshit and that's why she's dead today.

"But where was God in all of this? "Why did he let that bastard take her life? I'll tell you why. There is no God. If there was some sort of Father up there, how could he stand by and watch her suffer and watch the rest of us suffer now? It's all one big fuckin' lie, and the sooner you get that into your heads the better off you'll be."

Will's urge to kill grew as he pictured the gang members and their cowardly act.

"Here's the only thing you can count on."

Will reached around to the back waistband of his pants and pulled out his gun. The crowd gasped and those that were close to the door started to quietly slip out.

"An eye for an eye, a tooth for a tooth … isn't that what the Good Book says?" Will shouted, waving the gun in the air.

"Well, I think we should start that practice right here and now. God, here's one for you."

He pointed the gun at the rafters and pulled the trigger.

The shot ricocheted off the rafters and the sound echoed throughout the hall. The crowd bawled in fright and covered their heads. Lauren stood up and faced her husband.

"Will, put that away. You can go now," she said, with courage and conviction despite her overwhelming sadness.

"Thanks so much for dismissing me, dear, but you have to own up to your crimes. It's your damn fault we're in this situation isn't it?"

Will pointed the gun at Lauren.

"If you hadn't filled our baby's head full of lies, she wouldn't have been coming to church in the first place and this never would have happened."

Alton took a step toward Lauren, trying to protect her from her maniac husband.

"Back off, Alton. I mean it. We're having a little family discussion here and you're not invited."

George motioned Alton to step back and he did.

"So, do you admit it? Did you lie to our baby and tell her that God would save her?"

"Yes, I did, Will. I'm guilty. I told Emma that the universe is filled with love and that all you have to do is believe. If you believe, you are a part of it, your life will be filled with love and joy. Yes, I said that. Guilty as charged. So just shoot me now so I can be with her. I'm ready. Do it. I am totally serious. I forgive you. I love you. Now do it."

Lauren got on her knees and put her head in line with the barrel of the gun.

Will's knees buckled and he almost lost his balance as he started to comprehend what his wife was asking of him. He was enraged at the thought that Emma had died because of God. He wanted to punish Lauren for her part in Emma's death, but he had never thought of actually shooting her. Different parts of his conscience were debating what to do, drowning out all the other noise in the church.

"Will, kill her. She's the reason that Emma is dead."

"Will, you love Lauren. She has been the best part of your life."

"Do it, Will. You know she'll go to *heaven*. Besides, how could she ever love you again after this insanity?"

This last point really struck home with him. No one would ever love him again after the way he acted tonight.

"Maybe it's the kindest thing you could do, Will. Do you really want to see Lauren slowly starve to death over the winter?"

Will knew that was a very real possibility. They would probably all die a slow painful death. But the thought of actually shooting the woman he loved made him feel ill.

Lauren was still pleading with him.

"Do it, Will. I want you to. I'm done here. I want to be with God, with Emma."

She was on her knees with her hands clasped together. Tears streamed down her face. Will's hand shook so hard it caused his whole body to shake. The effects of a huge dose of adrenalin were taking their toll; beads of sweat poured down his forehead and his heart was pounding as if he had just run a marathon.

"*Do it now!*" she screamed at him.

Will wiped his brow on his coat sleeve and put both hands on the gun. It was time for both of them to go. Lauren first, then him. It was right. He squeezed the trigger. Only Will heard the click of the hammer in the barrel.

"No!" Matt bellowed from the back. He ran to the altar and bent down to hold his mother.

Will fell to his knees, shaking, sweat dripping from every pore in his body. He looked at the gun. He had pulled the trigger, but he was out of ammunition. He turned it on himself, but that was pointless without bullets.

Matt stared at his father in shock and disgust. He could see at a glance that his mother was unhurt but in shock. She choked as she struggled to catch her breath. Matt told her to breathe deeply and that she was going to be OK. He held her tightly and wouldn't let go.

He turned and glared at his father with more hatred and fury than the devil himself.

"Get away from us, you son of a bitch. Haven't you done enough?"

Will felt a strong shiver run through his body, and it was as if his eyes had just opened. He was awake. He had been in a nightmare and had just woken up. Only in this nightmare, he was the bad guy. He could see that his actions were totally insane, and he felt small and cowardly.

"I am *not* your son. I don't know you. *Get out of here!*"

Spit flew out of Matt's mouth as he screamed. He burst a blood vessel in his eye from the sheer force of his words.

Will stood there confused and ashamed. His eyes beseeched Lauren, not for forgiveness because that was too much to ask for, but for some sort of understanding that his grief had caused this insanity.

Lauren had buried her face in Matt's arms and Will realized he wasn't going to get the chance to explain. He had alienated everyone in his family, first his son, then his daughter, and now his wife. He had truly lost everything. He put the gun in his pocket and skulked to the back door.

Everyone exhaled in relief.

As he held his mother close, Matt saw Emma lying beside her. The dream must have combined the two events. He was too late to help his sister, but he was thankful that his mother was still alive. Matt loved his mother with all his heart and her pain was unbearable.

"Matt, I... I... I thought I would never see you again and, with Emma gone, I didn't see the point of—"

"I know Mom. I didn't know if I was going to come back, but I needed to see you, to make sure you were OK. I was worried about you and Emma."

He told her if there was a heaven Emma would be a first-round draft choice.

George smiled at Matt's sports analogy.

"He's right, you know, Lauren. Look, she left us a message."

He read it aloud. "I love you all. Be happy for me. I am one with ..."

Here the message trailed off.

# Chapter 35

## August 2012

*Dietrich's* pulse was racing and his palms felt sweaty as he drove away from the coffee shop. Maybe he was having a stroke or a heart attack. He pulled over and clawed at his chest. He felt extreme pressure there and was having trouble breathing. He reclined his seat and put his arms above his head.

"Slow deep breaths," he said, trying to reassure himself that he could get through this.

He started counting his breaths. With each one the pain lessened slightly. By the time he got to two hundred he was feeling a little better.

He thought about the girl in the coffee shop, Raspberry Lips. She was so beautiful and had such a good heart.

"I'm doing the right thing. I know it. I'm following God's plan."

He knew he just had to stay focused. Still, he remembered her round lips and sweet scent and thought about her future. He knew there was a good chance she would not make it through the winter.

Dietrich thought about the plan and was reassured. Only

God could have revealed it to him. God didn't want man to live his life as a slave to money and machines. What better way to get rid of machines than to poison their very source of energy – fossil fuels? Dietrich knew God had planted the idea in his head and made him a vehicle for his work.

Dietrich thought back to his Bible studies. He knew that God gave his disciples tough jobs, and that every one of them had struggled with the task assigned. Abraham was instructed to sacrifice his only son on a mountain. Dietrich thought about the pain and anguish Abraham must have endured as he prepared to kill his only son. And Moses had to lead his people into the desert in spite of their constant whining and complaining.

The Bible was full of great men who struggled against God's plan for them. That didn't make them any less remarkable but just showed that these heroes were human after all. The important thing was that, in spite of their weakness and incomprehension, they were able to complete the tasks that God assigned them. That's what set them apart from the others: they were strong enough to continue in spite of their doubts.

Dietrich compared himself with these men. If he was having a moment of weakness, all he had to do was remember that it was God's plan and it must be carried out.

It's a little late to be worrying about the plan now, he thought as he drove. It's done. It can't be reversed even if I wanted to. Besides, justice must be done for my mother and sister in heaven. An eye for an eye, a tooth for a tooth. That's how it goes.

Dietrich breathed easier. He must be doing the right thing. He continued driving. It was still safe to do so. It was early July and he knew that the effects of the bacteria would not start taking effect until September or later. He drove past refinery row and shook his head. Soon they will all see the light, he thought. God's plan will be revealed.

Although it was a relatively short drive to the colony, only about twenty minutes outside the city, Dietrich had not been there since he left at eighteen. He had often wanted to return home but knew that the plan would not be completed if he lived in the colony. He thought it was better not to go back until he could stay. That day had now arrived. He was driving home. Soon the modern world would be a thing of the past.

He pulled his car to the side of the road, got out, and looked over the fields. It was August and the hay fields were just at their prime. Swirling patterns of silvery green appeared fleetingly as a light breeze blew on the young fields. Dietrich breathed in the aroma of fresh vegetation and felt the warmth of the sun on his skin. In that moment he felt God was smiling on him, showing him the glorious bounty of the land.

"Excuse me, sir, this is private property."

Dietrich spun around and saw an old man walking toward him. He squinted in the bright sunlight, trying to see the man's features. As the man moved closer, Dietrich's heart pounded with excitement.

"Papa?"

The colour in the man's face drained to a stark white. He tottered over to Dietrich looking as if he had seen a ghost. "Dieter? I never thought I would see you again." He wrapped his arms around his son and cried.

"Dieter, it has been so long. I thought you were lost to the modern world."

Dietrich's eyes watered as he heard his father say his real name. He had not used it since he left the colony. Hearing it made him remember how much he missed his family.

"No, Father, I thought about you, Mama, and Amara every day. All of you, you were always in my thoughts. That's why I'm here now. I have completed the task. We will see justice for Mama and Amara."

When the old man heard Dieter say that, a shiver ran down his spine. He wasn't sure what Dieter meant. It was so long ago that the task was given to the seven young men. It was hard to remember what had been written. Memories came back in fragments. What he recalled best was Dieter's anger.

That last night Dieter had shouted, "Father, remember how Mama died? She was poisoned. That's why Amara was born without arms or legs. They both died because of the poison from the refinery that fills the sky every day. They died less than a month ago. How can you forget? Don't you want justice for that?"

"Yes, I do, but at what price? Will you be lost, all for the sake of justice? You are all I have left."

"The modern world has killed its last from this colony," one of the other fathers shouted. "I say that there is no price too great. We must stand up now or risk losing everything. We must protect our future to live on the land the way God intended. The modern world is slowly killing us. Its evil must be stopped."

No one really knew how old Waldemar was, but he was probably the oldest man in the colony. He sat in the corner listening to all of the arguments. When he cleared his throat, the shouting stopped.

"Perhaps the young men should wait outside. This is a decision the elders will make."

Like all teenagers, they grumbled and complained.

"It's our lives you are deciding on. Shouldn't we get a say?" they said as they were sent out.

*Patricia McConkey*

"Let us talk about the problems," Waldemar said in a thick German accent.

The men started listing the problems as if they were run-of-the-mill issues.

Gunter hung his head and choked back the tears as he recounted the events of only a few weeks ago.

"My baby was born with no arms or legs and lived only a couple of days. Her mother also died giving birth to her."

"My little boy, Wilhelm, has similar deformities," another farmer added. "He's two years old. However, he's weak and sick. I don't think he will last the year."

"The vegetables grow in strange forms, and sometimes the plants do not produce at all."

"We've lost more calves this year than the three previous years put together."

"What have we done to fix these problems?"

"We've talked with the oil companies and tried to explain that ash from their smoke is landing in our fields and making us sick. They haven't listened. We have no more options in talking to them."

All of the men looked at Waldemar as he sat, his face stern. The problems were very serious and must be dealt with. The question was how.

"I have listened and I see only one option," Waldemar said. "These men of the modern world, do they really think God is on their side? The machines they build are killing all of us.

"We must help them get back to the true, simple life of farming, raising animals, and growing crops. That's what men in the Bible did, that's what we must continue to do. It's our obligation to show others that our way is what God wants for all men. We must protect our way, and keep the modern men from poisoning our children.

"I believe we must send our boys into the modern world where they will go to schools and learn modern ways. Only then will they be able to find a way to show the modern world the error of its ways. They can make changes from within."

And so the decision was made. The young men were sent away with a bit of money and a scrap of paper that read, "An eye for an eye, a tooth for a tooth."

Now, Gunter thought about the instructions given long ago. How could anyone devise a solution from something so vague? He hadn't heard about anything happening to the refinery, so maybe Dieter's solution was something relatively small.

"Dieter, your mama and Amara have been gone a long time. I'm sure they are together in heaven. I'm so happy to have you here. I don't want you to do anything that would take you away from me again."

He stopped to hug Dieter again. He looked into his eyes and couldn't believe he was really seeing him.

"God has been good to me. He brought you back to me. That's enough. And God has been good to the colony. Look how well we've done since you left."

Gunter waved his arms at the fields.

Dietrich noticed for the first time that there were tractors and balers in the hayfields. He staggered back in shock. He thought he might be sick.

"Papa, where are the horses?"

"We got rid of those many years ago. Tractors are much faster, with air conditioning, too. Very nice to drive. Dieter, are you feeling OK? You look pale."

Dietrich was sick at heart. With all his foresight, he never imagined that the plan would affect the colony, too.

*Patricia McConkey*

# Chapter *36*

October 2012

*Will* left the church and walked around aimlessly. He couldn't go home.

Sometimes when a person has too much to drink, they know they're being a jerk but they keep on drinking and being a jerk. Then, the next morning, they think back to the night before with regret.

Will had this feeling in spades. His daughter had just been murdered and he had blamed his wife. Slapping yourself on the forehead and saying, "I'm really sorry honey," just wouldn't cut it. Having your husband point a gun at your head and pull the trigger, well, that was one of those things that you couldn't recover from. Ever.

The most disturbing part of this whole thing was that he pulled the trigger. He knew she wasn't responsible for Emma's death, but at that moment he wanted to make someone pay. It didn't matter who. He also knew that, after she died, he would have turned the gun on himself. He considered ending his life now.

He walked to the ravine. Before the Change this was one of his favourite places, to run, to walk, to be close to nature. He could feel the rhythm of life here. Now he felt

197

alone and isolated. In the back of his mind, he hoped he would run into a gang. He ran through the scenarios in his mind, thinking of ways he could end his life.

Will walked along the empty trails in a mindless daze. Something deeper in the woods caught his attention, so he left the trail and headed into the bush. He came to an abandoned campsite once used by a homeless person. There was a firepit with a few charred logs, some food wrappers, scattered tin cans, and a makeshift dwelling. This appealed to him now. He crawled inside a cardboard box covered with pine boughs, pulled the ends of the box closed, and lay there in the dark.

~

Matt, Sarah, and George stayed with Lauren at the church all night. She said she couldn't bear to leave Emma there alone.

Finally, after the long night, Alton returned. He and Matt covered Emma's body with a sheet and moved her to the back so Lauren could have some privacy. The two men decided to have a funeral service as soon as Matt could find a coffin. Of course, due to the many deaths over the past month, there were no coffins at the morgue or any of the funeral homes that would normally provide these services. Matt would have to build it himself.

"Mom, come on, let's go home for a while," Matt said. "Alton said he'd stay with Emma. You need to get some rest. We can come back later."

He put his arm around his mother and walked her to the door. She resisted slightly, but eventually she started the walk home with Matt on her right and Sarah on her left. As always, George was there, supporting everyone. He was a rock. Matt was grateful for his strength.

Once they arrived home, George made everyone sit at the kitchen table. He pulled out seven cans of food and opened them all. When Matt asked where he'd got them, he just winked. Matt really didn't care; he was hungry. Sarah suggested they save some for later, but George insisted. He smiled as if keeping a secret.

The family ate chickpeas, baked beans, tuna, peaches, vegetarian soup, and two cans of crabmeat. It was a feast.

After every last drop was licked clean Sarah helped Lauren upstairs and put her to bed. Sarah was quietly closing Lauren's door when Matt put his arms around her from behind. He pulled her close and squeezed her.

"Thanks for being so good to my mom. You know, I couldn't do this without you."

"Matt, I have to admit that, when you told me about your dream, I thought it was *just* a dream. I knew you were worried about your mom and I thought that was enough to explain your nightmare. I've no idea if that was some weird coincidence or if you really did have a premonition."

Matt hardly heard her. The reality of his loss was just hitting him.

"Emm, if you can hear me, I miss you, too," he said. "I wish I hadn't hassled you so many times when we were little. I wish I could have done a lot of things differently for you."

"Matt, I'm sure she doesn't care about that stuff," Sarah said. "I know she's very happy you're here to look after your Mom."

Matt tried to pull himself together.

"Yeah, I know you're right." Matt wiped his nose on his sleeve. "Well, if Emma were here, she'd kick my butt if I didn't get busy. You need some sleep though. Why don't you go sleep in Mom's room? I'm sure she will sleep better if you're there with her."

Sarah smiled and stroked Matt's face.

"OK, I am really tired. But promise me that you're going to get some rest later."

Matt ran down the stairs and headed for the garage to look for tools, wood – anything he would need to build a coffin. He didn't hear George come down until he came up behind him.

"Grandpa, don't do that. You scared me half to death."

"Sorry, mon petit crapeau. Did you think I was a ghost or something?"

Matt wondered if his grandfather had overheard their conversation.

"Are you starting on the coffin? I've got some beautiful cherrywood I've been saving for something special. C'mon, help me carry it in here and we'll get started."

Matt smiled at his grandfather. He was always one step ahead of everyone else. It's funny that Dad never saw that, he thought. He also smiled thinking about the crapeau nickname. Grampa knew he hated that name, an old French nickname for toad.

# Chapter 37

*W*ill had been lying in the box for hours, maybe days. It was hard to tell. The cold had seeped into his bones and he ached all over. He crawled out, squinting in the bright sunlight. His eyes hurt, his head hurt, everything hurt, and to top it off, the dried blood on his clothes was giving off a putrid smell.

He sat on a nearby log and stared, not knowing what to do.

There really was only one solution. Every idea that he came up with led back to that one thought. He must end his life.

Will examined all the ways he could do it. He looked at his gun, but he had no bullets, so that was out. Besides, it didn't seem like the right answer. It would be fast and painless, and he didn't think he deserved a death like that. The river was nearby but he thought it wasn't a sure thing. What if someone tried to rescue him? That was out. He didn't have a knife, or he would have considered stabbing himself in the abdomen.

All these ideas rolled around in his head and confused

him. The bright sunlight hurt his eyes. When he turned his back to get some relief, he saw it: a hundred-foot cliff with a sheer drop to the river below.

After a long slow crawl to the top, he stood on the edge and looked over the valley. The sun was shining and there was a fresh breeze blowing. He could see for miles. This felt right. This was the moment. Before letting himself go, he wanted to say a few words, even if he was the only one to hear them.

"Lauren, I'm sorry for so many things, mostly for not being the husband that you needed. You deserved more.

"Matt, I'm sorry that I always focused on your weaknesses and never praised you for your strengths.

"Emma, my baby, I'm sorry that I couldn't protect you when you needed it. I'm sorry that I wasn't there for you.

"Dad, I'm sorry that I haven't been the kind of son that shows his father love and respect."

Their faces flashed before him and he thought he could hear their voices in the wind, but he knew it was just wishful thinking.

He paused for a moment. A tear rolled down his cheek. He was done. There was nothing more to say or do. He could barely move, he was so tired – tired of living and tired of struggling. This was the moment. Time to end the struggle.

Will collapsed in exhaustion, letting his body fall from the cliff, waiting for the relief of death.

For a moment, it felt as if time had stopped. It reminded him of being a child on a swing. He had loved the feeling when he was swinging when he reached that moment really high when the swing ceases to go forward and starts to fall backward. In that moment, time seems to stop for an instant. That's what he felt now.

*Patricia McConkey*

Then Will felt an extreme rush of air on his body. Parachutists must feel like this, he thought. But something was different about this. The wind was so strong it was pushing him around like a leaf just fallen from a tree.

Then there was impact and everything went black.

Will opened his eyes and wondered if he was in heaven or hell. Is there such thing, he thought. Is this death?

He looked around and pieces of the puzzle started to fall together. He saw the same blue sky above him and about twenty feet of cliff on his left side and about eighty feet to the river below on his right. The right side of his body was jammed between a rock and the face of the cliff. Apparently, that crazy gust of wind had blown him against the rock face and he had rolled down the cliff and become wedged into his current position.

He was still alive. He had failed even at killing himself; just one more failure in the many of his life. When this realization hit; the floodgates opened and the tears flowed freely. He lay there and cried like he had never cried before.

Will thought he could hear voices. He stopped crying and looked around. It was quiet now. His mind was clear. He looked in the sky and saw clouds moving. He shook his head and tried to focus. He thought he could see Emma's face.

"Emma, is that you?"

That was crazy. Of course it wasn't Emma. Emma was dead. Still, something felt different. In the back of his mind he still held out hope. Perhaps death was not the end. Maybe Emma could be out there somewhere. But his rational mind brought him back to reality. He chastised himself. Don't be stupid. There is no life after death. If there was, don't you think some scientist would have proved it by now?

Will tried to free himself from the rock cleft imprisoning

him, but before he could pry himself out of his predicament, he noticed a tiny sapling curve itself over and dangle just above him.

"What the hell?"

"Will, climb up here. We need you."

George's face appeared at the edge of the cliff.

"I can't pull you up, so you're going to have to climb on your own. You can grab onto this tree."

For a minute, Will considered just rolling off his perch and continuing his journey downward. But hearing his father's voice weakened his resolve. He was in a fragile state of mind, and George's voice was more of a command than a request: firm and strong. He rarely heard George talk like this and was a bit shocked by it. He felt like a child being scolded.

"Will, did you hear me? Climb up."

"How'd you find me?"

"I just did. We'll talk about that later. Come up here."

That was just like George. Never a straight answer but he did manage to pull off some crazy stuff.

Will grabbed the sapling and pulled himself free of the rock that had saved his life. With both feet firmly planted against the rock face, and using the sapling as a rope, he tried his best to scale up the side of the mountain. Ordinarily, he could have done this easily, but today he was weak with hunger and hurt from his fall. He could barely hold his own weight. By sheer force of will he got to the edge of the cliff where George took his hand and pulled him up.

"Before we talk, I want you to have this."

George reached into a bag and pulled out a large can of kidney beans and a big bottle of blue Gatorade. To Will, they were like the best Christmas gifts he had ever received. He took the bottle of Gatorade and gulped about half of it down before taking a breath. George pulled out a Swiss army knife and opened the beans. There was a spoon attachment for Will to eat the beans with.

"Not so fast. You'll get sick," George said.

Will couldn't remember anything in his whole life that tasted better.

"Will … eat slowly. I'll talk while you listen. First, we need you at home, so no more jumping off any cliffs. Understand?"

George looked at Will sternly.

Will felt as if he was being reprimanded for crossing the street without looking, rather than for trying to commit suicide.

He stopped eating momentarily and stared at his father in confusion. He had no idea how he could help his family survive the winter. He was full of questions. The biggest one was whether Lauren and Matt would want to see him again.

"Well, they don't want to see you looking like this," George said.

"What are you talking about? I was just thinking—"

"Well, I know you've got some fences to mend, but Lauren and Matt still love you. Let's see if we can get you looking and smelling a bit better. Come with me."

George started off down the steep trail to the bottom of the ravine and Will followed like a child.

"It's sure a lot quicker to go down than it is to come up," George said. "I thought I was going to have a heart attack climbing up here."

George had some trouble going down the trail and stumbled more than once, but Will helped him back up. He thought it was odd being rescued by a seventy-four-year-old man, but nothing was making any sense these days.

As Will trailed behind his father, his mind revved up again. He couldn't imagine going back to the house. What would he say? How could he apologize to Lauren for nearly shooting her? That requires a little more than a bunch of flowers.

George took him to the edge of the river.

"Take off your clothes and wade in."

"Are you crazy? That water is barely above freezing. Besides, Dad, I really appreciate what you are doing, but I don't think I could ever go home. Maybe we should just say our goodbyes and move on."

"Will, why do you think I'm here?"

Will looked at his father and wondered about that. His brows furrowed as he tried to think of an answer. He knew that his father loved him, despite his shortcomings as a son. But he couldn't imagine that anyone would really want him around after what he had done recently.

"Will, I want you to do this one thing for me. Then if you don't feel differently, I'll leave you to choose your own path."

George placed his hand on Will's arm and looked at him with beseeching eyes.

"I brought you some clean clothes to put on when you come out. But you need to wash off Emma's blood and get clean. You need to make a new start, and you can't do that smelling the way you do. I know that the phrase 'make a fresh start' is a metaphor, but in your case it's also literal. When you go back to Lauren, you need to look like a new man."

Will started to undress. It did feel good to get those stinky clothes off. He walked to the edge of the river and stepped over bits of ice that had accumulated at the shore. He looked downstream. There was a big patch of ice where the current wasn't quite so strong. Just thinking about going into the icy water made his testicles rise a little closer to his body. He put his feet into the water and expected to feel burning cold but did not. It was cold, but felt good, like having an ice pack on a sore back.

Will gently edged his way into the half-frozen river until the water had reached mid thigh. He had to step carefully because the stones on the bottom were slippery and there was a strong current. He splashed water on his face, armpits, and groin.

He looked back at his dad, "OK, I think that's good enough."

Even though he was stepping carefully, one of the rocks came loose from its resting place on the riverbed. Both of his feet slipped out from under him and he fell back with a splash. His head plunged into the icy water and smacked hard on a rock on the bottom.

Will drifted off into another world. He saw visions of his life: pivotal moments from the past that had shaped his life, like the day he got married, the births of Matt and Emma, and a moment when he saved a young woman's life. There were a lot of happy moments like these, but there were also a lot of things he wasn't proud of.

He remembered the look on Matt's face when he was yelled at about the gang incident, the anger in Emma's eyes as she tended to her mother's concussion, his father's sadness when Will treated him like a crazy old man. All the images, good and bad, seemed so bold and vivid and struck him deeply. He knew he didn't want to die with the events of the past month defining his life. He wanted to rewrite the end of his story.

He suddenly became aware of where he was. The current had dragged him downstream and left his limp body under a patch of ice several centimetres thick. He didn't know how long he had been under, but the temperature of the water had made his arms and legs sluggish and his lungs were screaming for air.

Will thought about his life. Only an hour ago he was desperately seeking the release of death. Now he could easily drown in this icy pond, but he wasn't sure that's what he wanted.

Did he want to live or die? He had only seconds to make his choice. If he didn't move quickly, he would be too stiff from the cold to have a choice.

He thought about the scenes of his life with his family. He knew he didn't want to leave them with the image of the crazy man who tried to shoot his wife in church. He realized that his father was watching him drown. He couldn't bear the thought of seeing one of his children drowning. His body kicked into action, and he took joy at the thought. He was going to live! Years of saving lives and being a hero were just too hard to ignore; now he needed to save his own life.

Will tried to pound his fist on the ice, but swinging his stiff arm underwater was clearly not enough force to break it. He knew the covering of ice was not large. He'd have to swim against the current to get to running water. His arms and legs were slow to act and it was a struggle to swim against the current. He wasn't getting anywhere.

The pond was only about five feet deep, so he placed his hands on the ice and his feet on the stony bottom and walked upstream. In about ten steps he could feel that the current was stronger and the ice was getting thinner. He slid his hand along the sheet of ice, came to the edge, and pulled himself up. He sucked in a huge mouthful of air.

"Will! Over here. Grab my hand."

George had waded into the water and his voice was frantic.

"Will, hang on. We'll get you to shore."

He had never heard his father so frightened.

George dragged him closer to shore and pulled him up. He put his arms around him.

"Will, I love you. You're all I have left. I'm not ready to let you go."

He held Will in his arms and shivered, not from the cold, but from the thought of nearly losing him. Seeing Will have two brushes with death the same day was even more than the oh-so-calm George could handle.

Will could barely speak. He put his shaky arms around his dad and it felt good.

"I lllllove yyyyyyou tttttoo," he stuttered.

The two remained standing at the edge of the shore.

George was clearly shaken by the whole incident. He had had a vision of Will jumping off a cliff. In his mind, he saw Will climbing up to safety and somehow knew he was going to be all right. So when he had rescued him from the ledge, he was no longer worried.

He hadn't foreseen the incident in the river. He only knew that when he last saw Will he was covered in Emma's blood. He thought that if Will was going to reunite with his family, he would certainly need to look a little better. But when Will fell into the river, George thought he had sent him to his death. He was nearly hysterical when Will did not reappear for what seemed like an eternity.

George opened the bag of goodies he had brought with him.

"I thought you might need a blanket after cleaning up in the river," he said in a shaky voice.

Will was curled up in the fetal position. George wrapped

the blanket around him as tightly as possible and rubbed his limbs to improve his circulation.

"I'll get a fire going and you'll be warm in no time."

There were lots of dry leaves and small pieces of wood along the edge of the river. George gathered his fuel quickly and piled them into a tepee shape. He pulled a lighter from his pocket and within minutes had a small crackling fire going. He walked into the bush and found some larger pieces of wood to add to the blaze.

George positioned Will next to the fire and told him to open his blanket to trap some of the warmth from the blaze. Gradually Will's body temperature climbed to near normal. Will was impressed with his father. That was the second time in under two hours that he had saved his life. He saw his father's love and wisdom as he never had before. How could he have missed it?

"Dad, something happened to me under that ice. I saw different parts of my life – the good and the bad. I don't want to leave this world with the reputation I have created for myself, but I don't know how Lauren and Matt could ever let me back into their lives."

George's eyes watered with tears of joy. He knew that his son had to find the will to live and no one could force that into him. Now it seemed as if Will had taken the first step. He had made the effort to pull himself out of that freezing water. Patching up the rest of his life would be difficult, but George had some ideas about how they might be able to do it.

George couldn't remember ever having a real conversation with his son, one in which he was truly heard. Now he found it difficult to express how happy he was that his son was confiding in him. It was as if he had returned from the dead. George swallowed a lump in his throat.

"I've got something to show you at home. Something that will help us all get through the winter, but I need your help with it."

Will smiled. He had tried everything he could think of, but still had no plan to save his family. If his crazy dad had some harebrained idea, he was willing to try it. And Will had to admit that, once in a while, he did have some pretty interesting ideas.

Will put on the clean clothes his father brought for him, and they started to walk back to the house.

"Dad, I know I haven't been the best son," Will said. "Do you think you might be able to give me a second chance?"

"Will, we all get as many chances as we need. As long as you keep trying, there's always another chance to set things right. You don't need to ask me for another chance. I never gave up on you."

Will's frozen muscles thawed a little and he felt a warm glow inside.

# *Chapter 38*

*A*s George and Will approached the house, Will started to slow down, apprehensive about seeing Lauren again.

He loved her more than ever, but was afraid it was too late to ever win her back. George noticed his hesitation.

"Come to the back shed. I want to show you something," he said, trying to distract Will.

But just then Matt walked around the corner of the garage and ran right into his father.

"Matt, oh I'm sorry. I didn't see you there ..." Will said.

Although it was Matt who ran into Will, it didn't really matter at that point. Matt just looked at his father, angry and hurt. He wasn't sure what to do or say and had trouble getting any words out.

Will was equally tongue-tied. The two stood there dumbfounded. Then Will saw what Matt was doing in the garage. Emma's coffin was finished.

Will stepped inside the garage and knelt down by the coffin to look at it more closely. It was dark cherrywood, stained a deep cinnamon. Matt had added two rows of trim around the sides. The lid had the same trim pattern and a row of boards on the inside to secure it in place.

Will was very impressed with Matt's work, especially considering that it was done without the use of power tools. Will ran his hand along the outside edge of the coffin. He couldn't imagine saying goodbye to his baby and putting her into the ground. He gulped back his tears and put his hands over his eyes, as if he could hold the tears in.

"Matt, you've done a beautiful job," Will whispered. "Thank you so much for doing this for Emma."

Matt felt angry, sad, and confused. His father seemed like a reasonable person right now, but when he had pointed that gun at his mother's head, he was a raving lunatic. Matt was still trying to deal with his sister's death and didn't want to deal with emotions related to his father.

He just turned and left without saying anything.

Will was hurt and disappointed, but he had expected this. He wanted to reconnect with Matt, but didn't know how.

Just then, Lauren stepped out of the house.

"Matt said the casket was finished and I wanted to look at it."

She walked over and put her hands on it in a cool, calm manner.

"Matt has done an amazing job," she said, as if speaking to herself. After a long pause, she looked at Will.

"I hope you will come to the funeral, but if you do, I want your word that you are not going to make a scene."

Will looked like a frightened child. He nodded in agreement, completely submissive. She stared back at him with cool aggression, asserting her power.

"It's at seven tonight at the church. You know the one."

She turned and went back into the house, leaving Will to his thoughts about the funeral, only a few hours away.

George just sat quietly with Will in the garage. His surprise would have to wait.

At six-thirty the family assembled outside the house on the front walk. Matt had prepared a dolly for the coffin so it could be easily pulled to the church. The funeral procession consisted of a neighbour pulling the coffin, with Matt, Lauren, and Sarah following and George and Will just a few paces behind.

Lauren, her arms linked with Matt and Sarah, held her head high. She and George had talked at length about Emma's death, and he had convinced her that Emma was very happy in her new life. Lauren was much calmer now.

The procession wound through the barren streets like a train of courtiers passing through a war-torn country. Lauren looked every inch the beautiful strong matriarch, with her long dark hair flowing around the stand-up collar of her black knee-length wool coat. The hem of her coat brushed the top of her Gucci leather boots.

Each member of the family was impeccably dressed in dark colours and looked regal in their own right. They walked through streets lined with the skeletons of burned houses and cars that had exploded and been left to burn. The fire damage went on for many blocks. With the fire departments shut down, there was nothing to prevent fire from spreading through the whole neighbourhood once one house went up in flames.

The city burned and the residents burned along with it. If they didn't burn, they were dying from starvation, gang warfare, and infections. More often than not, dead bodies were just left to rot where they fell.

The small procession arrived at church and carried the coffin inside. The mourners went to the back room and found Alton praying over Emma's body. They gently placed Emma in the newly made coffin. Before they took it into the main hall of the church, George asked if he and Will could have a few minutes alone with Emma.

*Patricia McConkey*

"Will, I want you to know that this is only Emma's body. Her spirit lives and is filled with joy. She is happier now than you could ever imagine. Just close your eyes and picture her face. She'll give you a small taste of what it's like to feel the peace that she knows."

Will tried to do what George asked, but all he felt was extreme grief and sadness.

"Somewhere deep inside you, you must know that her spirit lives. Can't you feel it?"

George looked at Will to see if he could comprehend what he meant, but Will was becoming more distant. He was trying to block out his feelings rather than explore them. George realized that he wasn't making any progress, so he led Will out into the main hall so that the service could begin. Matt and a number of neighbours carried Emma's coffin behind them.

Alton started the service.

"We are here to celebrate the life of a young and vibrant member of our church, Emma Elizabeth Connor."

Will stood up and Alton paused briefly, not knowing if he should protect himself or offer comfort. Alton braced himself for an interruption. Instead, Will walked quietly to the closed coffin and draped his arms and torso over it as tears streamed down his face. Will lay there quietly, and Alton was not sure whether to acknowledge him or go on.

George walked over to Will, stroked his son's head, and held his hand. He nodded to Alton, indicating that everything was all right.

Alton was a bit flustered but continued his eulogy.

"It has been said, death is never an end. It is a beginning. Emma has begun a new chapter, and she is rejoicing, just as we all will when our time comes. Our time here is just a blink of an eye, and we must remember that our soul has a bigger purpose."

Alton could see he wasn't reaching them. He took a new tack. Matt, in all his thoughtfulness, had brought a beautiful framed picture of Emma, and it sat majestically on top of the coffin. Alton walked toward the coffin, hoping it would not cause Will to go off on another tirade.

George handed Alton the picture and smiled, reassuring him that all was safe.

"Emma was exquisite, was she not?"

He held up the picture and all of the gatherers agreed, smiling through their tears.

"As beautiful as a rare flower?"

Again the crowd agreed.

"But if we see the flower as dying, we will feel sadness. Yet if we see beyond the physical form and think about the process, then we can realize that in nature a tree will blossom, then the flowers die and fall off. But then the truly magical part of the process begins because soon beautiful sweet fruit grows in their place. When you understand that the blossoming and falling away of the flower is a just a part of the process, then you will understand life."

Will heard Alton, but his words sounded like a radio playing in a distant room. He thought about Emma and how much she meant to him. He couldn't imagine his life without her. He retreated deep inside his head and tried to work out the dilemma in his thoughts.

Baby, I miss you so much, he thought. I just can't let you go. I don't know how.

From somewhere in the dark, thoughts seemed to flow into his head. Although they were not words, just mental constructs, his mind translated them into Emma's voice.

Dad, it's time. You can let go. I'm happy and I'll live forever.

But I need you with me.

*Patricia McConkey*

And I'll be with you always. Just turn off your brain and let your thoughts go quiet. Listen to your heart and I'll be there. Whenever you experience joy, I'm there. So make your life about being full of joy.

Emma, you were the one full of joy, not me.

But you can be, Dad. Just make the choice to be joyful. Do it for me.

Anything for you, Cupcake.

You have all the pieces; just put them together and live your life one joyful moment at a time.

I love you, Baby.

I love you, Dad.

George patted Will's arm to get his attention. The tears slid down Will's face as he lifted his head to see what was going on. The service was over and it was time to take the coffin to the grave.

"Will, are you able to be one of the pallbearers?" George asked.

Will stood up immediately and took his place at the head of the coffin. The other five men took their places, and they started the procession out of the church through the parking lot to a nearby park that had been converted to a graveyard.

They walked past rows and rows of coffins of all shapes and sizes sitting on top of the frozen ground. This was the way it had to be done in Alberta in the late fall. There was no way to dig a proper grave with the ground frozen as hard as cement.

They reached the spot chosen for Emma and gently lay her coffin down on its winter resting spot. In the spring, they would dig a proper grave. Alton gave a short final speech, and those who had followed to the gravesite silently took their leave.

Lauren was the first of the family to say her final goodbye.

She leaned over and whispered some hushed words to Emma and pulled an old sock puppet from her coat and laid it on the casket.

"Goodbye, my love. I've brought your favourite friend so you will have fun in your new life."

She smiled through her tears and kissed the coffin.

Matt, Sarah, and George each said a goodbye to Emma, then the family turned to Will and looked at him with questioning eyes.

Will realized that it was his turn. For a minute or two, he was frozen to his spot. It was only a few steps, but they were the hardest steps he had ever taken. Finally he knelt beside the coffin.

"Baby, I wanted to say I'm sorry … sorry that I wasn't there for you when you needed me most, sorry that I couldn't protect you like a father should have."

Will's body trembled with emotion and he had difficulty speaking.

"You … You didn't deserve this. Emma, baby, sleep well."

Will leaned over and kissed the casket, sobbing loudly.

The family all exchanged glances, and Lauren gave Matt a look that said, "Help your father. He needs you."

Matt leaned over his dad and helped him to his feet.

"Dad, come home now."

Matt put his arm around Will's waist and directed him toward home. Will sniffed and tried to pull himself together. George took up the other side and the three generations, arm in arm, walked home.

As they were getting close to the house, George said, "I think I should show you guys something I've been working on for quite a while."

"You mean we actually get to see inside the bat cave?" Matt asked.

George led them through the back yard to his secret hideaway, the shed in the far corner. He had asked for the space in the summer and had the whole family promise that they'd give him his privacy and stay out of the shed.

At the time, Will saw it as just one more indication that his father was one brick short of a load. Actually, Will had been curious enough to try to get in, but George had it locked up so tight it wasn't possible.

George pulled the keys out of his pocket and unlocked the three padlocks. He pulled the old door open.

"Let me shed some light on things," George said.

He switched on a big battery-powered light.

Will blinked his eyes and stepped back in surprise. He examined the equipment closely. There was a metal container over an electric burner with a copper tube that spiralled to a second container. Even if you had never seen a still, the strong smell of alcohol gave it away immediately.

"Grampa, you dog. You got a shine factory here!"

George's contraption was not just for brewing a bottle or two for sipping. Will looked at the big blue water jugs in the corner, full of alcohol, and thought there must be over three hundred litres.

"Shall we have a toast?"

George took a couple of coffee mugs and poured them each a double. He handed out the mugs and held his up in a toast.

"Emma, may your days be filled with laughter and joy because that's what you brought to us each day."

Will's eyes started to water again. To numb his senses, he pounded back the whole snort in one gulp. He coughed and gagged. After about five minutes, he was finally able to choke out some words.

"Dad, are you sure you're not trying to kill me?"

"Well, it was designed for strength not for taste, and on that factor, I did pretty good. I think it's about one hundred twenty-five proof, which means you're gonna be hammered after only a few shots."

Matt had only taken a mouthful, but had the same reaction as his dad. It felt as if he had just swallowed a fireball and it was still burning in his stomach.

"You rock, Gramps," Matt said. "This is my kinda hooch. I think my balls are on fire."

He tried rearranging the boys.

Will and George laughed, but had to agree. One sip gave a warming effect to the whole body.

"Let's go inside and have a proper celebration for Emma."

George led the party into the kitchen.

"What are you three reprobates up to?" Lauren said. "No good from the looks of it."

It was a rhetorical question given the strong aroma coming from their general vicinity.

"What's a girl have to do to get a drink around here?"

George took a mug and poured a generous shot for Lauren.

"A careful word of warning, sweetheart," Will said with a wink. "This stuff could knock a charging bull off its feet."

"That sounds like a challenge if I ever heard one. Have you ever known me to back down?"

She raised her glass in the air.

"To Emma, the best damn daughter a mother could ever hope for."

She tipped back the mug, and her eyes went wide as pie plates. No sound came out of her mouth even though it hung open for a minute. She rested her hands on her knees and took a few deep breaths.

This must be how a dragon feels after breathing fire, she thought, then said, in a gravelly voice, Gimme another.

*Patricia McConkey*

"She's got more balls than you, Will," George said. He poured another round for everyone.

In less than an hour they were all well past drunk. Sarah wasn't interested in the high-octane shooters. That stuff tasted worse than gasoline and no one was making any sense so she went to bed. For the rest of the crew, tension gave way to laughter, and family bonds were somewhat re-established.

"You're an arrogant sonovabitch, ya know?" Matt said, looking at his father.

"I am, I am, no fuckin' doubt 'bout it. But aren't you the son of a bitch who gave me a fat lip when you punched me in the mouth?"

"Yeah, that was a grrrrreat shot, honey," Lauren said, and high-fived Matt.

"Glad you enjoyed that, Sweet Cheeks. D'ya want to take a little shot at me yourself? I promise not to move."

"Ab-so-fuckin'-lutely."

Lauren was definitely a non-violent person and in her right mind would never consider this. However, overproof moonshine can make a person forget their values.

"OK, lay it on me, honey."

Lauren was sitting at table with Will. Given her wobbly legs, she thought she would just remain sitting for this event. She balled her hands into fists and jostled around in her chair as if she was boxing sitting down.

"OK, Mom, make it a good one," Matt said.

"I'll make it easy for you, sweetie, I'll close my eyes."

Will closed his eyes and leaned in toward Lauren. He thought he was getting off easy if all she was going to do was hit him. He also thought this might substitute for the real punishment of not talking to him for weeks on end, which he would find unbearable.

Lauren put her chin down and her fists up and launched a right hook. Unfortunately, since Will had leaned in to give her a better chance, he was now closer than she had calculated. Instead of landing it right on his chin, her fist went around the back of his head, lightly brushing the back of his scalp. Since she had put a lot of muscle into her punch, her body followed through and she fell toward Will.

Will felt the punch on the back of his head and, when he opened his eyes, he panicked as he saw Lauren falling forward. He was afraid she would hit her head again. He reached out to catch her but slid off his chair. On the way down, he whacked his eye on the corner of the table. The two of them landed on the floor next to the table. Lauren was making a high-pitched squealing noise.

"Mom, are you OK? Mom?"

"Lauren, sweetheart, are you hurt?" Will said.

In another moment, they realized that she was laughing so hard she couldn't speak. Will was relieved.

Matt got up and tried to help them both back to their chairs. But he was so hammered he just ended up falling on top of them. That was just another reason for everyone to go into hysterical laughing fits.

"Group hug," George said. He piled on top of the crowd on the floor.

There were lots of "I love yous" being said, but it was hard to tell who was saying them. Everyone hugged and got teary-eyed for a moment before they tried to untangle themselves. The four of them now lay on the floor and stared up at the ceiling.

"This is a different perspective than I'm used to," Lauren said, looking up from the dining room floor.

"That reminds me of a joke I know about four people sitting together on a train travelling through the Canadian Rockies," Matt said.

*Patricia McConkey*

"A fella from Western Canada, one from Eastern Canada, a little old lady, and a young blonde woman with large breasts – really hot – were riding a train.

"The train goes into a dark tunnel, and a few seconds later there is the sound of a loud slap. When the train emerges from the tunnel, the fellow from Eastern Canada has a bright red handprint on his cheek. No one speaks.

"The little old lady thinks: That fella from Eastern Canada must have groped the blonde in the dark and she slapped his cheek.

"The blonde woman thinks: That fella from Eastern Canada must have tried to grope me in the dark but missed and fondled the old lady who slapped his cheek.

"The fella from Eastern Canada thinks: That fella from Western Canada must have groped the blonde in the dark. She tried to slap him but missed and got me instead.

"The fella from Western Canada thinks: I can't wait for another tunnel so I can smack that asshole from Eastern Canada again."

Everyone laughed. Even Will was happy it had worked out this way. A black eye was minor compared with what he thought he really deserved. He watched Lauren as she laughed hysterically and felt happier than he had in years. It was good to hear her and Matt laughing.

He remembered Emma's funeral and smiled because he knew she was with them at this moment. George saw Will's expression and knew that he had found some measure of peace with Emma's death. This pleased him, but he still was surprised that no one had put two and two together yet.

"OK, you Yahoos, if I can get your attention for a moment," he said. "I did all the work of brewing this stuff up because – well, because – I thought that's what the universe was telling me to do. Now I want you to think about the big picture for a moment. Did any one of you wonder why I brewed this stuff up in the first place?"

The room went silent as the three drunks thought about that very relevant question. Even in a drunken stupor, they managed to come up with some ideas.

Lauren, being one of the drunkest, came up with the first contribution.

"Oh, oh I got it. 'Cause even though we're gonna starve to death this winter, we'll be so drunk we won't notice. That's it, isn't it?"

George just shook his head. Maybe they were all too drunk and it would have to wait until morning.

"No, no. Nice try, Mom," Matt said, "but not right. Gramps, you are soooo cool. I could rejig the generator motor to run on this stuff and we could use it to keep warm over the winter."

"George, you dog you," Lauren said. "You are so right. Let's fill up the gas tanks of the SUV and drive to Florida. I'll get my bikini."

"Lauren and Matt, you're both right," Will said. "Matt, if you can rework the engine of a car, we could use this stuff to get out of here. And I think I know just the place."

He turned to his father.

"Dad, you're a genius. Here's to the great and powerful Oz, my dad."

Lauren and Matt raised their glasses, even though they didn't really understand what Will had said. They all drank to George's brilliance anyway.

"OK, the bar is closed," Will said. "We've got to save our supplies, and Matt, we've got a lot of work to do tomorrow. George, help me get these two drunken idiots to bed."

"Takes one to know one," George said.

# Chapter 39

*The* sun had been up for a couple of hours by the time Will woke up. Despite how he felt – pounding head, nausea, and sore eye – he was happy. He had spent the night in bed with Lauren. Even though she was practically in a coma from the alcohol, it was wonderful to be close to her.

And it was good to be talking to Matt again. Will was surprised at what he saw in Matt. He thought that it was too bad he hadn't seen all those good qualities years ago. Most of all, he was so happy to be back with the family. He felt as if he was getting a second chance at life.

He tiptoed down the stairs and just about had a heart attack when Matt tapped him on the shoulder.

"I was just going to wake you. Here, take these. Hurry up. We've got to a lot to do."

Matt handed him a couple of extra-strength painkillers.

"Oh, bless you, my son. You are a godsend."

It was just a figure of speech, but even Will was surprised to hear it come out of his mouth.

Matt looked puzzled.

"What happened to you? Did you find religion or something?"

Will smiled. He was thinking that having a second chance to make things right could make even a non-believer like him see the light.

"Let's go check the SUV and see if we can get it running on Grampa's hooch," Matt said.

He directed his dazed father to the garage.

After a quick check, Will found that it was loaded with the bacteria. There was no way they could drive that vehicle. In fact, they pushed it into the street, just in case it did blow up.

"You know, before all the craziness started, Mom asked me if I would fix up an old bus at the church. Maybe we should check it out."

Will looked at him with a smirk.

"In the words of your oh-so-wise mother, ab-so-fuckin'-lutely."

They walked to the church and found a parking lot containing ten to twelve cars, but no bus. After a quick search, father and son sat down.

"Maybe they moved it to a shop somewhere," Matt said.

Will shook his head with frustration; he didn't want to give up yet.

"Just take a break for a moment; I've got to piss," Will said. He walked to the corner of the building.

"Matt, Matt come here," Will shouted a moment later.

Matt ran, afraid a gang had a gun to Will's head or something worse. He turned the corner and saw his dad opening the hood of an old bus.

"This must be it. Look she's an old one ... the best kind these days."

"Shit, Dad, you scared me half to death. Now move over and let me take a look."

The bus had been out of service for some time, so it

*Patricia McConkey*

wasn't infected with the bacteria, but there were some other maintenance factors to deal with.

Matt wiped his hands on an old rag.

"There's a lot of crap we need to do to get this old baby running. For starters, the hydraulic system needs a lot of work, the cam shaft timing will need to be adjusted, and we will need to add a spacer in the pistons for the moonshine to work with this old engine."

Will was impressed.

"Well, you're in charge. Just tell me what I can do to help."

Matt looked at his dad with a bit of hesitation, but smiled. It felt weird to order him around, but good, too. He had just started listing off the items that Will would need to remove from other vehicles when a noise from the corner of the building distracted them.

Within seconds, Will had both hands on his gun and the barrel pointed at the newcomer's head.

"Will, Will, it's just me," Doug said, his hands in the air.

"Doug, I thought I was seeing a ghost. I'm amazed you made it out of the plant that day."

Doug put his hands down and approached Will cautiously.

"Well, I was lucky to be near some of the underground holding tanks, so I jumped in and was able to wait it out until most of the explosions had stopped. Anyway, I went to your house and your wife told me I would find you here."

Will walked up to Doug and hugged him. A look of shock and confusion came over him, but he got over it quickly. Matt excused himself to continue work on the bus as Doug and Will continued to chat.

"Will, I've got this situation, and I'm hoping you can help me out with it. Do you remember the guy you brought with you to the plant that morning?"

"Yeah— Zain. But I'm sure he didn't make it. He was about ten feet behind me when the building went up. When I looked back, I saw a lot of blood."

"Well, you're right about one thing, he did get pretty torn up. But when I was heading home that day, I found him with a big piece of metal stickin' in his back and just 'bout dead. I didn't know what to do, so I took him home to my wife. She's a paramedic. I thought she could give him some painkillers just till he passed away. But the son of a bitch lived."

"No shit! Well, you know what they say: You can't kill the devil."

They both laughed.

"Well, he told me a crazy story about having food and supplies. I didn't know whether to believe him or not, but we're desperate so we kept him alive to see if we could get hold of this food. But there's a catch. He says that he has a girlfriend who is pregnant and he needs to find her. He said that if I find her he'll tell me where the food is and we'd have more than enough for the winter."

"Son of a bitch. Just like Zain to pull something like this."

"He said you have connections with the Premier and his people and that you might be able to find her. Zain thought that the Premier's police force might be keeping tabs on her to find Zain and his crew. That's why I came. If you can help me find her, I'll give you some food to help you and your family."

"Doug, I'd love to help you, but I don't know if it's possible. Tell me a bit about her and maybe I can go talk to the boys at the Premier's office."

"Zain said her name is Kabira Maarteen, and she is small, with long dark hair, and has a big tattoo on her back that looks like angel wings."

Matt had been pulling apart the brake system while listening to them talk.

"Dad, I might know this girl. I don't know her name, but I know a girl who has a tat like the one he described. I used to buy stuff from her."

Doug's face lit up like a light bulb.

"D'ya know how we can find her?"

"Well, she quit selling a while back, but I know where she used to live, maybe she still lives there. We could check it out if you want to."

"Matt, why don't you and Doug go check out this girl's place?" Will said. "Maybe we can find her and score some food? Who knows? It might make some other people happy, too. Just tell me what you want me to keep working on while you're gone."

Will couldn't believe that he was actually helping Zain get back together with his girlfriend. The old Will would have said, "Fuck that, the guy's an ecoterrorist," but the new, second-chance Will thought differently. He tried not to think about it too much because the logic of the old Will might just start making noise and win the argument.

"Dad, I expect those brakes to be done by the time I get back," Matt said.

"Yes, sir."

Doug was like a kid just before Christmas. He had trouble standing still. He'd been really worried about how he and his wife would survive the winter, so if there was even a small chance that Zain was telling the truth, he was going to take it. He was almost pushing Matt to get going.

"I don't know what you guys are up to," Doug said, "but I can help. I have tons of tools and am pretty handy with old jalopies like this one. I'll take a look at it after we get this thing with Kabira sorted out."

"Sounds good, Doug," Will said.

"Matt, be careful out there. I need you."

"The whole world has gone crazy, don't you think?" Doug said, as he walked along with Matt.

"It sure has, but somehow I think we're going to make things work. I don't know exactly how, but I think it will be OK."

Matt was beginning to wonder if he had inherited some of George's sixth sense.

~

Matt and Doug headed to the dangerous downtown area. Of course, these days everywhere was dangerous. Gangs roamed all over the city. They owned the deserted blood-stained streets. Most of the windows were broken in the storefronts and burned remnants of buildings were everywhere. It seemed so long since things had been normal. In fact, it was only slightly more than a month.

Matt found the alley where he remembered seeing the girl with the angel wings tattoo. He and Doug saw a young woman come out of the building carrying some bags. Even though she was wearing bulky clothes and a heavy coat, she looked pregnant.

"Hey just a minute, can we talk to you?" Matt yelled.

She spun around, gun drawn, and fired a shot above their heads. Matt and Doug fell flat on their stomachs, and put their hands above their head.

"Back off, you sons of bitches. The next shot will be right through your fuckin' brains."

"Wait, wait, we just want to talk to you about Zain, Zain Bedow. Do you know him?" Doug called out to her.

"Don't move, I have the gun pointed at your head. Did you say Zain? What about him?"

"Are you Kabira? He sent us to find you. We're not here to hurt you, only to take you to him."

"Yeah, why didn't the bastard come himself?"

"He can hardly move. He was in a big explosion and got hurt pretty bad."

She put the gun in her pocket and came over.

"Is he all right? Is he going to live?"

"My wife says he'll live, but he looks pretty bad, something like the Phantom of the Opera only without the mask."

Doug and Matt got up slowly, taking care not to make any sudden moves. Kabira stood wringing her hands, not knowing what to do. She was cautious, but needed to know the truth.

"Can you take me to him?"

"Sure, but you have to promise me you're not going to shoot me."

Matt decided to head back to the church. Doug gave him a big hug and shook his hand. He said he'd come back to the church shortly with some supplies that might get the old girl running again.

Kabira was too worried about Zain to talk much to Doug on their walk together. She wondered what she would do or say when she saw Zain. Shooting him was a good possibility, she thought, but that would be the back-up option.

Zain had disappeared just about the time all this madness started and Kabira was furious that he had left her in this mess, pregnant and with no food. She thought he had left her because of the argument they'd had about the baby. That he'd taken off to the hideout he had stocked with food and supplies. He had told her that he had a safe house in reserve in case he got into trouble with the law and needed to stay out of sight. But only he knew where it was.

Kabira wrapped her hand around the gun in her pocket, deciding that if he denied this baby again, she would shoot him on the spot. Pregnancy was making her more extreme than usual – which was pretty extreme to begin with.

Doug opened the front door and was surprised to see Zain standing. He generally spent his time lying on the couch snoring.

Kabira walked in behind him and gasped when she saw Zain. He stood there in his boxers with at least half of his body covered in bandages. The areas of skin that weren't bandaged were covered with cuts of various sizes. His torso was almost completely bandaged due to the huge gash in his back. His head was shaved on one side, clearly revealing a deep cut that arched from his temple to behind his left ear. The right half of his face had been burned but was healing. To top it off, he had an IV in his right arm hooked to the curtain rod.

Zain knew he must have looked a bit like Frankenstein, so he gave her a second to adjust. He pulled his IV bag along the curtain rod so he could get closer to the front door where she stood. He moved very slowly and stiffly and with a great deal of pain. With great effort, he knelt down in front of Kabira. Zain pushed back her coat, put his massive hands on her belly, and leaned his face in close.

"Hello, little one," he whispered. "Look how big you've gotten. I've been thinking about you a lot."

Kabira's eyes watered as she swallowed a huge lump in her throat. Her hands shook as she reached out to touch Zain, but she hesitated because she didn't know if there was a spot on him that wouldn't hurt him. He guided her hand to the left side of his face. He stared up at her with a look that would melt the coldest heart.

"I didn't think I was going to make it, and more than

once I was hoping I would die because the pain was so bad," Zain, told her. "The only thing that kept me going was the thought of you and the baby. I had to stay alive to tell you how much I love you and to see my baby."

Zain held out his hand and showed her the angel wings. Most of the detail was gone as he had rubbed it smooth during his convalescence.

Kabira was speechless. She wanted to be angry at him, but it's hard to push away a broken man on his knees telling you how much he loves you. She leaned over and kissed him gently.

"It's a good thing you look as bad as you do, 'cause I was ready to come in here and twist your balls off one at a time for leaving me," she said. "But you obviously had a good excuse, so I'm going to let you off the hook. This is a one-time deal, though. If you ever leave me again I will hunt you down and kill you."

Zain laughed. That was the Kabira he knew, as sentimental as a mercenary. He loved her just the way she was, but he also knew that she really wasn't joking about the killing thing. He wrapped his arms around her belly. As he pressed his face against her stomach, he felt a solid kick. He pulled back in surprise.

"Did you feel that?" he said in amazement. "That little bugger is as strong as an ox. He takes after his dad."

"What? It's not a boy, it's a girl, just as sweet and cuddly as her mom. She was just telling you that she won't take any shit from you."

Doug gave Zain and Kabira time to reconnect before he asked about payment. About fifteen minutes later he poked his head in from the kitchen.

"Zain, we need to talk about those supplies you were going to contribute."

"Yeah, c'mon in and we'll talk about that. Doug, I want to thank you and your wife for taking such good care of me over the past weeks. Both of you, you saved my life. And for finding Kabira; that means more to me than you could ever know. As I promised, I can only try to repay your kindness with food. I have about a ton of dried beans, rice, canned food, spices, candles, and books, lots of books, but there's one catch. It's in a safe place … about one hundred and fifty kilometres northwest of here."

Zain was waiting for Doug to start swearing or take a swing at him or something because he hadn't told him up front that the food was so far away. But Doug was calm and paced back and forth.

"This might work," Doug said, rubbing his beard. "I'll get back to you on that. Right now I have to go help a friend with something."

Doug kissed his wife and told her he'd be back in a few hours. He told her to pack blankets and lots of winter clothing because they were going on a trip.

"Really? You have a ride?" Zain said in surprise.

Doug didn't hear the question because he had already headed into the garage to get some tools.

*Patricia McConkey*

# Chapter 40

*D*oug, Matt, and Will worked on the bus all that day and the next and finally got to the moment of truth: turning the key to see if it would run on the new fuel.

"Matt, I want you and Doug to go around the corner of the building and take cover. If this thing is going to blow, I need you to look after your mother."

Matt rolled his eyes.

"For God's sake, Dad, it's not going to blow. Quit being so dramatic."

To Doug, he said, "There's no chance it's going to blow, but just humour my dad and come with me."

As Matt turned the corner, Will picked up a huge metal bucket of screws and climbed on the bumper of the bus. He lifted it as high as he could and let it drop. It came down with a huge bang.

Matt came running around the corner as white as a ghost. Will was standing there laughing his ass off. Doug had been in on it from the start, and he was rolling on the ground with laughter.

"OK you shitheads, very funny. Cut out the pranks and let's get this old hunk of junk running."

He sat in the driver's seat, crossed his fingers, and turned the key. The motor hesitated for only a moment and then started to chug along.

"Just needs an adjustment on the timing, but I think it's gonna be OK," Matt said proudly.

Doug and Will clapped and cheered and danced around like three-year-olds.

While Matt was doing some final engine tuning, Will and Doug talked about the plan.

"Leslie's got all our stuff packed and we're ready to go," Doug said. "Ya know we're going to have to bring Zain and his girlfriend. You're OK with that?"

"A week ago I wouldn't have been, but now … I guess I am. Maybe he deserves a second chance, too. There's still part of me that wants to take a swipe at him, but I'll wait till he's fully functional."

"I think this whole experience might have changed him, too, but that's just a hunch," Doug said.

"We're leavin' at ten a.m. tomorrow," Will said. "Just get him and Kabira here by then, and bring whatever you can for hunting, fishing, and keeping warm in the snow."

Word had spread through the church community that Will had a bus and was driving north to a hunting camp. The plan was that everyone would go to his friend's camp and live off the land. There would be lots of fresh water from the lake, fresh meat from hunting wildlife, and the cabins, equipped with woodstoves, would keep everyone warm on those long winter nights.

Will lay in bed and waited for the sun to peek over the horizon. He couldn't remember a time in his life when he felt more excited, more alive. Every cell in his body was buzzing. When he saw the first streams of light, he bounded out of bed and layered on as many clothes as he could. He leaned over the bed and kissed Lauren to wake her.

"Time to get up, my love. Today's a new day: a new start for all of us."

Will had barely spoken to Lauren since the big incident at the church. He was afraid of what she would say. However, today felt different. Will was hoping this new day would be a fresh start for the two of them.

Lauren stretched and smiled. She was not a morning person, but she was intrigued with the whole idea of this new life they were starting. She wasn't sure about her feelings for Will. She knew he would be a part of her life whether she liked it or not, but she didn't know if she could let him into her heart again. The only thing she knew for sure was that time would sort it out.

Over the past two days, she had been making preparations of her own. One thing she just couldn't live without was spice. She had some left in her cupboards, so these were definitely coming with them.

She also found some books on edible native Alberta plants. She was looking forward to spring when she could seek out as many sources of flavour as the forest would offer. Until then, she'd heard that she could rely on some of Zain's spice supplies to get them through the winter.

Lauren had also gathered how-to books on canning vegetables and sewing, something she knew nothing about but guessed she would need to learn in the coming years. So many things had been taken for granted before the Change. The simplest thing like making soap was a lost art, but now would be critical to their back-to-the-earth way of life.

Over the past couple of days, Will had been looking for Keath. He'd been to his house and his work but there was no sign of him.

Will wanted to tell him about the plan to live at his hunting camp. Before George's moonshine, it would have been next to impossible to get there. It was over three hundred fifty kilometres northwest of Edmonton, and winter snow could fly any day now.

He felt anxious about going to the camp without Keath's permission, but he didn't have any other options. Heading south was even riskier. Most people headed south to get away from the cold winter, but food would be very scarce, and shelter would be on a first-come, first-served basis – and they certainly weren't first.

All the wandering souls created by the Great Change would be clamouring for shelter and eating everything in their path. Will knew that their range of destinations was limited by the amount of fuel available, so given the critical variables of food, shelter, and fresh water, the camp seemed like the most logical place to go.

It did have one major drawback – the weather. Winter in northern Alberta was tough even with modern conveniences. Minus forty Celsius plus wind chill is harsh even by hardy Canadian standards. Trying to survive in that climate by hunting for your food and keeping warm with a woodstove was a daunting thought, but it was their only chance given the chaos that had descended only a month ago. Will thought that the men and women who settled out here one hundred years ago must have experienced the same fears.

If they made it, so can we, Will decided.

He, Lauren, and George arrived at the church just after nine in the morning. Matt and Sarah had promised they would be along shortly after making a quick stop at Sarah's former home for some necessities. Other members of the church started showing up, dragging bags and bundles and boxes of items they wanted to bring. Will asked Lauren to go to each family and make sure they brought only essentials because space on the bus was limited.

*Patricia McConkey*

Doug arrived with Leslie, Kabira, and Zain. Will turned his back for a moment and tried to get control of himself. He closed his eyes and tried to think of his father's wise words. What was it he had said? That everyone should get a second chance? He tried to relax.

"Will, Will, over here. Come and meet my wife," Doug called to him. Will braced himself and tried to think of something to say to Zain.

"Will, this is Leslie, and I don't think you've met Kabira. Kabira, this is Will Connors."

Will held out his hand; Kabira grabbed hold of it and shook it harder than Will would have imagined for such a small woman.

"And this is the little one I was telling you about when we last spoke," Zain said. He rubbed Kabira's bulging belly.

Kabira jerked her head around. She was surprised Zain had told anyone about the baby.

Will realized that he and Zain were more alike than he wanted to admit. Both were passionate, dedicated men who excelled in their fields, even if Zain's profession was terrorism. Second chance, second chance, Will kept saying to himself. And he did relate to Zain's feelings about the new baby. It reminded Will of how he felt when Matt was on the way.

Then there was the guilt he felt for not trying to save Zain in the explosion. The old Will would have thought he deserved to die in that blaze and would even have cursed the fact that he didn't. This new side of Will confused him and he didn't know what to say.

"Hey man, I thought you were … I mean I thought …"

"Yeah, I thought I was a goner, too. But I got a second chance, and I see you did, too."

Will gulped. It was true, but not the way Zain thought.

"You don't look like you're going to be helping out with firewood duty any time soon, so we're gonna need all that food you've been talking about. At least you're useful for something."

Zain laughed. "You're right. It'll be a few weeks before I can split logs, but I'm pretty handy with an axe. And once we get on the road, I'll have to show you how to get there. My place is pretty well hidden."

Zain and Will chatted about the route north so it would be as efficient as possible, but Will excused himself when he heard the engine start. Matt had started up the bus and was pulling it around to the front parking lot where everyone had assembled. The crowd backed off, a little nervous, wondering if it might explode. Matt turned the engine off and bounced out the front doors.

"Purrs like a kitten, don't she, Dad?"

"You did a fantastic job, Matt. Better than I could ever do."

While everyone else was packing the bus, Will asked Matt to get his mom and then come with him.

Will gathered up a few more men and asked them to help. He also got Alton to come along. He, Lauren, Matt, and the men walked across the parking lot to the graveyard. Will stood there for a moment, not knowing what to do.

"Will and Lauren, if it's all right, I'll just say a short blessing and then we can move Emma's coffin," Alton said.

Lauren gave Will a look he understood perfectly.

"Of course, Alton. Please do," Will said.

After Alton had said a few words, the pallbearers lifted the coffin on their shoulders and headed toward the bus. Everyone bowed their head in respect. Someone in the crowd started humming "Amazing Grace," and soon the whole crowd joined in. The men carefully lifted Emma's

*Patricia McConkey*

coffin onto the roof of the bus, almost in rhythm to the music. Will was on the roof, tying it tightly, securing it in place. As Will stood up, everyone stared at him, not knowing what to expect.

"I just want to say a couple things before we start. Firstly, I am sorry for the way I have behaved. There was no excuse for it." He paused for a moment and bowed his head. "But today is a new start, for all of us."

Will put his hand on the coffin.

"I know Emma would want us to celebrate, so let me hear how thankful we all are to get another chance!"

He raised his hand in the air and shouted with joy. Everyone whooped and hollered until their throats hurt.

"Let's hit the road!" Will bellowed.

The crowd of about thirty people piled into the bus. Half the bus had been loaded with treasures and necessities, leaving the other half for people. They sat three or four to a seat, with some sitting in the aisles.

Everyone got a place, even Finnigan. He sat right behind the driver's seat and looked very proud of himself. He certainly was special; he was the only dog on the bus. No one would admit it, but all the other pets had been eaten. Finn was lucky that the bus trip came up when it did, or he might have been on the menu, too.

Lauren, Alton, and Zain sat in the seat right behind the driver with Kabira, Leslie, and Doug right next to them. Kabira reached across the aisle and held Zain's hand as Will started the engine. Matt was sitting on the steps to the door with Sarah on his knee. He smiled with pride as Will put it in gear.

They were only about twenty minutes outside of town when they saw some people in a field picking pumpkins. Lauren noticed them first and asked Will to stop. She thought she could trade something for fresh pumpkin. She rooted around, found a couple of cans of tuna and bustled out of the bus, excited by the thought of fresh vegetables. She walked across the field with Will following.

"I was wondering if we could trade some tuna for a couple pumpkins," she said. She held up the cans.

The man she spoke to was on his knees cutting pumpkins off the vine with a small curved knife.

"No, no, we don't want any ..." he said.

Lauren's face and her beautiful full lips caught him by surprise. His mind raced to think where he had seen her. He couldn't place her face, but then it came it him. He had seen a younger version of her, perhaps her daughter, in a coffee shop only a few months ago. Raspberry Lips. There was no mistaking the resemblance.

"We ... don't need any ... any ..." he stammered.

"Or perhaps we can offer you some other canned goods?"

Lauren kept trying to barter with the man, but he kept giving excuses. Will looked at him closely; he was also having a kind of déjà vu feeling as he looked at him. He recognized him from somewhere, but couldn't place him. Finally it was his accent that gave him away.

It struck Will like a bolt of lightning. This was the man from GEO. He remembered his German accent and the comment "someday I'll be a farmer again."

Will pulled out his thirty-six and pointed it at his head.

"Will, what are you doing? Put that away."

"Lauren, you might change your mind when I tell you who this man is. This is the man responsible. The man who created the bacteria, who created this chaos that killed millions of people. This is the man who killed our baby."

Lauren looked at Will in disbelief, but Will didn't flinch. His eyes met Lauren's and she knew it was true.

In anger, grief, rage, and a host of other emotions,

Lauren spun around with a back roundhouse that hit the man square on the chin. He had been concentrating on Will and was totally taken off guard when Lauren hit him. He was thrown to the ground and knocked unconscious for a few seconds.

Lauren held her fists up and was bouncing up and down ready for more. She looked at Will holding the gun and screamed, "Do it, Will, he deserves it. Do it. Do it."

When the bus had first pulled up, the other workers in the field were afraid of what could happen. Gangs had approached them before, but never a busload. One of them had run off to get help. Now about a dozen men marched toward the scene, each carrying a rifle.

The bus passengers saw the scene quickly degrade from a harmless request to a life-threatening situation involving a dozen armed men. They were not about to let one of their own be overtaken by some farmers.

Both sides were somewhat equal in force. The Jacob colony had about a dozen or so rifles with more and more unarmed farmers showing up by the minute. The Edmonton Universal Church group had more guns, bows, baseball bats, and even a chainsaw (which didn't have any fuel but looked effective). They had men and women of all ages, including the very pregnant Kabira wielding her handgun. There was no way she was going to stay in the bus, despite Zain's pleas. Tension was building as both sides eyed each other and yelled insults.

Alton was trying to take control of the situation. He asked everyone to be quiet for a moment until they figured out what was happening.

"Will and Lauren, what's going on?"

Lauren was still jittery from the adrenaline running through her veins.

"Alton, he did it. He's the one. He killed everyone. He killed Emma, Emma."

"Alton," Will said in a calm, guttural voice, "this man is responsible for the way the world is today. By the end of this winter, millions of people will have burned or starved to death. *This* is the man responsible. *This* is the man who started the whole war on modern society by injecting fuel sources with an explosive bacteria."

The churchgoers gasped in horror. They had never expected to find the person who started this nightmare. Now that he was standing right in front of them, many had the same reaction as Lauren. Alton tried to keep control of the mob.

"Sir, is this true?" Alton asked the accused man.

An old farmer stepped forward.

"This is my son and he is my only son. Please be on your way. We do not want any trouble."

He stood in front of Dietrich, ready to die for him if necessary.

Will looked at the man and knew how he felt. He stared back at him,

"That was my daughter, my only daughter," he said, pointing at the coffin on top of the bus.

The old farmer and Will shared a moment of understanding. Despite their common ground, it was clear that neither would change their position and each was prepared to die for their family.

A low grumbling from the churchgoer side grew louder. Every one of them had lost friends and loved ones from this insane plot. They wanted answers.

"Are you responsible?" they asked Dietrich.

Dietrich was still wobbly, but he walked to the front line of farmers and held up his hands.

"Let me speak for a moment."

*Patricia McConkey*

Both sides went silent. Dietrich surveyed each side. Will still had a gun pointed at his head while Dietrich's family and friends had their guns pointed at Will and the church group.

"For many years," Dietrich said, "I prayed to God and asked for justice for my family. I asked my mother and sister in heaven to guide me and show me God's way. Then God revealed his plan to me. I was his servant. I had no choice but to carry out his wishes. As we see in the Old Testament, many must die in order for God's people to survive. It was meant to be."

One of the men from the Universal church was fuming. He couldn't believe the man was using God's name to justify his actions.

"How can you say this nightmare was God's plan? God is love. God's not about destruction and death. You're a coward, killing innocent people in God's name. When will people learn that God is not about killing?"

The church crowd roared in agreement. They started shouting, calling Dietrich murderer, killer, and Hitler.

"Everything that was done was predicted long ago in the book of Revelation," Gunter said, "where John tells us that the fourth angel was permitted to burn humanity with fierce heat and fire. Only the worthy shall enter God's kingdom."

Despite having carried out one of the most successful extermination schemes in the history of mankind, Dietrich did not want to lose any of the colony members to violence. He knew that, once it started, the violence might not end until they were all dead.

He searched for a way to end it before it got started. Dietrich was standing fairly close to Lauren and looked deep into her eyes. She stared back with a fierceness she had never felt before.

She reached toward Will and put her hand on the gun. She eased the gun from his hand. Will didn't know if he should let her have it. He didn't want her to have to live with the murder of a man.

Lauren held the gun in her hands. It felt cold and heavy as she aimed it at Dietrich's head. Her hands trembled and her breathing was raspy as she thought about her next move.

Will was sure she was going to shoot Dietrich. But instead she raised the gun straight in the air and pulled the trigger. The crowd silenced.

"I want to say something."

She stood face to face with Dietrich and pointed to the coffin on the bus.

"You took my beautiful daughter from me, and I'll miss her every day for the rest of my life. That's my cross to bear.

And look at the rest of this crowd," she said, sweeping her arm over the churchgoers. "Each one of them has lost family and friends, and like me, each one will grieve their losses for the rest of their lives."

The crowd nodded in agreement and some of them started to cry.

"You don't deserve to die. That would be too easy, too quick. Instead, each day, whenever anyone feels pain and sorrow, we will picture your face. We will release our misery and move on to a better life. But you won't. You'll receive our grief on top of your own guilt over what you've done. You'll suffer a long, long, slow death each day as you feel our pain."

Dietrich looked at her with fear in his eyes. He knew she was right. His insecurities had grown since that first panic attack in the car. He'd already spent countless hours reassuring himself that he was God's disciple. But a voice in the back of his head kept telling him it was all just revenge for his mother and sister.

Dietrich knew the voice in the back of his mind was the truth. This was not God's plan. It was *his* plan. His plan to get back at the men who took his mother and sister. He had justified it to himself as saving the colony's way of life.

Lauren continued her monologue to a captive crowd.

"And all of you," she said, pointing to the Jacob people, "all of you have to live with him among you. How can you do that? He's like a cancer. Doesn't he sicken you?"

The farmers hung their heads. Dietrich was a disgrace. There were no words to describe his wrongdoing. Months ago, when Dietrich first arrived in the colony, he had told the elders what they must do to prepare for the coming Change. The community was sickened by the revelation. They couldn't imagine the devastation that Dietrich's actions would bring to the world.

Even though Dietrich had explained what would happen, no one in the colony had really believed the outcome would be a worldwide massacre. Now some of the victims of Dietrich's plan stood before them: a crowd of thin, dirty, grieving souls trying to survive any way they could, reduced to begging for vegetables.

When the matter was first brought before the elders, Gunter had pointed out that Dietrich was only following their orders from long ago. They had to concede it was true. They allowed Dietrich to remain in the colony, although no one spoke to him except his father.

Lauren got the answer to her question. She saw that the colony people detested Dietrich. She looked into his eyes and knew that he was afraid, afraid that he would live a long life of guilt and anguish over what he had done.

Lauren knew there was nothing left to say. She knew she could let go of her anger and move on. She felt the cold metal of the gun in her hand and wanted to be rid of it.

She passed it to Will and turned toward the bus. The other members of the church community saw that the fight was over. Lauren was right. The worst punishment they could inflict was to leave Dietrich alive. Everyone started back to the bus.

Dietrich's heart pounded as he thought about the many years ahead of him and the millions of deaths he was responsible for. A panic attack struck him like the one he experienced that day in the coffee shop. He could barely breathe. He couldn't imagine living life this way. He saw Alton and knew he was the group's minister. In a desperate attempt at absolution, he grabbed Alton's sleeve and fell to his knees before him, pleading for forgiveness from the one man who could bring him some peace.

As a spiritual leader, Alton felt it was his duty to bring peace to those who needed it most. Clearly, Dietrich was admitting his wrongdoing by kneeling in front of him.

But Alton was not a traditional minister. He refused to absolve sins merely by waving his hand over the guilty party and pronouncing some sort of blessing. In fact, he refrained from any sort of judgment. He believed that wasn't his job.

As Dietrich pled with him, he closed his eyes and tried to hear his inner voice, guiding him in what to do. There was nothing. No thoughts or feelings on what he should do. He thought that he should show forgiveness, but he had none to give. Alton thought of the many, many funerals he had presided over and a wave of anger and disgust swept over him.

"I have nothing to give you," he said. He pushed past him.

"Please," Dietrich begged in a whisper. He grabbed Alton's leg as he walked past.

"Take your hands off me, you filthy, disgusting man," Alton said, wrenching his leg free. He shivered in disgust.

*Patricia McConkey*

Dietrich's face fell to the ground and he lay on his stomach trying to breathe. His heart was palpitating and his chest burned with pain. He couldn't go on. He had to end it here.

Dietrich gripped his knife in one hand as he crawled to his feet. He saw Lauren about twenty feet away and ran toward her. He wrapped his arm around her neck and held the knife to her throat.

Will spun around and had the gun pointed at his head in mere milliseconds. Feelings of helplessness flooded him, reminding him of how he felt holding Emma's lifeless body.

Lauren saw Will's reaction and looked him square in the eyes. She didn't want him to shoot Dietrich, because that's what he wanted. He was looking for an easy death and she didn't want to give it to him.

"Will, don't. He doesn't deserve death."

Dietrich wanted to end his life now. Pain flooded throughout every cell of his body and he wanted to make it stop any way he could. From the first moment he saw Lauren, he had guessed that Raspberry Lips from the coffee shop was her daughter and the man protecting her must be the girl's father. He goaded Will, trying to get him to shoot.

"Did your daughter go to Ottawa to deliver some money for a water project? Do you remember the last donation she received? I think it was two thousand dollars, wasn't it? I wanted her to complete her water project before ... Well, I guess we know how the story ended."

He smirked, looking toward the coffin on top of the bus.

It was as if he had struck both Will and Lauren in the gut. Will staggered slightly and dropped to his knees but still had the gun pointed at Dietrich. Lauren burned with rage.

Dietrich should have known from her earlier back roundhouse that choosing Lauren for a hostage was not a good idea. Lauren was very skilled in self-defence techniques. She used her Tae Kwon Do moves to grab the arm around her neck with both hands, placing her right hand on the meaty part of Dietrich's thumb.

By applying pressure, she was able to peel Dietrich's thumb back and twist his wrist. Within seconds, she twisted his whole arm to apply pressure on the wrist and elbow joints. To avoid getting his arm broken, Dietrich had to rotate his body until he was face to face with Lauren.

She looked at him with revulsion as she thought about his involvement with Emma. With as much force as she could muster, she kneed him in the groin, caught the knife as he dropped it, and sliced through his forearm. Dietrich collapsed to the ground.

Lauren ran the few steps from Dietrich to Will. She put her arms around his neck and held on tight. He pulled her behind Doug, who was standing next to him with a shotgun. He dropped his own gun so he could use both hands to hold her. Will knew Doug would cover them.

Although Lauren was clearly capable of defending herself, she needed Will's comfort. She shivered as she thought about Dietrich's words about Emma. It was sickening to think that this monster was somehow part of Emma's life. She knew Will was thinking the same thoughts and they reconnected in their grief.

Matt's heart almost exploded when he saw Dietrich's knife at his mother's throat. He held his ground only because he thought his mother might get hurt if he tried to rescue her. Within a few minutes it was over, although the adrenalin was still pumping madly through his veins. He moved toward Dietrich, still writhing on the ground from the groin kick, and stepped on his neck. He wanted to stomp down and crush him like a bug.

Sarah tugged at Matt's arm, trying to keep him from doing anything more. She leaned down close to Dietrich's face.

"See this face? I want you to remember the pain you caused me. I lost both my parents. I hope you rot in hell."

Sarah spat on his face. She held Matt's arm tight as they headed toward the bus. She was shaking all over.

Gunter, standing nearby, looked at his son and thought it would have been better if he had never come back. Instead of defending him again, he turned his back and walked away. He knew he was the only one who would ever speak to Dietrich again. That would be his cross to bear.

The farmers headed back to their fields and the churchgoers hung their heads as they started back toward the bus. There were no winners. The farmers had to live with the monster they had created, and the churchgoers had come face to face with their enemy but had failed to find closure. There was no punishment, no justice that could be meted out for such an appalling crime. Both sides were left with a gnawing ache that felt worse than a sickness.

Will took a few quick steps, and caught up with Matt.

"Matt, can you drive? I want to sit with your mom."

As they were making final preparations to pull away, a young woman from the Jacob colony ran in front of the bus. Matt got out and went to her. She held out a basket full of fall vegetables: squash, zucchini, sweet potatoes, and a couple of pumpkins.

She looked at Matt sadly. Matt nodded and took the basket. As she let go, she paused to put her hand on his. Then she turned and walked away, not looking back. Matt saw her wipe her eyes with her sleeve.

# Chapter 41

*Matt* drove with Sarah next to him, letting go of her hand only when he changed gears. He gently kissed her fingers, trying to comfort her. He knew the incident had reopened wounds of grief for her and his mother.

The happy mood of the group had muted into an almost palpable quietness. The thought of the quivering coward who had created so much pain and suffering was hard to understand and even harder to move past.

For her part, Lauren had an intense headache. Will was sitting in the aisle on a box of supplies. He convinced her to lie down and put her head on his lap so she could relax.

Will stroked her hair as she rested. He couldn't shake the image of Lauren with a knife at her throat. He tried not to squirm, but Lauren could tell he was upset.

"Will, it's over. I'm OK."

"Lauren, no matter how hard I try, I can't always protect you."

"No, you can't, Will, but you can be there when I need you."

"Lauren, I love you more than anything in this world. I would do anything for you."

"I know you would. But what I need you to do is relax, have fun, and not worry about me. Be the goofy guy I married."

Will snorted with laughter and tears.

"OK, if you want that guy, then you …"

He paused because Matt was sitting right in front of them. He leaned over and whispered in her ear, "Then you have to be ready for sex three times a night."

"I'm *up* for it. Are you?"

"Dad, hold on!" Matt shrieked.

There was a loud thud and the bus came to a screeching halt.

"I couldn't help it, Dad. It jumped right in front of me before I had a chance to react."

Will got out, saw the blood on the front of the bus, and followed it around to the middle of the road. About sixty feet back lay a huge eight-point buck, still alive but obviously struggling with a broken leg. It squirmed and heaved as it tried to pull itself up. Will pulled out his gun and gave it a quick shot to the head.

"Fresh venison tonight!" he yelled.

Everyone forgot their worries for the moment and cheered. Their hunger was almost as strong as their grief.

"You don't think you're going to take credit for that kill when I flushed him out of the bush for ya?"

Will whirled around, gun drawn, and saw Keath, his hunting buddy.

"Hey, don't shoot," Keath said. "Awww, on the other hand, go ahead. I'm sure you couldn't hit me anyway. I'm at least twenty feet away."

Will ran up to him and hugged him hard.

"Man it's good to see you. What the hell are you doing way out here?"

"Well, I started walking about a week ago. I got sight

of this beautiful buck two days ago. I've been tracking him ever since, trying to get a shot. Then your bus comes along and bam. But you're not getting away with it. I'm taking credit for this one."

"Yeah, but where are you gonna skin and cook him? I know this place a couple of hours from here. Got a good set-up for that type of thing. Are you interested in a ride?"

"How are you going to find it?"

"I was going to use my keen sense of direction."

They both laughed. Will's sense of direction sucked. Whenever they went hunting, they stopped letting him go out anywhere on his own because they would always have to organize a search party just to find him.

Will looked a bit worried as he mentioned the next point.

"Keath, as you've probably noticed, I've brought a few friends with me."

"I can see that, but I'm sure we can fit everybody in. The more people we can save from this madness, the better." His voice cracked as he spoke.

Keath told him he had lost track of his parents. Will could see the pain from his loss was still fresh. He gripped Keath's shoulder, then turned his attention back to the bus.

"Matt, any damage?"

"Broken headlight and dented grill, but nothing serious. We should be fine to keep going."

"OK. Let's get this beast loaded onto the hood. He's comin' with us and gonna be lovely steaks later tonight. I can just taste it now."

"I've got some great spices to make it even tastier," Zain said. He poked his head out the bus window. "Will, we're not far from my stash. Let's get going."

"Who the hell was that?" Keath whispered. Zain still looked pretty strange.

"Mad Max. Didn't you know that the whole damn world is now one big episode of Mad Max the Road Warrior?"

Keath nodded.

It took four men to load the huge buck onto the hood of the bus and strap it down. Once they got moving again, it was only about twenty minutes before Zain said they should pull over. He walked along the side of the road peering into the thick brush. To anyone driving along the highway, there was no sign of an entrance. Zain kept walking and looking. After about ten minutes, he called to Will.

"It's about two kilometres in here, but we'll have to walk. We should take about ten men with us to carry it all out."

Will went back to the bus and got the troops organized.

"Kabira, I need you to stay here with a couple of sharp-shooters and look after everyone in the bus. I don't want any more surprises. I also need some strong men to come with me to help carry out the food and other supplies."

A small group of men followed Zain into the bush. He made everyone follow close behind him because there were booby traps set along the way. Zain actually set one of them off himself about twenty feet ahead of the group. No one was hurt, but Will was more than ticked off.

This better be damn well worth it, he thought.

They reached a group of undersized shrubs growing together in front of a small hill. Zain instructed the men to cut through them. Within minutes, they exposed a door. Zain discharged all the traps and pushed the door open, motioning to the others to follow him inside.

It was surprisingly big inside the bunker under the hill. It was one big room, with a bed on one side and shelves loaded with supplies on the other. Will walked up and down the two rows of shelves and nodded his head. It definitely was a worthwhile trip for all the dried food and other useful supplies here.

Zain was busy organizing who would carry what, when something caught Will's attention. At the end of the bed were four tiny framed pictures. Will bent over to get a closer look. There was a picture of Zain with no hair and what he assumed was his mother. That must have been the time when Zain had chemotherapy. There was another picture of Zain as a young boy with his mother and a younger child, probably a sibling. There was one of a man, perhaps his father, and finally one of a tiny old Chinese man standing next to Zain.

"Awww, you saw my pictures," Zain said. "I wanted to bring those to show Kabira. Can you take them in your box?

"Sure," Will said, feeling as if he'd been caught looking into someone's medicine cabinet.

"That's my mom, as you may have guessed, and that's my brother, who was killed when he was four when he got hit by a car. And that's my dad, the bastard. He left right after my brother was killed. Couldn't handle it or something, I don't know. So I never really knew him, or what having a dad was like. Maybe you can give me some pointers? Seems like you've done a good job with Matt."

Will winced at that.

"Matt turned out great *despite* my efforts," he said. "I'll let you talk to *my* dad. He's a pretty smart man, a great dad, and has learned a thing or two over the years. He might even be able to help you with some of those injuries. One question, though."

"Who's the Korean guy? He was my Tae Kwon Do instructor. Very wise old man. Closest thing I had to a dad. Taught me to respect myself, a very important lesson."

"You and Lauren will be good sparring partners, once she's feeling a bit better. She was just training for her black belt when all of this craziness started."

Zain smiled at the thought. He couldn't wait until he was healthy again. He felt as if he had been lying around for a year.

"Here, this is for Lauren. Seems like she's had a hard day."

Zain handed him a big bar of Toblerone chocolate.

"We'd better get this stuff back to the bus before Kabira shoots someone," he said with a smirk.

Will laughed and nodded, but the scary part is that it was true. It was as if there was an army general hidden inside that pregnant body of hers. If she wasn't pregnant, Will would have suspected she'd had a sex change at some point in her life.

They had boxed all of the supplies and were carrying them out when they heard three rapid shots. Will dropped his boxes and ran the last kilometre. Kabira was standing in front of the bus cursing at some coyotes that were sniffing the buck.

"Nothing to worry about. Those little bastards were trying to steal our supper, but I got rid of them. They almost got your dog, too, but he's safe."

Finn was standing behind Kabira, which he knew was a safe spot. Finn always ran for cover in any dangerous situation.

"Finn, you are the biggest coward I have ever met," Will said, puffing to catch his breath. He reached down to scratch the dog behind his ears.

He jogged back to the rest of the group and told them about Kabira's run-in with the coyotes.

Shortly afterward, the men carrying the supplies reached the bus and started loading everything on. Zain trailed along at the end of the line. He walked slowly to the front of the bus where Kabira was standing, leaning against the front bumper, clutching her belly. His face went pale when he looked into her eyes. It was the first time he had ever seen fear in those beautiful blue eyes.

"Shit, Zain. Look at this," she said, pointing to her wet jeans. Her water had broken. "You'd better get Leslie. I think we need her."

Leslie was helping to load supplies when Zain nearly yanked her arm off and pulled her to the front of the bus.

"What the hell are ya doin' to me, man?" she growled at him. Then she saw Kabira.

"OK, dear, I'm going to have to check and see what's going on down there. Zain, get me a blanket and my black bag. It's right at the front of the bus."

Leslie did an internal exam on Kabira as she lay on a blanket at the front of the bus.

"How far along are you?" Leslie asked with concern.

"Thirty-two weeks and two days. The baby is not supposed to come for another eight weeks. It's too early isn't it? It's too early."

"Dearie, yes, it's a bit early. We are going to try and keep this baby from coming right now, so I need you to stay as calm and relaxed as possible. Zain, stay with her and talk to her. I'm going to get a spot on the bus ready for her."

Leslie prepared the seat behind Lauren with blankets and pillows. Leslie talked to Will and said that they should get moving so they could get Kabira to camp where she could lie still.

Once they had all the supplies loaded up and everyone else was on the bus, Kabira got on. She had removed her jeans for the examination and Leslie had asked her not to get dressed again because she would need to keep checking her. So now she wore a blanket wrapped around her bottom half as she bobbed up the bus stairs. Given that her belly was so big and the blanket was too long, it wasn't surprising that she stepped on the corner of it and exposed her naked belly and bottom half to Alton and the rest of the bus. What was surprising was her reaction.

"What the hell are you looking at, preacher? Never seen one of these before?"

Alton turned about six shades of red and had no idea what to say to her. This was not the time to try to reason with an angry, half-naked pregnant woman.

Zain got Kabira lying on her side, with a pillow between her knees and all her parts fully covered with the blanket. Zain had moved Will's boxes and sat in the aisle with Kabira's feet on his lap. He told her to take some deep breaths, trying to calm her, as Matt started the bus. Zain knew that telling Kabira to remain calm was like telling a pit bull to be a nice puppy, but he had to try. It could mean life or death for the baby. They lurched forward and they were off again.

After a few minutes, Kabira took Zain's hand and in a quiet voice said, "Hey, tell that guy I'm sorry. I really didn't mean it. I'm just ..."

Zain knew exactly how she was feeling. She was scared. So was he, terrified. But he had to try to remain calm and look as if everything was OK.'

"It's OK, angel. I'm sure he knows you didn't mean it."

Zain glanced at Alton, sitting a few seats away, who nodded.

"Can you ask him to say a prayer for the baby?" Kabira asked. She was not a religious person. Her mother had dragged her to church for years, but she had never felt comfortable there. Now she would try anything that might help.

"I already have, but I'll keep on praying. Don't you worry."

Alton could see how stressed Zain was. He looked around the bus for George. They didn't need to speak. George made his way to the front of the bus. It wasn't easy: he had to climb over boxes, bags, and people. Finally he was able to tuck himself a space behind Kabira. He peeked over the seat and introduced himself.

"Hi there. I'm George."

Kabira looked a bit startled but nodded. He held out his hand and she shook it awkwardly. George then held his hand out to Zain, who seemed to know who he was.

"Will told me about you. He said I should talk to you because you're a great dad."

George got a bit choked up for a moment. It wasn't like Will to say something like that but it certainly was welcome.

He tried to put them at ease with small talk, but could feel the tension in the air. He tried to lighten the mood a little by telling them the story of Will's birth. It got funnier every time he recounted it. It was quite a story because Will had been born on a streetcar atop the high-level bridge in Edmonton. George was a good storyteller and he soon had them smiling and laughing. Afterward he told them the real reason he had come to them.

"Kabira, I was wondering if I could help you relax by using something called Reiki. It's really just moving the body's energy around using my hands. Would it be OK if I placed my hand on your belly?"

Kabira was starting to feel better, but she could still feel her groin muscles tightening, which was not a good sign. She was not a trusting person, and her first instinct was to tell George to piss off. But she saw how hopeful Zain had looked and said yes.

George placed his hand on her belly and could instantly feel the energy of both baby and mother.

*Patricia McConkey*

"Oh, the baby is doing fine, very healthy."

"Really, really? You can feel that? Zain, did you hear that?"

George continued, "I want you to close your eyes and breathe with me, slowly and deeply."

George and Kabira breathed together. Zain found himself breathing along with them, not knowing why, only that he wanted to help, too. The three of them breathed together and it became a moment of bonding. George let the energy flow from Kabira's muscles into his hand.

For some reason, Zain's pain was temporarily lessened, and he felt light and free. This connection continued for what seemed an infinite length of time, then George lifted his hand. Kabira opened her eyes and stretched. She felt as if she had had a long sleep. She was rested and relaxed. She took George's hand and held it firmly. Kabira wasn't the type to give thanks or praise easily, but she felt George's magic had really helped.

"Thanks, man." She wanted to say more, but was lost for words. Saying thank you was very rare for Kabira.

"Glad to have helped. I'll be around whenever you need me."

Keath moved up front and sat next to Matt to give him directions. It was a very twisty road into the camp and difficult to find once you had left the highway. The trees were so thick it was sometimes hard to see the road. Branches brushed the top of the bus as they drove, making a loud scraping noise. If Keath hadn't been with them, it could have taken hours to find the right combination of turns.

"It's just around this clump of trees," Keath said.

"Look, we're here," Matt yelled to everyone on the bus.

It was as if everyone had stopped breathing in anticipation. As they pulled up, there was a huge sigh of relief mixed with a feeling of excitement and hope for the future.

The road had opened up into a clearing in front of a beautiful lake. Set neatly around its edges were six small cabins and one large building used for communal gatherings. The camp looked like a picture from a storybook. It had charming log cabins with flower boxes under the windows and painted gingerbread trim around the eaves. There was a beach area in front with a roped-off area for children. A canoe and a motorboat were pulled up in the sand.

The passengers filed off one by one and thanked their Creator for their new home. Even those like Zain with no particular spiritual persuasion felt an overwhelming sense of gratitude and thankfulness. Finn knew for sure this was a special place. He ran around in circles barking with delight. After the hell they had all experienced, it felt as if they had arrived in paradise.

"Keath, Keath, over here," someone shouted as they walked toward him from across the compound. Keath ran toward them.

"Mom, Dad, you made it. I looked for you in the city and, when I couldn't find you, I thought ..."

He couldn't finish.

"Keath, we were out here closing up for the winter when all the explosions started happening in Edmonton," his mother said. "We started to drive back and the car broke down. We talked to a farmer and he told us that we should probably wait it out until some of the craziness died down. We prayed every day that you would come here. God answered our prayers."

"I see you brought some friends," his dad said, giving Keath a hug.

"C'mon, Mom. We've got some patients for you to look at."

Keath's mom had been a family doctor for over thirty years before she retired.

*Patricia McConkey*

Leslie relayed all the medical details to Keath's mother, Catherine. She grimaced as Leslie told her that Kabira was only thirty-two weeks pregnant.

Catherine was a take-charge kind of person and started giving orders to make sure Kabira was looked after.

"Keath, can you help us please? Carry Kabira over to your Uncle Wayne's cabin. It's the closest. She needs to lie down and I need to check on her progress."

Keath scooped up Kabira in his arms and carried her toward the cabin. Zain walked beside them holding her hand. He was embarrassed that he couldn't carry her himself.

"I'll take a look at you after we get your wife settled in," Catherine said, noting Zain's wounds.

Once Keath saw that his mother had everything she needed, he headed out to organize the rest of the group.

His father, Rick, was making quick work of the buck, carving it up with an expert hand. Every piece of meat would be used and the hide could be tanned and used for winter clothing. Nothing would be wasted. Even the intestines would be saved for fish bait.

Keath got some of the men to start gathering firewood for the big barbeque pit in front of the main hall.

The women were trying to organize sleeping arrangements. Each cabin had two small bedrooms and a loft where children usually slept. There was enough room to accommodate everyone. It was just a matter of who bunked with whom. The whole place was buzzing with activity and everyone felt a renewed sense of hope.

After a big meal of venison stew with rice, fresh squash, and sweet potatoes, the whole group decided to have a big bonfire on the beach to celebrate their new life. Sarah had brought her guitar and was strumming and singing familiar songs. She had a beautiful voice, but it was soft and was often drowned out by others who were not so musically gifted. It didn't matter. The laughter was contagious.

Lauren, still feeling shaken after her encounter with Dietrich, was not going to miss the festivities. Will spread a blanket on the sand just a short distance from the crowd and she lay there watching. Will noticed how moonlight edged the tops of the trees, turning them into silvery candlesticks. The moon was reflected on the surface of the water, more beautiful than he ever remembered.

It was too bad it took so much pain to wake him up, he thought. He stroked Lauren's hair and was so thankful she was here with him.

"My love, I want to spend the rest of my life making you happy, learning how not to be the biggest asshole on the planet. And, ummm, what was it you wanted? A goofball? I can be that, too."

Lauren took Will's hand and traced some letters in it, which he said aloud.

"I, heart, U," he said with a smile.

"I heart U 2, my love, always."

Will and Lauren were just heading off to their cabin when Lauren ssshhhhed Will and pointed to her ear. Will strained to hear but couldn't make anything out above the rowdy singing, hooting, and hollering. Will caught Sarah's eye, and she stopped for a moment.

"Everyone, stop for a moment. Listen, I think I hear something."

Everyone hushed then and listened, and there it was, clear as a bell – a newborn's cry, loud and lusty. There was a moment of awe when everyone realized that this was the first child to be born into their new world. It hit each person differently, but everyone felt hope. The crowd cheered and hooted and everyone hugged.

Sarah started to play Happy Birthday to you, and everyone joined in and sang as loud as they could. "Happy Birthday, dear baby, happy birthday to you."

Alton gave George a questioning look. George said he thought everything would be fine, but you could hear concerned whispers in the crowd, wondering if the baby would be OK, given its early arrival.

After a while, the cabin door opened, and Zain slowly emerged carrying a tiny bundle in his arms.

"It's a girl!" he said with tears of joy in his eyes. The crowd cheered and clapped. "The doctor says she's seven pounds and healthy as a horse. She's a fighter like her mom."

More clapping, cheering, and hugging.

"Have you got a name for her?" someone called from the crowd.

"We do, but just a minute …"

Zain stepped off the porch and walked through the exuberant group to where Lauren and Will were standing. Lauren looked at the baby with tears in her eyes.

"Do you want to hold her?"

Lauren nodded, and Zain awkwardly transferred the baby to her.

A wave of emotions flooded over Lauren. She remembered vividly the moment she first held Emma. Will stood behind her and steadied her as the tears streamed down her face.

"Kabira is doing really well," Zain said. "The doc is just sewing her up right now. She says she thinks the baby is only four weeks premature, not eight. Kabira must have been pregnant longer than she thought."

Will looked at Zain and remembered their conversation at the plant. Zain had said that he wasn't sure it was his baby for two reasons. One was that he been told he was sterile and the other was the timing. Will's thoughts must have been obvious because Zain answered his unspoken question.

"Yeah, that means she's my baby," Zain said to Will. "All mine."

"Congratulations, Zain. She's beautiful. I think she looks a bit like you, but in a good way."

"Thanks, I think. The reason I came over here is about her name. Kabira wants her first name to be Zoe, sort of after me, but I'd like her second name to be Elizabeth. I wanted to ask if you were OK with that."

Lauren gently passed the baby back to Zain and kissed him on the cheek. She nodded. Elizabeth was Emma's middle name. Lauren wondered how he knew that. It was a nice thought. Will was also touched at the gesture and choked back a few tears, shaking Zain's free hand.

"I'd better get the baby back to Kabira. She'll be wondering where we ran off to."

Will swallowed hard to regain his composure.

"Hey everyone, the baby's name is Zoe Elizabeth," Zain said in a proud papa voice.

More clapping and cheering. Sarah started another round of Happy Birthday and now inserted "Zoe" at the appropriate spot. Zain thanked everyone and walked back to the cabin.

Will and Lauren were just heading back to their cabin when Matt grabbed his dad's shoulder.

"Dad, wait a minute. I got a little bit of Grampa's hooch. It didn't all go into the gas tanks. Let's have a toast."

"You go ahead, Matt. Your mom and I are heading off to bed. It's been a busy day."

"No, really, you've got to stay for this." Matt put his arm around Sarah. He looked a bit self-conscious. "Maybe we should toast to the next generation of Connors?"

Lauren put her trembling hands over her mouth, and looked at Matt with questioning eyes. He put his arms around her and said, "Yep, Mom, it's true. We're gonna have a baby, and you're gonna be a grandma."

Will wrapped his arms around Sarah and held her close. He lifted her off the ground and spun her around so fast her feet lifted off the ground. He couldn't remember feeling more joyful than this moment. He felt a warm breeze on the back of his neck, and smiled. He knew Emma was smiling with him.

# Epilogue

*T*he first winter was tough on everyone, but with the food and supplies they had from Zain's hideout, they managed. They learned quickly that surviving in northern Alberta required everyone to depend on each other and work together.

The most important change for the group came during their first summer together.

On one of their many fishing trips, Will and Matt went to the far end of the lake and saw a boat pulled up on the shoreline. It was a surprising find. They weren't aware of any other inhabitants on the lake. They pulled their boat ashore to investigate. After walking past the first row of trees, they were astonished to find a huge building built into the side of the cliff.

A log A-frame structure protruded from the rock face, and the rest of the building was almost flush with the cliff as if it had been hewn out of the rock. To the left of the A-frame was a long row of windows that stretched around the side of the cliff. It was an impressive building, yet blended perfectly with its natural setting.

They walked through the front doors and realized it was some sort of hotel. The front lobby had beautiful greenish-gray slate floors. Big cedar beams gleamed from the sunlight that poured through skylights. It had a stunning stone fireplace surrounded by leather couches and chairs, and a chandelier made from elk horns hung in the centre of the room. A baby grand piano sat in the corner. It seemed like a posh getaway with every comfort that money could buy, but there was no one here.

Both Matt and Will noticed how warm and humid the air felt. They walked down a hallway that went deep into the hillside.

"Check this out," Will said. "I think it's a hot spring."

The pool was lined with slate and had water trickling out between the layers creating a waterfall effect. Matt had his clothes off in under a minute and waded into the warm water. He wanted to touch the back wall of the pool.

"It's warm water. I bet this is a natural hot spring and that's why this fancy place was built. You know, so the rich and snooty could have a warm bath."

Will and Matt soaked in the warm water until their curiosity got the better of them and they went to explore more of the complex.

They discovered guest rooms, each with a small sitting room, a queen - or king-size bed and a beautiful bathroom with all the amenities. Will's heart pounded with excitement as he counted the rooms. There were more than enough suites for each family. As they continued wandering, they came across an industrial-size kitchen with an attached greenhouse, kept warm all year by an in-floor heating system, compliments of the hot spring. Will opened the fridge; it was full of food. Someone had obviously been here recently, but there was no sign of them yet.

"Matt, have you noticed that all the appliances are running? Where is the electrical source?"

"I think we should go to the roof. It must be up there."

They went out the back door of the kitchen area and scaled a grassy hill. As they reached the top of the embankment, they found two large banks of photovoltaic panels, more than enough to supply the whole compound with electricity. But if that wasn't enough, there was also a micro wind turbine, presumably meant as a backup if something went wrong with the solar panels. Matt was fascinated by the mechanics of the green technology and was too absorbed to notice Will's discovery.

Will had found a large glass dome barely above ground level. He knelt down and cautiously leaned on the edge of the dome, not sure how safe it was. He cupped his hands around his eyes to block out the reflection of the bright sunlight and peered inside. He found the resident of this beautiful haven.

"Matt, follow me. I've found him."

Will ran down the hill and through a hallway he thought would lead to the room he just saw. He threw open the double doors, and there he was, hanging from the rafters. Will picked up the stepladder he must have used and climbed up to cut him down. He lowered the body to Matt. Will shook his head at the senselessness of it. The body couldn't have been there very long; it had not yet seized up with rigor mortis.

It was ironic that the man had chosen to take his own life in the room labelled Spiritual Centre, though Will thought maybe that was the perfect place for it. Sun streamed through a huge domed skylight at least thirty feet above the floor. The centre of the room sunk three steps below the main level and was decorated with a huge tile mosaic in the form of a yin-yang symbol.

"I wonder who he was," Matt said, looking at the thin, dark-haired man in his late fifties.

"Me, too. More importantly, I wonder why he did this, living here with everything that he could have ever wanted."

"It would mean nothing without your family," Matt said, giving Will a meaningful look.

Will's heart swelled with love for Matt. His son was wise beyond his years. He wrapped his arms around Matt and lifted him from the ground.

"This would make a beautiful spot for a wedding, don't you think? And did you see that wine cellar? We could have one hell of a party."

"The baby's due any day now. Sarah's as big as a house. She'd look like a huge marshmallow in a white dress."

Matt laughed at the thought.

"And if you tell her I said that, I'll kill you for sure."

~

Shortly after the group moved into their new accommodations, they held a memorial service for the man who had taken his own life. They built a large rock monument to honour his life and thank him for providing them with their luxurious new home. During the ceremony, they thought it was appropriate to name their bountiful new home Eden.

The man had made this haven as self-sufficient as humanly possible. Solar and wind power ran all the lighting, appliances, and water and sewer systems. The hot spring provided more than enough heat to keep the building and greenhouse warm through even the coldest winter. Hunting wild game, fishing, and gardening provided more than enough food.

Zain's shortwave radio allowed them to communicate with the outside world. They were able to locate a few

*Patricia McConkey*

other small groups like their own, families that had bonded together to make life possible in this new world. They and their contacts estimated that only twenty percent of the population had survived. The small groups kept in touch and exchanged ideas, but travel between groups was limited to once per year during the early summer months.

Gabe, Matt's son, was born on the day they moved from the hunting camp to Eden, so the wedding was postponed for a few weeks. By then the bride was back to her normal svelte figure. She looked nothing like a marshmallow in her beautiful wedding dress, ingeniously created from linen tablecloths and lace doilies.

Will cried like a baby at the wedding, and was the butt of jokes for years to come.

George, who was loved by everyone in the group, lived two years more after the Great Change. He died peacefully in his sleep with a smile on his face. Everyone knew he was smiling because he was reunited with his beloved wife.

Matt became Chief Engineer and knew every nuance of each mechanical system in the compound. Sarah kept busy looking after Gabe but still found time to teach music lessons to anyone interested. Will was her first student. He learned to play the harmonica.

For those who had survived, it was a transformation. As was his intention, Dietrich had created a new way of life, one focused on family and the basics of food and shelter. The purpose of life was no longer to accumulate wealth and goods over the course of a lifetime. It was very simple. It was about living in harmony with nature and appreciating every breath, every moment, because that's what we are truly here for – to live with each other in peace and joy.

# *About the author*

*Patricia McConkey* earned a Bachelor of Arts degree from Carleton University in Ottawa and a Master's of Business Administration degree from Queen's University in Kingston. Her business, Wastaway Services Canada, promotes technology that converts municipal waste into a clean fuel, reducing the need for fossil fuels and preventing many of the harmful effects of landfills. She has two children, a son and daughter, and hopes to make their future a little brighter by getting the message out that if we all make small changes, we can keep our environment beautiful for generations to come. McConkey is involved in promoting an education project for girls in Uganda sponsored by a Canadian Rotary Club.

www.patriciamcconkey.ca

CPSIA information can be obtained at www.ICGtesting.com
Printed in the USA
LVOW112315160312

273455LV00006B/1/P